P9-BUS-708

CAMINATA
A Journey

Lori DiPrete Brown

Copyright © 2013 by Lori DiPrete Brown
Global Reflections Press
All rights reserved.

This is a work of fiction. Names, characters, businesses, places, events, and incidents are either the products of the author's imagination or used in a fictitious manner. Any resemblance to actual persons, living or dead, or actual events is purely coincidental.

Cover photo © 2009 by Evan DiPrete Brown.
Book designed, formatted, and edited by Evan DiPrete Brown.

Please direct any inquiries to:
Lori DiPrete Brown
dipretebrown@gmail.com
globalhealthreflections.wordpress.com

ISBN-13: 978-0615863818 (Global Reflections Press)
ISBN-10: 0615863817

For my mother

Once I took a long walk that changed my life.

In Spanish a long walk is sometimes called a *caminata*. It can mean a walk to the river on a Sunday afternoon, a journey into the mountains, or the long walk home after a day in the coffee fields. A *caminata* can also be a spiritual journey, a pilgrimage to a place where God dwells and miracles happen. People pray and fast; they sing together, sometimes in bare feet, sometimes on their knees.

When I think about my walk, it's the Spanish word that comes to mind. I was just twenty-two. I wanted to try myself out, to walk in the world, to heal its wounds if I could. My *caminata* took me to the far corners of another country, places you wouldn't think to go unless you were walking with someone who was born there. There were times when the journey stopped being mine.

We walked until the road ended, then followed footpaths to places further on. Walking that way is slow. Not that you don't see mountains and waterfalls and other natural wonders. You do. But you walk for a long time first. You get thirsty and tired and scared. You almost never end up in the place you set out for, but in spite of taking the long way around, in spite of the detours, or perhaps because of them, you get to the place where you needed to go.

I made the other kind of *caminata*, too. It was the funeral procession of someone I cared for, someone I had walked with, someone I might have been able to save if I hadn't wanted so much to believe in her. I know the *caminata* is a ritual out of step with modernity, but as I headed toward the shrine of the Virgin of Suyapa, grieving with the others, I felt the truth of its pulse.

I expected the Virgin to be a large statue. I hoped some of the mourners would take her up on their shoulders so she could lead us, her robes casting a protective shadow over us all. I wanted her to extend her arms to me, to speak my name.

But the Holy Mother of Honduras, housed in a small chapel against a dark mantle of embroidered stars, was small enough to fit in the palm of my hand. Her indigenous features were pure, child-like. The crown was larger than her head, and she seemed surprised to be wearing it. You had to move in close to see her, to be comforted.

A walk in the world. A search for God. A path to the self. My *caminata* was all of these. And more.

La Casa de los Niños
January 1983

I

I saw my reflection in the window as I got into the taxi. I had hoped I would blend in here, but somehow my dark brown eyes and hair looked lighter than they did at home, and my olive skin seemed almost white. I'd never left the States before, not even for a two-week vacation to Europe, but now here I was in Honduras, where I'd be staying for a whole year. I showed the driver the letter that explained where I was going. It said *La Casa de los Niños*, three blocks south and two blocks west of the *Iglesia de San Juan*.

The city rolled past the closed windows of the taxi like a slide show. The buildings of Tegucigalpa stood close and low, as if they were about to tumble down on the narrow street. A row of bright storefronts passed — yellow, green, blue, with bold red letters — the Spanish words passed too quickly to read. I rolled down the window and took a shallow breath. How long would it be until the dusty heat tasted like air? The taxi zigzagged through a maze of cars and pedestrians until it was held up behind a bus at a crowded stop.

"Dondé estamos?" I heard my voice crack. I'd studied Spanish for years, but now that I needed it, now that I had no choice, it felt like I was inventing every word I spoke.

"This is the *Parque Central*," the driver answered.

I leaned forward to get a closer look. The Central Park was bounded by streets on three sides and a large cathedral on the other. A woman in high heels crossed herself as she passed the church. Another who carried a basket on her head knelt and did the same. A one-armed beggar by the door lifted his cup and mumbled an appeal to each passerby. In front of the church an old man laid out sheets of lottery tickets on the ground, securing them with small stones. A young man bent over the tickets, searching for a lucky number in the random array. *"Compra-juega-gana,"* the ticket seller called out, repeating it with the rhythm and timbre of an auctioneer. Buy-play-win. Buy-play-win.

Pigeons pecked around the ground and hovered restlessly in the trees, filling the air with dry notes. Two ragged shoeshine boys chased each other in a game of tag, and an armed soldier stood guard at the corner, his back to a tree. I knew there would be a strong military presence — I'd expected big arms and a belligerent stare — but this soldier had the face of a boy.

Suddenly a hand reached into my open window and tugged at my sleeve. I jumped, then laughed at myself — it was just a little girl. Her face, darkened by dirt and overexposure to the sun, was framed by black matted hair. Her dress was the color of dirt, too, with raw hems at the neck and sleeves. She carried a rose, its red petals black around the edges.

"Señorita, un cinco." She demanded five cents.

"Váyase. Get out of the street." The driver shooed the girl away as if she were a stray dog, then sat back and resumed glaring at the bus in front of him.

The girl moved in closer and pointed to my purse. Then she took a step back, straightened her shoulders. *"Un canto para la señorita."* She was going to sing me a song.

She stood at attention and directed a series of flat tones and syllables to a point on the ground near the front of the taxi. The only words I could make out were *"por el amor de Dios"* — for the love of God. When she finished she reached in the window again and forced the rose into my hand. She grabbed onto my purse and wouldn't let go. I saw my reflection for the second time that day in her shiny dark eyes.

"Monee, plees."

I didn't know what to do. I didn't have any Honduran money yet, and anyway, the girl clearly needed a home, not a handout. The bus at the stop was just about full, and the taxi idled in anticipation. We were about to pull away from her.

I could have taken her into the taxi, brought her to *La Casa* with me. Saving children like her, after all, was what I had come all this way to do. But there in the taxi, seeing the truth of her at close range for the first time, this simple act of salvation seemed impossible. I fumbled through my purse, pulled out a U.S. dollar bill and pressed it into her hand.

"That's why we have so many children climbing into our taxis," the driver shouted back to me as we drove away. "Do you think your money will buy bread for that alley cat? Her *papi* is probably around the corner, ready to beat her if she doesn't give him your dollar. He'll buy enough rum for the whole afternoon, and then he'll beat her anyway. Ha. You *gringos*."

I turned my face toward the window. I had tried to prepare myself for the realities here, but I hadn't expected a little girl to reach into the taxi and touch me. Now the driver's scorn made me feel hot, ridiculous. A salty tear ran down my cheek and fell to the flower in my hand. I took a deep breath and tried to compose myself. I would be at *La Casa* soon.

After a mile or so the urban bustle gave way to rows of modest stucco houses with iron gates and well-kept gardens. Then the paved road ended; the houses were made of wood and flanked by an occasional vegetable garden, and, inevitably, a pile of trash on the edge of the dirt road. *La Casa* was further out than I had expected.

Finally we came to the *Iglesia de San Juan*. A few blocks beyond the church a large house sat up on a hill. There were a number of smaller cinderblock houses on the fenced grounds around it. At the entrance a wooden sign hung on a black wrought-iron frame. *La Casa de los Niños*. The driver honked at the gate.

When the gate was opened the taxi driver left me at the front door of the big house. The houses below buzzed with life. Giggles and cries rose up from all directions, and children darted in and out of the houses like stray bees around a hive. I watched the cab rumble away, then reached for the knocker on the front door.

After a moment a woman in an apron answered the door. "Mother Maria's not here," she said. "She won't be back until tomorrow."

"I'm Beth Pellegrino, from the United States." My voice came out a little higher and louder than I'd intended. "She's expecting me."

"Come in and sit down. I'll call Sister Paula."

The house was relatively simple by American standards, two stories with wood floors and an oriental rug in the front hall, but here in Honduras this complete and orderly house was an oasis of luxury. I sat in the straight-backed chair by the front door and waited. I hoped the Sister knew something about the plans I had made with Mother Maria. I didn't want to have to go back into town, find a room in a hotel, then come back tomorrow...

Instead of descending from the stairs as I expected, Sister Paula approached from outside the house, leaning into the doorway from the front step and placing a gentle hand on my shoulder. She was tall, with a wide wingspan. The round yellow brim of a straw hat framed her face. She wore a light blue cotton skirt, a white shirt with a clerical collar, and a small wooden cross around her neck. She seemed cool in spite of the heat.

"You must be Beth." She spoke Spanish with a slight French accent. "We heard you were coming." She leaned forward and kissed my cheek, careful to keep her dirt-covered shoes on the step outside. "I hope you haven't been waiting long. We were in the garden behind the *casitas*. The children are planting their own tomatoes this year."

Sister Paula's face was exuberant with the promise of fleshy tomatoes and child gardeners. Hers was a prayer-fed smile. There was peace in it, certainty.

"You'll be staying down there," she said, still fixed in the doorway, pointing to a house at the bottom of the hill. "That's where we keep the young ladies." She smiled affectionately. "They're almost all grown up, but Mother Maria thinks they need a little help from you."

I didn't answer at first. I was expecting to work with children, not "young ladies." That's what the letter had said... Or had it? I reviewed the assignment again in my mind. "To counsel and assist residents of *La Casa de los Niños.*" I had assumed it referred to young children, but of course orphans grew up eventually like everyone else... What would it mean to be a grown-up orphan, I wondered, on your own still, but without the armor of childhood? I thought about the games and crafts and hugs I had prepared. They were probably not going to be very helpful.

Sister Paula saw my hesitation. "We were told that you had offered to live with them, but if you've changed your mind a place could be made for you here in the big house."

"No, it's okay." I made myself smile. "Which house is it?"

"I'll show you." Sister Paula called in to the woman who had answered the door, "Mercedes, we're going down to the *Residencia de las Señoritas.* Could you send Filiberto to help us with the bags, *por favor?*"

Filiberto packed himself like a mule, with my suitcase hung over one shoulder, a box in one hand and another balanced on his head. He kept pace a few steps behind as we walked down the hill.

"This group has been together for three months," Sister Paula explained. "The youngest is sixteen. They organize their own chores and cook for themselves. They're preparing themselves for life on the outside."

I felt worried. It sounded like they were all grown up. What if there wasn't anything for me to do? "That's great," I said aloud.

Sister Paula opened the door and called out in a singsong voice, "*Buenas tardes.*"

As we crossed the threshold into the *sala,* I saw a sweep of brisk movements at the perimeter of the empty room. All the girls had scurried away. Then I heard low voices from the hall. I strained to listen but could only catch a few phrases over the hushed whispers. "Let's get out of here." "They're coming." "It's Sister Paula and the *gringa*."

I looked around the kitchen. There were dishes in the sink, and two large pots turned over to dry on the counter beside it. A metal spoon, a ladle, and a knife lay in a row by the stove. The wooden table in the middle of the room was marked with scratches and gouges, and there were no curtains on the windows. The pantry closet was wide open with a padlock slung through the latch.

"Come out, girls," Sister Paula called. "Come out and meet Beth."

There was an awkward silence, then one of the girls came out of the hallway and stood before me, her head down. "*Bienvenida,*" she said in a low voice. Welcome. I couldn't tell if she was sullen, or just shy.

"Thank you, Luz." Sister Paula squeezed the girl's hand. "You're going to like Beth."

This was so different from what I had been expecting, but I managed to get out a greeting and a small smile. Luz was dark and short with jet-black hair. She looked up at me. Her sad eyes were such a deep brown that they looked black. They made her pupils look large, as if they could soak up all the light around her.

"*Señorita* Luz is our gracious lady today," mocked a heavyset girl who came forward from the hall. She had a square face and bright red lips. She looked like a painted man, and her thick layer of make-up looked pasty from the heat.

Sister Paula put an arm around her. "This is our Katia."

"Don't be fooled by good manners," Katia said to me. "You have to watch out for Luz. She's *lunática*. A crazy Indian. She disappears like a witch and when she comes back she doesn't know where she's been."

I wasn't sure how to respond, so I looked to Sister Paula, who took the remark in stride and glanced at me in a way that let me know we could talk about it later.

Before I could say anything, Katia threw her big arm around my shoulders, guiding me away from Sister Paula. "Are you going to take care of us? Are you our new housemother?"

"Actually I'm more like a counselor." I looked to Sister Paula, who smiled encouragement but said nothing. "I'm not going to take care of you the way a housemother does," I said, thinking this through for the first time myself, "but I'll be here to talk with you, and to help you when I can."

Katia shrugged. "There's a dance at the *Club Siglo 20* next Saturday. Can I go, housemother?"

Before I had to answer Sister Paula stepped in. "There'll be time for that later. Let's show Beth her room."

Sister Paula led me to the room at the end of the hall and opened the door. The room was empty of furniture, and there was no bed, just a dusty foam mattress in the corner. The cinderblock walls were discolored by grime in places. The window was not small, but it had no screen or pane, just wooden shutters. I could tell that the cement blocks had been faded by the sunlight that streamed in, because dark rectangles marked spots where furniture had been placed in the past. The musty odor made my eyes water.

Filiberto entered with my bags and set them down in the middle of the floor.

"Goodness, it's not even clean," said Sister Paula. "I'm so sorry, Beth. You can stay in the guest room in the big house for tonight."

"Once she sleeps there she won't come back to us," said Luz from the doorway.

"The food in the big house is better," Katia added, "and they bathe in *agua caliente*."

I was tired and the hot bath sounded tempting, but something in Luz's voice made me want to stick with the girls. "I can sleep on this mattress on the floor until a bed can be found. It won't take long to clean up — it's just dust." I went to the window and opened the wooden shutters to let in some fresh air.

Sister Paula came over and gave me a light hug around the shoulders. "I'll introduce you to Don Pablo. He'll get you everything you need." She turned to the girls. "Perhaps one of you could come with me to help Beth?"

"I'll go," offered Luz. She looked to Katia and shrugged. "She can't carry everything by herself."

Sister Paula walked with us to the storage shed. Once we got there she cupped my hands in hers and said goodbye. "It's time I got back to the garden. If you need anything the girls know where to find me." I wasn't ready for her to leave just yet, but I did have enough pride to pretend it was fine.

Don Pablo greeted me kindly from under a worn *sombrero*. He seemed pleased that he had what I needed as he placed things on the counter: a roll of toilet paper, a plastic bucket, a broom, a mop, a scrub brush, and a fat bar of all-purpose cleaning soap. "Anything else?"

"The room needs a bed and a dresser. And would it be possible to have a small writing table for my work?"

"A bed." He furrowed his brow as if he were solving an algebra problem. "I can have one for you tomorrow. And I'll put a lock on your door this afternoon. With all your American things you'll need that. The other things, no. But I can tell you where to buy."

"Thanks." I nodded. "That would be fine."

As we spoke Luz leaned on the wall and picked up a paintbrush. She held it up and rubbed the dry bristles against the wall.

Don Pablo looked at me and raised an eyebrow. "Would you like some paint?"

"Oh, yes." The cleanness of freshly painted walls was just what the room needed.

"Give her two brushes," said Luz. She turned to me. "I'll help."

"Thanks. We can do it first thing in the morning."

Back in my room I opened my suitcase and started to unpack the neatly folded T-shirts that lay on top, but there was nowhere to put them. Unpacking would have to wait. I was tired, so I thought

I'd put the sheets from home on the old mattress and take a nap, but the floor was filthy. I'd have to wash it before making up my bed.

I took the bucket that Don Pablo had given me to the kitchen sink, but when I opened the tap nothing came out. Katia happened to be walking by.

"We only have running water in the morning, Beth. In the afternoon you have to get it from the *pila*."

I went out the back door to the large cement water storage tub. It was wet at the bottom, but empty. I wouldn't even be able to wash my face until morning.

I could sweep, at least. I started in the empty corner. Once a small area was clean, I placed my bags there. I planned to sweep all the dirt toward the doorway, but I had to move the mattress first. I lifted it from its place in the corner to find a cluster of large roaches. They were startled into activity by the light. I jumped back. The roaches scurried toward and away from me, disoriented. Some crawled into a hole in the wall, while others flew at me. One landed in my hair. I screamed and shook it out, then swatted at the roaches with my broom until all of them had either escaped into the hole or were dead.

My heart was still pounding as I swept up the roach carcasses, keeping an eye on the hole in the wall. I hoped no one had heard me scream. The thought of hundreds of roaches crawling around inside the wall filled me with a spasm of revulsion, then another when I thought of it again. I wondered if I should find Sister Paula and ask to sleep in the big house?

I knelt down on the floor and thought a minute. Of course, I had to stay. After all, the girls didn't have the option of going somewhere else for the night. I would close the hole somehow. There was some masking tape among the art supplies in my suitcase. That would hold things until I could patch the hole.

After sweeping the floor I set up the mattress in the middle of the room. For this first night I'd sleep with the light on to keep the roaches away.

I made up the old mattress and lay down for a nap, lulled to sleep by the familiar feel and smell of the sheets I'd brought from home.

I had grown up in Providence, not far from Boston, in a quiet neighborhood with parents who loved each other, and two younger sisters. My father was Dr. Pellegrino, pediatrician, an Italian-American success story. He was proud, loving, devoted to his family, and completely dedicated to his work. From a young age I understood that my father's mission in life was to save sick children, and that he could be buzzed or beeped away from me at a moment's notice. I accepted the parting kisses on the forehead with grace, and got used to lending my father to other children until they got better.

My mother was a music teacher who chose to keep working after she married but quit when she became pregnant with me. She had been adopted when she was five, by a good and loving family. Those were the bare facts, and she never said more, never spoke about the time before. When it came to her three daughters she was loving and willing in every way. Rather than resenting the extra weight she carried because of my father's work, she seemed uplifted by it. When he was called away she'd conjure pajama parties and art projects and sing-alongs to amuse us. It was joyful, the four of us, waiting for someone who we thought would always come home.

Then one night he didn't. When I was twelve, my father died in a car accident. His death left a huge hole in our lives, and it broke my mother completely. I remember the days following his death, tip-toeing around the house caring for my sisters and my mother, who stared vacantly over her coffee for hours at a time.

When my father was alive whatever unspoken sorrows my mother suffered stayed in the background. We were the Pellegrino family, healthy and whole, and my mother was at the core of that. But after the accident I realized that in addition to being a wife, my mother had also been, like so many others, a child that my father had saved. He'd saved her from abandonment, filled her life with love, and then, through the accident, without meaning to at all, he had abandoned her again.

During that first year after his death, my mother slowly became herself again, but she had lost her faith. My grandmother took it upon herself to take us to church on Sundays. She prayed for us silently, her lips moving as she held her rosary beads tight, and she made sure we were enrolled at St. Cecilia's School for Girls, where I would eventually be fortunate enough to find Sister John.

Until I met Sister John, God had a quiet place in my life. Conventions were observed, like Sunday Mass and Easter hats, but God wasn't mentioned much at table, except through the rote words of Grace. Sister John, however, talked about God a lot — his justice, "her" unconditional love. She excited me with ideas about social action and service, and her lessons brought something of my father's spirit into my life.

None of the girls at St. Cecilia's made fun of Sister John's name because she was the prettiest nun at the school. She had chosen a boy's name, she told them, because John was the one who had loved Jesus most, had walked closest to him. Sister John wore street clothes, not a habit. It was known that she shopped at the thrift store on Washington St. and she never spent more than a dollar on an item of clothing. The rest of her clothing allowance went to the church school in Central America where she had taught for five years before coming to St. Cecilia's.

Sister John taught Spanish. She told me I had a gift for languages, which, true or not, became a self-fulfilling prophecy. I took Sister John's classes for four years and was active in the Spanish Club as well. The Spanish Club at St. Cecilia's was not a place where girls learned to make *paella* and Mexican coffee. Instead, Sister John engaged us in meaningful community activities. We took a pledge, in Spanish of course, to "use our talents to love

11

and serve the poor." We tutored children from a low-income school in Chelsea, we had fund-raising drives for Sister John's old school, and we learned Spanish songs of resistance from places as far flung as Chile.

I came home singing one of these songs — Victor Jara's lyrics were unbearably beautiful in Spanish, I thought. I sang them for my mother, then tried in vain to translate. "He's taken the call to work for justice and woven the Lord's Prayer into it," I said, flushed and breathless. "It says we can end misery, that we can turn today into the tomorrow that we dream of."

My mother seemed worried. "It says in the Bible that the poor will always be with us," she said. "Don't they teach that anymore?"

"No," I said. "They don't."

My announcement that I intended to go to Central America after college graduation brought my mother to tears. A year was too long, she said, and she feared for my safety. Couldn't I go to Europe for the summer, like some of my friends, she wanted to know. When I made it clear that I wasn't interested in visiting castles or strolling the halls of famous museums my mother turned the conversation to Jake.

"You could lose him. What about that?"

She approved of Jake, I knew. He was steady and responsible, and not likely to roam far from Boston. He was the college boyfriend who shared everything with me. He'd been a faithful friend, study partner, biking buddy, confidant. He made me happy. He made me laugh. But the lifetime of quiet contentment that he promised... I didn't want that now.

"I love Jake," I said. "But I need to do this first."

My mother shook her head, speaking to herself as much as to me. "Sara will be sixteen. Pammy starting school in the fall..."

I knew what she was thinking. Teaching Sara to drive would have been my job. And Pammy always listened to me. My mother was counting on me to make sure she got started on the right track at college. I was sorry, sort of, but I didn't see why I should let ordinary things like my sisters' driving lessons and freshman grades keep me from living my own life. Still, it was hard to find words that told the truth gently. 'I want to go.' That simple wish, when spoken aloud, implied disobedience — something I had never allowed myself to do — and pronounced abandonment.

Before I had to defy my mother's wishes, she relented. "I know children have to leave home," she said. "I know that's what you're supposed to do."

Still, she held Sister John responsible for my going off to Honduras. No amount of common sense, she said, not even four years of college, could erase the ideas that she had put in my head. But Sister John hadn't put ideas in my head. The feelings had been in my heart all along; Sister John had just shown me how to speak and act accordingly. At college I studied literature, but stayed involved in social service projects and continued with Spanish. Childish as it may sound, I was keeping my pledge, which guided me like a compass, and landed me at *La Casa*.

I awoke from my nap to the sound of a knock on the door. I opened the door to find a slender girl in an apron. Her light brown hair was pulled back in a tight ponytail. She said her name was Rosa. I was glad that at least one of these girls knew how to smile.

"You must be hungry after traveling. Dinner's just about ready," she said.

I followed her to the kitchen table, where four places were set. Three were identical, with a plastic cup and two tortillas. The fourth place was set with a cup, a paper napkin, a fork and knife, and two slices of white bread.

The coffee had been brewed in a large uncovered pot, and now Rosa poured it into plastic cups with a soup ladle. "We have beans and rice, some meat, and bread." She stressed 'bread' as if it were a delicacy.

"Thank you, it looks wonderful." I knew that tortillas, not bread, were the staple here. "You were so kind to get bread for me."

"The *señora* who is teaching me to cook has a *comedora*," said Rosa, "She sells bread. When I heard that you arrived I went to her and asked her to put some aside for you." She pointed at the bread with the casual air of someone who has connections.

A young woman who I hadn't met yet came and sat down at one of the places. Her name was Felicia, and like Rosa, she seemed friendly.

"*Quién más?*" called Rosa.

A girl in a neatly pressed school uniform hurried in and sat down beside me. "We worked late. I barely had time to change," she said to Rosa. Rosa introduced her as Vera.

Vera bent her knees in a small curtsey. "They told us you might come today."

"Here comes Dina. Make way for the queen," called out a voice from the hall. I recognized the voice to be Katia's.

The young woman that she announced was prim and fair-skinned, with short black ringlets around her face. She stood before me and extended her hand. "Dina. Pleased to meet you."

"Hi, I'm Beth."

"I'm the oldest of the *chicas*," the girl said quickly, looking at the others. "I live here, even though I have graduated, as a favor to Mother Maria. I keep the girls organized, and make sure the chores are done..."

"Yeah, and her shit is chocolate," chided Katia from the sidelines. The other girls, even Rosa, muffled their giggles.

Dina gave Katia a smug look. "We're not all ill bred. Some of us are respectful. We have jobs. We've made the best of our circumstances and we show our gratitude to Mother Maria, who saved every one of us."

"What kind of work do you do?" I was curious, and it seemed a safe question.

"I have my teaching certificate. I expect to get a job in a *colegio* soon."

"Do you have any leads yet? Let me know if I can help in any way." I was supposed to be a counselor, after all.

"That won't be necessary." Dina sat down and asked Rosa for a napkin. "Mother Maria herself is helping." She spread the napkin in her lap and returned her gaze to me. "When are you leaving?"

"I'll be here for a year."

"For what? Are you here to learn Spanish?"

The girl named Felicia rose to my defense, "She already speaks Spanish. Where did you learn, Beth?"

I minored in Spanish in college. And I had a chance to practice with some children I tutored. I was helping them with math. Most of them spoke Spanish at home, so the work was easier for them when I explained things in Spanish."

"I always got A's in English," interjected Dina, "But I don't like foreign languages much. It's something that's easy for me, but not interesting."

Rosa served the others, filling each plate with beans, rice and a chunk of stew meat. After all the plates were full she counted out what was left in the pot and placed an extra piece of meat in my dish.

The girls ate quickly with little conversation.

"The dinner is delicious," I said after a few minutes.

"*Frijoles* Honduran style," said Rosa. "We eat them every day."

"Don't tell her that. She won't want to stay with us," Felicia giggled.

"Oh, but I like beans," I said.

"*Permiso*," said Vera, with an apologetic smile, "I have to hurry or I'll be late for class."

Vera stood up and took her plate to the sink, and Felicia and Dina followed right after. They each rinsed their plates with water from a small bucket that sat on the counter.

I was left alone at the table, my dinner only half eaten. Some of the other girls hung around the front steps and went in and out of the kitchen without saying anything. Then I heard giggling and a jumble of Spanish sprinkled with the word "Beth." What had happened? Had I done something to offend them or to embarrass myself?

I looked down at my food. I'd expected to be in the company of children hungry for affection; I'd imagined holding them close, telling them stories. But these girls looked almost like women and they acted indifferent. I knew enough about teenagers to know they probably weren't. Teenagers were complex, sometimes angry, easily hurt, and difficult to reach. This wasn't what I'd signed up for at all. I wished I could have a tortilla instead of stale white bread. I finished eating, pretending to be absorbed by the sunset on the horizon. When I brought my plate to the sink Rosa took it from me.

"I'll wash it for you."

"Thanks, but tomorrow I'll wash my own." I lowered my voice a bit. "I wish the other girls would come and eat."

"They're waiting for these plates," said Rosa, embarrassed.

I watched the next four girls sit down. This was their dinner routine, then, not a major conspiracy against me. I felt foolish, but also relieved. Maybe I could make plates and cups my first project. I would talk to Mother Maria and see to it that the *Residencia de las Señoritas* had enough for everyone; nothing fancy, heavy-duty plastic would be fine. Or maybe Mother Maria thought that was something they should take care of themselves. If so, I could help them find a way to earn the money. Then they could all eat together, and drink their coffee as slowly as they wanted to.

After supper I went to my room. I was jittery from the coffee, and my mind wouldn't stop working. I thought of the things I could have talked about at dinner. What kind of job did Rosa plan to get as a cook? What were her specialty dishes? What was Vera studying? And how did she manage to work all day and go to night school too? I could at least have showed that I appreciated how difficult that was. Felicia had wanted to make a connection, she'd sent a few shy smiles my way, and she'd made a joke about the food. But I'd been so eager to show my willingness to eat beans

16

that I didn't even laugh — I acted like a person with no sense of humor.

I turned on the lamp, then lay down on my mattress with my head facing the hole in the wall. I was tired, but it didn't keep me from a pointless vigil, watching for roaches.

I thought of home. How appalled my mother would be by the conditions here. Pammy and Sara would see humor in the situation. I could hear them now: "Beth battles three hundred roaches in an attempt to save the world." But their laughter was over two thousand miles and one year away...

My father was with me, I supposed, watching over me as best he could. He would have approved. He would have been the one who understood.

And there was Jake. I'd said goodbye to him just last night, but already his love seemed to belong to another world.

"You're sure this is something you have to do?" he'd asked, when I told him that I'd signed up for a year with Mother Maria and the Sisters of the Living Cross. "I'll be okay," he said finally, "I have a lot of work to do on the house."

The "house" was an empty lot on Holden Lake in rural Massachusetts. Jake bought the land himself. He planned to build the house during his summer breaks from architecture school. On the day he took me to see the lot he showed up with a small oak tree tied to the top of his car. He wanted to plant it next to where the front porch would be. It would take time to build the house, he said. In the meantime, the oak would mature. We carried that tree around the imaginary house instead of cutting through it. We laughed, but we both knew we meant it.

We spent the summer after graduation pretending that I wasn't leaving. We knew the day would come, but we had an unspoken agreement not to talk about it. We rode up to the lake on the weekends, feeling the summer sun against our wet skin. Jake's embraces were like clean ripe fruit. Then in late September we were faced with the reality of a plane ticket to Honduras. I was to leave in January, and now here I was.

Alone. Away from all I loved. I had no choice but to leave, because this work had called me...but had I wanted to get away, too? From my narrow foam mattress in a foreign country, I finally admitted to myself that the answer was yes. I'd wanted to leave them, to find a time and place of my own. A place where no one could hear my thoughts, and where I might summon the courage to look deep inside myself, deeper than I had ever looked before.

I forced myself to close my eyes, leaving my vigil to the lamplight, and waited for sleep to erase time until sunrise.

II

I set the cup of wet plaster on the floor. Don Pablo had mixed just enough plaster to fill the hole in the wall. I crouched down and spread the thick paste into place with the edge of Don Pablo's small putty knife. Just as I finished, there was a knock on the frame of my open door.

At first I did not recognize the young woman in a faded housedress who stood in the doorway. If she had any hair it was completely tucked under a red bandana. Her eyes were dull and downcast, and her dark cheeks looked puffy.

"Luz?"

"I'm here to paint," Luz said.

"Thanks for remembering." I went over to the small ladder and the paint can in the far corner. "I was just about to start."

Luz picked up a paintbrush without a word.

"Is something wrong?" I said. "You seem upset."

"This is how I am," said Luz without looking up.

"Are you sure? We can do this later."

"Later will be the same as now."

Luz didn't seem to want to help, or was her reticence a backward way of reaching out? I pried open the lid of the paint can with the key from the padlock that Don Pablo had put on my door. I stirred the white paint with a wooden stick until it was smooth, thick cream. The smell of paint cut through the dust in the air.

"I'll start on this side of the door and you can you start on the other. We'll meet up in the far corner, okay?" I said.

Luz dipped her brush, turned her back to me, and began to paint. I was focused on painting too, looking to Luz now and then. Soon we settled into a pattern of thick broad strokes to cover the gray cinder blocks, followed by dabs with the end of the brush for the rough grout in between. We worked in silence for almost an hour, mirroring each other in pace and technique, stopping only to pass the ladder back and forth to reach the high parts.

We reached the far corners of the room and began to work toward each other. I caught Luz's eye and smiled. "Where are you from, Luz?"

Luz stepped back, tipped her head to one side, and looked at the wall as if she was creating a picture there. "I was born in the *campo,* outside a town called Juntapeque."

"Where's that? What's it like?"

"It's near the Guatemalan border. All I remember is a house in the woods."

"Really? Nothing else?"

"Just that. And the taste of my tin bowl. My mother couldn't understand why I liked to lick my empty dish. But there was still a taste there, of bean broth and then just salt. I didn't stop until I could taste the bare metal. My mother never had to wash that bowl."

I was careful not to look up. "It must have been a hard life."

Luz shrugged. "We managed to survive. Until my father left us."

"Where did he go?"

"Another woman ⸺ a *bruja.*" Luz looked at me out of the corner of her eye. "Do you believe in witches?"

"I can understand why people might be afraid of them," I answered carefully, "but no, I don't believe in them myself."

"Because you've never been cursed by one," Luz challenged. "I have. The spell that she cast on my mother ruined us."

"What happened?"

"The rain didn't come. The grass turned brown. The chickens started dying. Then there was a fire, and we had to patch the wall with a plastic sheet. When the rain came it poured so much the tomatoes rotted on the vine before they were ripe. We had nothing to eat. My mother came to Tegucigalpa. She couldn't get work; the spell was too strong. No one wanted to help a poor Indian who barely spoke Spanish. After the money ran out we lived in the street. Finally, she left me here."

"Where is your mother now?" Luz was silent a moment, then looked me in the eye. "Did you come all the way from the United States just to watch us suffer?"

"I didn't come to watch you suffer, Luz. I came to help — I wanted to be with you."

Luz put on a bored look, but it seemed to be covering something else. "What for?"

I wanted to move closer to Luz, but I knew I should step back instead. "I know it can be hard to be alone. And I thought maybe you girls could use a friend. That's all."

"Some of the others have been through a lot," Luz admitted. She started to paint and looked at me again.

"Tell me more about the farm," I asked lightly. "What else do you remember? What's the first thing?"

Luz didn't speak for a while. She kept her eyes on the wall she was painting. "Sleeping in my hammock," she said finally. "I remember waking up in the night. My father was yelling at my mother, *gritos* that could raise the roof. He was drunk. Then he pushed her. He had her down on their bed, his hands around her neck, and he shook her until she couldn't even cry out. He wouldn't stop. I was afraid he would kill her."

I was as shocked by the story as by Luz's matter-of-fact tone. "What did you do?"

"At first I didn't know what to do. I thought if he heard a noise he might let her go, so I threw myself out of the hammock."

Luz held her head up as she recalled this, almost proud of herself.

"Then what happened?"

21

"He let her go. She came over and picked me up. I was crying. She was, too. He left the room and by the time we were calm he was asleep in the kitchen chair from the drink."

Luz stepped back to decide where to put the next stroke.

Intent on Luz's story, I had stopped working, but now I took up my brush again. "What about you? Were you hurt?"

"My head was bleeding, but I was okay. My mother always said it was that fall that made me *tonto*. Stupid. But I think I must have been stupid already..."

"Luz, you shouldn't think that way about yourself. You're not stupid. I bet you're good at a lot if things."

Luz considered this. "There are some things I'm good at. No one can embroider the way I do. Flowers, birds — I can make pictures with a needle. In sewing class I'm the best, too. I can copy any dress. I just look at it and cut. They try to teach me to measure and make paper patterns, but my dresses come out better without one. I have the *magia* of the Indians with a needle.

"But math and reading — that's another story. It's my third time in sixth grade. When I first came to *La Casa* the teacher made me stand up in front of the class to show them a malnourished Indian."

Then Luz was quiet, painting toward me, intent on her strokes. After a while I spoke again.

"What ever happened to your mother, Luz? Leaving you here must have been the hardest thing she ever did. Does she ever... Do you ever see her?"

Luz shook away the question. "I don't know where she is. Anyway, she's half crazy — afraid of my father. By the time he left she was already lost. My mother is dead, Beth, but the poor thing still has to get up and walk around every day."

"What about your father? Have you seen him since he left?"

Luz was silent for a moment. "He came here looking for me. It was a long time ago. He wanted me to go to live with him, but I refused."

"I can understand why. You must have been angry."

"At him? I don't waste any feelings on him." Luz laughed. "But I'd kill him if I could. Without a single regret."

"Do you mean that, Luz?"

"I know it would be a sin," Luz said, staring at the wall, "but sometimes I'd like to go crazy for a day. God forgives *los locos* — they don't have to burn in hell for their *locuras*. They do what they do."

"What would you do if you were crazy?"

"If I were crazy and I knew God would forgive me? Ha. I'd kill my father for what he's done. Then I'd rob a bank or some *rico*, and give all the money to my mother, so she would never have to work again. She could buy a *casita* in Juntapeque and hire a servant. She could keep her garden.

"Then I'd kill myself, too, so I'd be sure that I'd never have to suffer again. After I was dead I'd float down to my mother's garden to visit, and I'd bring rain to refresh her."

We both reached the corner; our white strokes touched each other. "It's done," said Luz. The spell was broken.

Before I could say thank you, Luz put down her brush, backed away from the bright white walls, and mumbled a goodbye.

The day that I painted my room was also the day when I first met Lola and Theo. I was still thinking about Luz's story while I cleaned the paintbrushes, then I went out for some fresh air. I heard children talking and laughing over by the vegetable garden. And someone was singing. The voice was so beautiful and full of love... It seemed almost out of place here, as if these orphans had a mother after all, at least for the moment. As I got closer I could hear the children's voices more clearly. Their chatter was punctuated by guttural sounds, thick words, and slurs, between the giggles. Then I saw them, an awkward, ragtag bunch. I gathered that they were all handicapped in some way, but it didn't seem to matter as they played in the dirt under an umbrella of song. In the midst of them Sister Paula knelt over a row of freshly turned soil, continuing her song as she carefully placed a tender plant in the center.

When she saw me Sister Paula smiled up at me from crouched knees and offered me a spade. The leaves of yesterday's tomato plants had already lost their limpness, and the fragile stems were standing firm. Now they were putting in a row of cilantro in front of the tomatoes.

I joined the gardening party, and the children gathered around to meet me and shake my hand. We made a game out of letting them all try to pronounce my name, with its foreign sounding "th."

"Bef," they said. Then "Bet." Then "Betti."

I shook each hand until I had greeted all but one, a little girl who knelt beside Sister Paula. She was tiny, but from her demeanor I guessed that she was about four. The children went back to their games but the girl stayed. She watched Sister Paula, then mimicked her, placing one stem at a time in the soft earth, pressing them into place with her fingers.

That's how it is, I thought. There's always that one child who understands.

I knelt down to speak to the girl. "What's your name?"

"This is Lola," said Sister Paula. "She's one of God's special ones."

"I like your garden, Lola. Can you say my funny name?"

"She doesn't speak," Sister Paula explained.

"Do you know why?"

"Early trauma maybe. Or simple neglect. We really don't know. She was brought to me by one of the *encargadas* when she was two. She wasn't walking or talking. They called her 'retarded.' I thought she seemed fine, just quiet, and told them so, but Mother Maria insisted that I take her in with mine." Sister Paula turned to Lola and caressed the top of her head. "So I made her my special helper."

Lola smiled and kept at her work.

After we had worked for about a half an hour more, Sister Paula invited me to the *casita* she shared with the children. "Ophelia will have lunch ready for the children, and we can have a lemonade and get acquainted."

All the children but Lola ran ahead toward a house that was set apart from the others by a chain-link fence. I presumed that the fence, the separateness, must have been for the safety of the children. A women, who I assumed must be Ophelia, come out of the house to open the gate.

As we got closer to the house I heard an ape-like scream coming from inside. Then I saw a full-grown boy on his knees in the doorway, swinging his fists. His straight dark shoots of hair were matted around his head, and his eyes were wild with anger. The boy had only one leg. The stump of the other leg was propped up on a narrow skateboard.

"Is he—"

"That's Theo," Sister Paula said.

He started to propel himself toward us on the skateboard. Lola, who had been by Sister Paula's side all the while, began backing away from him.

Theo flew after her, pushing the skateboard forward with his hands, his face reddened with rage and the force of his angry shouts. The housemother chased after him, almost caught up to him, then backed away as he swung his fists wildly at her.

Lola ran to one side to avoid him, then changed direction and headed back through the gate toward the *casita*. She tried to close the gate, but when she couldn't secure the latch she left it ajar and ran for the house. In the meantime, Theo had turned around and propelled himself toward the gate. He charged through it and caught up with Lola at the front door, skated a circle around her to block her entry, then grabbed her by the leg and dragged her down. Just as he was about to strike her with his fists, Sister Paula, who'd been running toward them, reached him, blocked the blow, and caught Theo by the arm in one smooth movement.

"Theo, look at me." Sister Paula took his head between her two hands, and held his face close to hers, as if she were reaching inside him with her eyes. "Let me help you calm down."

25

She embraced Theo, chest to chest, taking slow deep breaths for him, then with him, until he was calm. Then she guided him over to the garden, where he slid off his skateboard and crawled over to a bush to pick a red hibiscus flower.

Sister Paula walked along beside him as he skated over to Lola.

"Theo's sorry," Sister Paula said to the girl, then she bent down to Theo, her face close to his. "Theo's sorry," she said, entering him through the eyes again. "Now give her the flower, please."

Theo presented the flower. Then, of his own volition, he gave Lola a gentle kiss on the cheek. A few moments later the housemother guided the children back to the yard and Sister Paula returned to my side and approached the house.

I still had my eye on Theo. He seemed dangerous, and I wondered if he was mentally ill. "How did he lose his leg?" I asked.

"We don't know for sure. He was begging in the street when I found him. An accident, one hopes, although sometimes these injuries are inflicted intentionally..."

"By the military?"

"No, by desperate parents who think a maimed beggar-child brings in a better daily sum."

I crossed my arms, trying to brace myself against this awful reality. I looked at Paula again. "But isn't he dangerous? For Lola, and the others."

Paula's eyes crunched as though the sun were suddenly too much for her. "He rarely strikes out at the other children like that...and he's truly sorry afterward." She paused. "I keep a careful eye on him."

"You're good with him," I said. "How long has he been here?"

"It will be ten years this April. Goodness, Theo is almost fifteen." She looked up at the sky to check her math, then opened the door and gestured for me to step inside. "He's hard to love at times, but I'd rather leave this world altogether than stop loving Theo."

III

When I pulled myself out of bed it was still dark outside. Five-thirty. I splashed my face with water and combed my hair. By the time I was dressed the room had filled with orange light. It was my third day at *La Casa* and I was finally going to meet Mother Maria. Mercedes had brought me the message yesterday afternoon. I was to meet Mother Maria in her office in the big house just before six.

I found Mother Maria behind a large desk. Her clean neck bulged where it met the clerical collar of her navy blue dress, and an electric fan blew cool air on her as she read her morning correspondence. When she saw me she smiled warmly.

"I've been waiting for you, dear." She held onto my hand as she spoke. "How are you settling in? Do you like my daughters?"

"I like your daughters very much."

"That's good." Mother Maria looked me in the eye. "There was a time when I knew every one of them by name. But now, with so many children coming...I spend my time raising the money to provide for them, to build more *casitas*. They're in my prayers every day of course, but they need someone down, there, with them." Mother Maria stepped around the desk and took me by the arm in a way that let me know she was counting on me to be that some-one.

"It's almost six," she said. "The *padre* should be here."

"So you start the day with Mass every morning?" I asked.

"When the *padre* can come, yes. But this isn't how I start the day. We begin with matins, usually just Sister Paula and myself. You're welcome to join us, Beth."

"Oh, thank you," I said, hearing my words ring false. My faith was based on helping those in need, not morning prayers before sunrise.

Mother Maria smiled. "I know it seems boring, praying the psalms year in and year out — but they deliver a wellspring of strength, my dear."

Before I could answer we were at the chapel door. Mother Maria ushered me in and sat in the row behind me.

Daylight filtered into the chapel through the stained glass. The room glowed with soft light and muted colors, and I could feel the warmth of the light on my face. The simple altar of dark wood was dressed with a brightly colored hand-woven runner. A stout candle emitted a steady flame.

On the wall behind the altar hung a life-sized crucifix. I had been to church all my life, but I had never seen a crucifix like this before. This Jesus, drawn in Honduran colors, had his head turned to one side, his jaw set against the pain. His blood was painted on in bright red drops the size of pennies.

Dina and a few of the other girls came in and sat in the row behind Mother Maria. Then the *padre,* with padded steps, took his place at the altar. He cleaned the glazed clay chalice scrupulously with a linen cloth, then set the cup by the candle, folded the cloth in front of it, and bowed his head.

Sister Paula entered with Lola, who hung onto Sister Paula's leg while they walked. When Sister Paula knelt down, Lola took a place beside her. She folded her hands the way Sister Paula did, then peeked into the space between her thumbs, as if she was making sure that she had some of what Sister Paula had.

As the priest spoke, I tried following along in Spanish, but I soon gave in to the English version, which, when prompted by the familiar rhythms and gestures, recited itself in my head.

After Holy Communion, Mother Maria led the prayers and meditation. Her voice came out soft, sweet and high as she said a simple prayer for strength and holy guidance. She offered God the obedience of all those present.

Then we sat in silence. I had to admit that the stillness felt good. I pushed aside the words that were forming in my mind, things I wanted to say to Mother Maria: a program in independent living...self-government by the young women...freedom earned through responsibility...

"It's all there in my notes," I told myself, "put it away."

Finally my mind was quiet and I felt the silence of the others amplify my own. Our prayers faced each other like mirrors, creating an infinite progression of mute hope until the air was thick with the serene silent words of God.

After a while Mother Maria rose to her feet. The Mass was ended. We should go forth in peace.

After the others had filed out, Mother Maria led me to the dining room and invited me to sit down. Mercedes poured coffee and served us beans, tortillas and sweetened rice with milk.

Mother Maria tore off part of a tortilla and used it to pick up a mouthful of beans. "So tell me, Beth, why have you come here?"

I didn't have a ready answer. I had prepared to talk about the girls, not myself.

"I've had so many blessings in my life," I began, "I guess I wanted to give something back." I groped for words in Mother Maria's language. "As a way of thanking God, I guess."

Mother Maria nodded understanding and smiled. "And my girls? What shall we do with them?" I pulled my notes out of my bag and set them on the corner of the table. Mother Maria listened as I described my ideas. Some of the girls needed counseling — probably all of them did — and I would offer that to the girls who seemed receptive. Many of the girls had job skills, and the basic education that *La Casa* had provided, but they needed to make a transition from living by the rules at *La Casa* to being out on their own. I outlined a plan for a gradual approach to independent living that would teach them to make responsible choices.

Mother Maria listened, and seemed to take a real interest in the details, so I took out the chart that I had sketched out the night before, and unfolded it on the table.

"Each girl will be assigned a level — white, yellow, orange, green, blue. She earns privileges by taking on increasing responsibilities. For example, when a girl gets a job and pays for her clothing and food expenses, she's green. That means she can come and go as she pleases during the daytime, and she can use the sign-out sheet in the evening. The privileges act as rewards, but they also teach the girls to make decisions. They'll learn about working, managing money ... when they turn eighteen you could offer them the option of paying rent to stay on in the *Residencia* for one more year, or they can rent a room somewhere on the outside. Either way, they'll be ready to take care of themselves." I looked up, expecting a smile and nod from Mother Maria, who had seemed in agreement with the whole idea so far.

She scanned the chart. "What about Mass?"

"I guess I didn't include that," I said slowly, knowing the chart would betray me if I tried to pretend otherwise. "It seemed to me that their spiritual lives are private, that only God can judge that."

"Yes, that's true." Mother Maria thought a minute. "But they can't be allowed to reach the highest level." She tapped her finger on the blue bar at the top of the chart. "Only those who come to daily Mass can do that."

I measured my words carefully. I wanted to show respect for Mother Maria, but I knew the program would fail if the focus were obligatory daily Mass.

"It's not that I don't think religious faith is important," I began, "but there are other ways to foster that. The levels I've developed focus on the practical skills that they'll need to survive."

Mother Maria shook her head. "But these girls need prayer more than anything..."

I wrote *"Misa"* down on my notepad with a question mark beside it. I'd have to figure out a way to make this work.

Mother Maria rose to go. "I'm sorry to leave you, Beth. I have an appointment at seven."

The meeting with Mother Maria was over? My face gave away my surprise.

"Don't worry," said Mother Maria. "You can finish your breakfast."

"It's not that," I said, caught chewing on a tortilla. "It's just that I had a few more things to talk about..."

Mother Maria put a hand on my shoulder. "It's all clear to me, dear. The levels will be fine. They may even help."

"I was planning to have a house meeting for all the girls on Sunday," I said quickly. "I'd like to present the program to them, and explain my role. It would help so much if you could come and show them that you support this."

"Of course I'll come." Mother Maria turned to go again.

"Just one more thing," I said. "The girls want to go to a dance at the *Club Siglo 20*."

Mother Maria raised a cautious eyebrow. "Going out without permission, now dances? I don't know, Beth. I don't see how dancing will teach my girls to keep themselves pure."

"I see it as an opportunity for them to learn to handle freedom responsibly. They'll have a curfew..."

Mother Maria shook her head and sighed. "That's not how we've done things in the past. We've been strict. Even then we've had girls getting pregnant," she lowered her voice, "even prostitution." She looked at me, relenting a bit. "You say you can teach them... Maybe you can. I'm going to leave this up to you. You're in charge of the *Residencia de las Señoritas* now."

I spread my soapy towel over the washboard that was built into the cement tub in the backyard. I didn't want special treatment, and I was determined to wash my clothes by hand like the girls did. I held the towel taut with one hand and, with the other, turned a small bucket of water onto it with a quick flat splash. The soap rose about the towel and settled again.

The clothes I had already washed hung from a clothesline that was tied to a pole on one end and a papaya tree on the other. The heels of my socks held their stains, and my white undergarments were a bit stiff, but at least they were germ free and fresh. It was the best I could do with cold water and a hard cake of soap.

I thought again about the meeting with Mother Maria. I had admired her so much — the way she saved the children from the fire. I remembered finding the pamphlet in the file marked "International Volunteer Opportunities" at the university employment office. The image of young Mother Maria, bent over a tent full of children, was what made me write to *La Casa* in the first place. It was hard to reconcile the image that had inspired me with the nun who seemed only to care about attendance at Mass and virgin status for the girls. I wasn't being entirely fair. Mother Maria was obviously a sincerely prayerful woman. Religious in the old-fashioned way, with all its contradictions... And she had been open-minded enough to agree to try things my way. Still, I couldn't help but wonder if I had made a mistake in coming here.

I was worried about Luz, too. She seemed to be suffering so. What had Katia meant when she said that Luz was *"lunática,"* crazy? As the word stretched itself out in Spanish, I saw the root was *luna*, the moon. Was being controlled by its cycles what made a person crazy? Or were those cycles and moods what made us human, able to feel?

I didn't think Luz was crazy. It was just that she was born with nerve endings on the entire surface of her soul. And she couldn't stand to see her mother hurt.

I wrung the towel one last time, but it was still dripping when I unrolled it. Meanwhile, Katia came out with a pile of laundry. Without makeup her skin looked gray and she had lines around her eyes. Still, I thought she looked better like this.

"Look at Beth," she said, even though there was no one else nearby. "She even washes her clothes in the *pila* like us." She pointed to my towel. "It's still soapy. Let me show you how to do it."

She took the towel and stood beside me. "You need to get all the soap out first," she said.

She scooped the water from the *pila* with the plastic bowl and raised it up high, cutting the flow with her fingers, so that it fell in three forceful streams. As she rinsed several times she gently moved the towel back and forth — letting it ripple, easing out the soap. Then she expertly wrung the towel, and hung it on the fence to dry in the sun.

"See? It's easy. Use your hands, not your whole arms. You looked like you were doing exercises. It's too tiring that way."

She pointed to my underwear that hung on the line, "You weren't going to wear those like that, were you?" She rewashed them on the washboard with swift strokes that made lather. Then she rinsed them and handed them to me.

"Thanks, Katia." I laughed at myself uneasily.

"And what about the dance on Saturday? Everyone is wondering if you're going to let us go."

"I'm still thinking about it. I'll let you know tomorrow, OK?"

Sister Paula led me down the hall. "We can talk in here."

I knew from my previous visit that the house where Sister Paula and her children lived was identical to the *Residencia de las Señoritas*, and Sister Paula lived in a room just like mine at the back. Now she went into the room ahead of me and stood in front of the open window, where a row of potted herbs thrived in the sun. Her desk was tidy. A leather-bound French Bible and a Spanish-French dictionary stood between two bookends, and a notepad with a half-written letter lay on the writing blotter. The wall around the desk was covered with pictures the children had made, drawings of flowers with bright waxy petals, lines and scribbles with a child's name printed carefully in the corner, even a crayon portrait of Sister Paula that bore an uncanny resemblance.

Sister Paula pulled the rocking chair from the corner and offered it to me. She sat down across from me on her wooden desk chair.

"What did you want to see me about?"

I hesitated. "I want to ask your advice about the dance on Saturday. The girls really want to go. Mother Maria said it was up to me, but I can tell she doesn't approve."

"What about you? What do you think?"

"Well, my approach to working with them is supposed to be based on trust." I looked up at her. "I think they should be allowed to go."

"I agree with you about trusting them. Eventually they're going to live on the outside. And unless we believe that they're all called to be celibate nuns like me," she said, holding up the ends of an imaginary wimple with a laugh, "we'd like them to be like ordinary girls — go to dances, and marry someday. I'd be inclined to let them go. Just be sure to give them some guidance about how to behave."

Now that Sister Paula agreed, the decision seemed simple. They would go. My feet stuck to the floor. I didn't want to leave just yet.

Sister Paula started to rise, but caught my hesitation and sat back down again. "So how is it going otherwise?"

I recognized that look; I had given it to others enough times. Sister Paula was worried that I wouldn't be able to make it here.

"Fine. I worked at a camp for teens a few summers ago. Some of them had run away, been mistreated... I know what to expect." I saw Sister Paula seeing through me. "Could be better," I admitted, "but fine."

"That's good. I remember how difficult my first days here were." Sister Paula got up and poured some water from a plastic pitcher into an electric hot pot. "I can offer you some tea in a little bit."

We sat through an awkward silence then smiled at it together. From the *sala* I heard a loud guffaw and the sound of wheels rolling across the floor.

Sister Paula saw the question in my eyes. "That's Theo."

"You really found him in the street?"

"Yes, or he found me. It was the day I arrived here. I had stopped in the *centro* to buy some fresh flowers to bring to Mother Maria. I was about to get back into my taxi when Theo scooted over to me and pulled on my skirt. He asked for money and a candy." Sister Paula shook her head. "He lives for sweets. I would love to meet the person who gave him his first piece of candy."

"Then what happened?"

"Once he caught my eye I couldn't look away. I tried to get into the cab, but he was still there, holding onto my skirt from his skateboard. Finally, I lifted him into my lap. He cried out at first, so I set him down. I thought he didn't want to come with me, but all he wanted was the skateboard. Once he had it he reached for me again. I asked him his name and fed him lemon drops all the way to *La Casa.*"

I remembered the flower girl I'd left in the street. "You saved him," I said aloud. "You changed his life."

"And he changed mine. Completely. Mother Maria didn't want a beggar-child who had already spent several years in the street. She refused to be responsible for him."

"Didn't she want to help him? Saving orphan children is supposed to be her calling."

"The children at *La Casa* are abandoned and orphaned, often terribly poor, but they haven't been on the street alone like Theo had. She didn't think he could ever adjust to life here."

"But she was wrong."

"Not entirely. She was right about the skateboard. I tried for a year to get him to use a wheelchair. He'd crawl out as soon as my back was turned. The skateboard is unsafe and filthy, but it's fast. And he still sneaks down to the city and begs. We can tell because he comes back covered with dust and his face is sticky from eating lollipops and gumdrops. But he always comes home at night. He knows he belongs here and he knows he's loved."

"What made Mother Maria change her mind?"

"She didn't. She said he could only stay if I agreed to live here instead of in the big house. I don't think she thought I would do it. Even now, after ten years, she still doesn't accept him entirely. She says that he'll have to move out when he grows a beard — that he'll be a danger to the girls in the house because he can't control his impulses." Sister Paula rolled her eyes. "She forgets that he's a child inside."

"From what I read about her I thought she'd be more understanding," I said, "more committed to the children."

"Well, she's given her life to them, that should count for something." Sister Paula raised her eyebrows in a stern peak then let them go soft again. "She's a good woman with a wise heart, Beth. You'll see that when you get to know her. My differences with Mother Maria aren't as big as they seem. And none of us would be here without her. Not even Theo."

"Still, he's lucky that he has you. They all are. What made you decide to come here?"

"I didn't. This was a random assignment."

"You mean you didn't choose this? But you're so perfectly suited to it."

"I did choose. I chose to do whatever God asked of me. My order believes that we are servants of God before everything. We pledge poverty, charity, and obedience like the others. But for the Sisters of the Living Cross that means dying to yourself, your wants, your life. The willingness to accept a random assignment expresses that." Sister Paula looked down at her hands and smiled. "And some of us believe that the random assignment leaves a little room for the hand of fate."

It was a lot to take in, but beautiful in a way.

Sister Paula turned her attention to the tea. She unplugged the pot and dropped a tea ball full of loose leaves inside it. She left it to steep and sat down again across from me.

"What about you, Beth? What made you come here to *La Casa*?"

I shrugged. "I believe in what *La Casa* does. I wanted to contribute something."

"You could have sent a check," Sister Paula teased.

I laughed, "That's what my mother said, but I had to come."

"So you're like me. You had no choice."

"I didn't feel like I did — with so much suffering in the world... I thought I could change things somehow, as foolish as that may sound."

"Never mind about sounding foolish. What would you change if you could?"

"I'd make the world safe." As I uttered the word 'safe' I felt a weight lift from my chest. "A safe place to be born into, so that wherever you were — the Boston projects or the slums of Bangladesh or a place like here — you'd be sure of the basic comforts, a loving pair of hands." I wasn't used to saying these things out loud. "I guess I have a morbid obsession with the suffering of others."

"Some of us call that compassion," said Sister Paula with a small smile.

"It feels more like fear."

"Of what?"

"I don't know. Of not being able to make a difference, maybe. Or of being born again myself. Or even in this life, I want to be able to walk in the world, to survive, no matter where I end up..."

Sister Paula poured the tea and held the cup out to me, not letting go until she was sure that I held it with my two hands.

I took a sip of tea. I was talking in circles, making things sound like some personal quest, as if it wasn't about the girls at all. "I'm probably not making myself clear..."

"I'm afraid that's as clear as it gets." Sister Paula sipped her tea and was quiet a moment, assessing me again. "You've come here to *La Casa,* to walk with our girls. How's that going? Are your feet sore yet?"

I smiled. "Yes, and my heart is aching a bit, too."

"Why is that?"

"I painted my room on Tuesday. Luz helped me. It gave me a chance to get to know her a bit."

"She's a lonely girl."

I nodded. "I'm worried about her. Do you think she could be suffering from depression?"

"I guess we're all a little depressed now and then. Do you mean clinical depression?"

"Yes."

"Why do you want to know?"

"As a counselor I should be finding out what her problems are, trying to help..."

"I know how you feel. When I first came here I kept imagining cures that might be available for my children. It took me almost five years to stop diagnosing them. I wish that they had the good fortune to be born in France or the United States, but they're here, and they have no one. We give them the best care we can. But the main thing they need is love."

"Are you saying it doesn't matter if Luz is mentally ill or not?"

"No. It matters. But ask yourself what you would do differently if she were. *La Casa* can't afford the treatment she needs, even if it were available here. You don't necessarily want people looking too closely at her situation, her age. And the label certainly won't help her."

"I'd thought of that. But what can I do for her?"

"Do what you would do if she were your sister. Think about what you would want, if you were Luz."

I had been taught that a good counselor helps people without getting too emotionally involved. Now, Sister Paula was saying that getting deeply involved, caring as much as I could, was the most important thing.

Sister Paula sighed. "I don't mean to confuse you, Beth."

"You're not. I can see that you're right about Luz. I wasn't going to suggest medication or anything like that. I was thinking that it might help her to get in contact with her mother though, even if it's just for a brief visit."

Sister Paula looked down. "You're right to think there might be some healing for her there but, oh, poor Luz. She's had a tough time. A number of years ago her father came looking for her. She pretended not to recognize him — she even told Mother Maria that her parents were dead." Sister Paula shook her head. "And Mother Maria believed her and sent him away. Since then Luz won't even admit that her parents are alive."

"But — " I checked myself before I said more. Luz had trusted me with the truth. "I still think it might be worth a try."

"It may be. I'll help you any way I can."

"Thanks." I put my cup down. "I know I have to figure things out for myself, but what would you do if you were me?"

"You're already doing it. Listen to them. Live beside them every day. Love them if you can. I think that's all."

Sister Paula studied the crayon drawings on her wall for a moment. "There is one other practical thing that you can do. Many of the girls don't have their identification papers. I know Felicia has a scholarship that's been held up for a month because she's been unable to get the papers she needs to register. If it's not taken care of soon she'll lose her place.

"It's been a problem for a number of the older children. Nowadays every child admitted to *La Casa* has papers. It's required for their protection, and it makes it possible to process adoptions quickly. But in the early days, when your girls came to *La Casa*, Mother Maria just took whoever showed up on her doorstep.

"The girls need their papers to apply for work, to vote, and now the political situation makes it even touchier. They're checking IDs everywhere, stopping whole busloads to find refugees from Nicaragua or El Salvador. With your dark hair and eyes you should carry your passport at all times, too. The police — soldiers really, it's just one armed-force here — could give you trouble. Last week one of our boys was picked up. He mentioned Mother Maria and they called to verify who he was. But we won't always be that lucky. Of course the girls are vulnerable in other ways, if the police are allowed to cart them off like that. And when they are on their own they won't have Mother Maria to protect them."

"What exactly can I do?"

"You can help them go to the birth registry and look for their names. It's difficult because they don't always know their exact birth date or who their mothers and fathers are. There's a lot of bureaucratic red tape. And if a girl is from a smaller town, they're not likely to be registered here in Tegucigalpa."

"What then?"

"The only record would be in the towns where they were born. They should be listed in the town register or on the baptismal records at the church. Church documents are recognized, as long as the town clerk has signed them."

"So if their papers aren't here in the capital we'd have to go all the way to their birthplaces to get them?" I couldn't believe the system could be so archaic. "Like Joseph and Mary?"

"At least you wouldn't have to ride a donkey all the way." Sister Paula laughed then turned serious. "It's not something they should do alone. Our children don't know how to get around in the rural areas, even though many of them were born there. They could get picked up or be challenged by the police. The presence of a representative of *La Casa,* especially an American, would make the trip much safer."

I sat back and thought a moment. Leaving the city was the one thing I had promised my mother I wouldn't do. "Stay near the Sisters," she had said, when she found out that Honduras was described by the State Department as a moderate-risk country with a heavy military presence. "Don't go looking for trouble."

"What would the trips involve?" I asked.

"Uncomfortable bus trips, long lines, rudimentary lodging. It would be difficult, but I think you'd be up to the task. Don't you?"

IV

I sent the girls off to the *Club Siglo 20* with a few simple rules: come home at eleven, walk together in groups of three or more, and don't take the *Camino Viejo*. According to Sister Paula that old walking path wasn't safe, not even in the daylight.

Just before eleven o'clock the girls returned from the party. Through the front window I saw Vera and Rosa saying goodbye to their boyfriends. They came inside smiling. Vera had forced Rosa to let her hair down for the party. Now their matching hairstyles made them look like sisters. Felicia followed still catching her breath. She must have hurried to make the curfew.

Dina sauntered in a few minutes later. "Oh, I missed curfew," she shrugged.

"Where are the others?" I asked.

"I didn't see Katia coming home. She may have taken the *Camino Viejo*." Vera frowned. "She does that sometimes..."

"And what about Suyapa and Luz?"

"Suyapa follows Katia," said Felicia. "Luz could be with them...but she wanders at night, too."

"I don't think I saw her dancing," said Rosa aloud to herself.

"The dance is over at midnight," Felicia offered, "so they can't be too long."

After an awkward silence the girls said good night and shuffled to their rooms. If they knew more they weren't telling.

I sat down at the kitchen table to wait.

At about three in the morning I woke with a start. I had fallen asleep at the table and now my neck was sore. Where were the girls? Could they have come home and gone to bed without my hearing them? I hoped against reason that this was so, but found three empty beds when I checked their room.

Before I'd fallen asleep I'd been irritated, even a little angry, that the girls had disobeyed curfew. But now I was scared, and worried about their safety. Katia could be up to no good at this hour, and I hated to think of her leading the others into trouble. If Luz had wandered off on her own it could be even worse... Mother Maria would blame me if something happened, and she had every right to. I was about to go and wake Sister Paula when I heard the sound of muffled voices and scrambling feet at the back of the house.

I looked out the back door to find Katia and Suyapa trying to pry open the wooden shutters of the bedroom window. They were all right, and Luz was with them.

I stepped outside, letting the door slam shut behind me.

Luz and Suyapa jumped, but Katia giggled. "We're sorry we're late, Beth. We didn't have a watch."

Luz and Suyapa walked carefully around me, but Katia came close, brushing my shoulder in a way that felt like a shove as she passed.

"We were at the dance." Her large body swayed and her speech slurred. "We didn't know it was past eleven, that's all. Good night, Beth."

"Not so fast." I placed a hand on Katia's arm. "The dance ended at midnight. I want to know where you've been."

Katia slapped my hand away. "Don't touch me. Nobody is going to tell me what to do." She went to her room and slammed the door shut.

My hand smarted. I resisted the temptation to follow Katia. It would be better to let her sleep it off. I'd talk to her in the morning.

I turned to Luz. "Where were you? Why weren't you home at eleven?"

Luz looked down at her feet and burrowed deep into her silence.

"The other girls didn't see you at the dance or on the way home. You took the *Camino Viejo,* didn't you?"

"Katia and Suyapa were going that way. We were three — I had to stay with them." She looked up at me. "And now you're angry. You're through with me." Luz ran to her room and closed the door behind her.

"I'm not through with you, Luz," I called after her. "I was worried..."

I closed my eyes. I knew I was handling this poorly, making a bad situation worse. When I opened my eyes Suyapa stood before me, waiting to be noticed.

"Do you want to tell me what happened?" I asked.

Suyapa's eyes were smudged with eyeliner and swollen with fatigue. She was dressed in the same style as Katia, tight jeans and bold makeup, but instead of looking cheap she looked like a chubby little girl playing dress up. Her arms hung at her side as she sniffed to clear her sinuses.

She began speaking in a slow monotone. "Katia wanted to stop and visit one of her friends on the way to the dance. She said we could make some money. She said it would only take a few minutes.

"When we got to his house there was a party going on — Katia's friend Gerardo and some other men. Luz said not to go in, that they were drunk, but Katia went anyway. A few minutes later she came out. She said Gerardo would give us some money if we came inside for a drink. Just one drink. And she promised she would take me shopping tomorrow for American jeans," Suyapa paused to looked down at her borrowed jeans, "a pair of my own."

"But Luz said no. She told me to stay outside with her. After a while Katia's friend came out. He said I could have five *lempiras* if

I let him kiss me. Just one kiss. But Luz said no, and pulled me across the street.

"Luz and I were scared, but we didn't want to leave Katia, so we waited there all night. Then she came out. She had twenty *lempiras* and she said we could each have one for waiting so long. That's all. We didn't go in the house, Beth, I promise."

Suyapa looked down. She was too slow-witted to realize what had happened. I could hardly believe it myself.

I put an arm around Suyapa. "I believe you, Suyapa. Now get some rest. We'll talk more in the morning."

Katia was late for Mass the next morning. She slipped in just before communion, and got in line behind the girls. She was still wearing her clothes from the night before and it looked like she hadn't even washed her face. As she took the host in her mouth, all I could think of was her pulling on Suyapa's arm, trying to trick her into kissing a stranger with the promise of new clothes. Katia knelt and made the sign of the cross. She kept her head down. Prayer was convenient, I thought, when it hid bloodshot eyes.

After the closing hymn I hung back and waited for Sister Paula. We filed out together in silence.

"Beth, you look terrible. Are you feeling okay?" Sister Paula asked when we got outside.

"Just tired. I was up until three last night waiting for Katia to get home."

"From the dance?"

"She didn't go. She talked about going all week and then she visited some boyfriend instead. She's really out of control. And she took Suyapa and Luz with her." Somehow I couldn't bring myself to use the word prostitution with Sister Paula. "I don't think she belongs with the other girls."

"Do you want to throw her out?"

The intention sounded cruel when Sister Paula said it out loud. "No. But I can't let her —"

Sister Paula put an arm around me. "Katia's a hard one, I know. She's built herself an armor so thick it's easy to forget she has a heart inside. But she's scared, Beth. She's been through some terrible things."

I felt my shoulders relax and accepted the embrace. "She has to take responsibility for her actions," I insisted. "I want to help her, but I can't let her put a girl like Suyapa in danger."

When I got back to the house the girls were gathered in the *sala*, filling it with laughter and excited chatter.

"Rosa's making pancakes with honey," announced Vera.

"We were talking about the meeting this afternoon," said Felicia. "Do you think Mother Maria will really come?"

"She has never come before," said Luz, still sullen from the night before.

"What is the meeting about?" asked Vera.

I sat down at the table across from Vera. "It's a house meeting. We'll have one every week, to talk about how we are living together — chores and house rules. And we'll work on plans for the future, when you'll be out on your own."

I paused to test the response to this. The girls were quiet. Then Vera nodded, and Felicia and Rosa exchanged smiles.

Rosa hummed as she reached into the back of the pantry closet for the baking ingredients. She pulled out a box of baking soda and then dropped it on the ground. "Ach!" she exclaimed as she shook off several roaches that were crawling on the box of baking soda. "What a disgrace. Mother Maria will see how dirty this kitchen is."

I seized the opportunity. "Why don't we clean up the kitchen after breakfast? It won't take long if we all pitch in."

"Are you going to help?" Felicia asked me.

"I live here, don't I?"

After breakfast we lined up every bucket, broom, scrub brush and sponge that we could find. We would empty out the cupboards, refrigerator and pantry, sweep then wash every surface, and put everything back again. After the girls had emptied the refrigerator, I got my radio and set it up on the kitchen table. Felicia turned the volume all the way up and clapped one hand against her soapy sponge as she made her way back to the refrigerator. They probably could hear the music all the way to the big house, but I didn't care. The girls danced and laughed as they worked.

Everything was piled up on the kitchen table and the girls were washing the insides of the cabinets. I stepped back to do a head count. Katia was missing.

I found her in the back yard standing underneath the mango tree, peeling a green mango with a knife.

"Don't worry, Beth. I'm helping. I'm preparing a *merienda*. They can't work so hard with nothing to eat."

"What are you making?"

"Green mangos with salt." Katia took the salt shaker from where she had set it on the *pila* and unscrewed the top. She poured a small mound of salt into the palm of her hand, rubbed a slice of mango in it, and handed it to me. "Hondurans love to eat it this way. Watch out, it's sour."

I took a bite. "Wow, it *is* sour, but I like it. I'll get a plate so we can slice some for everyone."

I returned with a glass plate. Katia was searching the low branches of the tree, absentmindedly slapping the knife blade against her palm as she looked for suitable fruit.

I stood by her and looked up, not sure what she was looking for. I pointed to the largest mango I saw. "How about this one?"

Katia squeezed it and shook her head. "No, it's too hard. It has to be green, but soft enough to bite."

I reached for another mango and tried squeezing it myself. "Katia, I wanted to talk to you about last night..."

"Last night's over." She found a mango that she liked and picked it. "I can do what I want, Beth."

"I know that, Katia." I took a deep breath. "But when a man invites you to a drinking party, and you're the only woman … when he pays you to come—"

46

"He didn't pay me. Who said that?" Karla's eyebrows rose sharply then relaxed as she began peeling the mango. "Gerardo lends me money when I need it," she said in a measured tone. "I was the only woman at the party because I'm his girlfriend. He loves me. Do you have a boyfriend, Beth?"

I dismissed the question. "I know it may seem like he loves you. But he tried to buy you — and your friends."

Katia glared. "I am not a whore," she shouted.

"I wasn't calling you a whore."

Katia dismissed me with a wave of her knife. "Jealous *gringa* bitch. Your breasts are so small no *gringo* would want you. So you come here to find a man who will love your white skin. Did you know you have a pimple right here on your nose — it looks like it's going to explode." She looked up at me. "You don't think Gerardo loves me? How would you know? Who would want you?"

"He loves you, does he?" I shot back. "I suppose that's that why he offered Suyapa five *lempiras* if she would kiss him?"

I wanted to take my words back as soon as I realized what I was going to say, but the message had already been sent to my angry tongue, and all I could do was listen to the wrong words pour out of my mouth. I had attacked a vulnerable, difficult girl, and I had betrayed Suyapa's confidence.

Katia's eyes narrowed. "Suyapa's a stupid bitch. Telling the *gringa* everything. As if you give a shit. I'll fix her ass, too."

"You're not going to fix anyone's ass." I was surprised to find myself shouting now. "And you're not going to take Suyapa or anyone else to parties like that again. If you do, you're out. Do you understand?"

My words had an immediate impact. Katia's face froze. I'd won the battle, but it didn't feel good.

I wished I could start over. I extended a tentative hand to Katia. "Look, I can see that you're hurting. Maybe if we can talk about that, the things that happened when you were a child..."

"Stop." Katia lifted her hands to her ears and accidentally knocked the fruit to the ground, breaking the plate. "Just leave me alone," she whispered, as she knelt to pick up the slices with her hands, separating the fruit from the shards of glass.

As I arranged the chairs in a circle in the middle of the *sala,* the girls gathered at the perimeters of the room, looking in and turning to each other with curious whispers. They entered slowly, as if they meant to be late but were too eager to pull it off.

Katia came in. She had washed off her mascara from the night before and combed her hair. She looked out the window as she stood beside me.

"I'm sorry for what I said before. Please don't throw me out," she said flatly.

"That's okay, Katia." I knew she wasn't sincere, but I wanted to give her a break, to try again. "I already knew I had a pimple."

Katia looked me in the eye and chuckled.

"I'm sorry, too," I continued. "I lost my temper. I said things I shouldn't have."

I decided to get a head start on the meeting, rather than waiting for Mother Maria and Sister Paula. I walked the girls through a description of the system of color and levels, and talked with them about my role. I was going to be a counselor and a facilitator, not an *encargada.* I didn't want them to obey me, I said, I wanted them to think for themselves and make good decisions. Soon I had gone through almost everything on my agenda. I started to assign the chores for the week, hoping that the sisters showed up in time.

"Here they come," called Katia, just as I was assigning the last chore.

The girls straightened their shoulders and folded their hands in their laps. When Mother Maria and Sister Paula entered, the girls stood up in unison and said, "*Buenas tardes.*"

"Good afternoon, girls," said Mother Maria. She made the sign of the cross and led them in reciting the Hail Mary.

When she finished the prayer, she looked up. "Tell me about your meeting," she said to me. Then she turned to the girls. "Beth is the *encargada* of this house now. I want you all to obey Beth as you would me."

The girls hid amused smiles and looked at me.

Mother Maria sat down and Rosa served her a cup of coffee from the large tin pot while I told her what we had talked about so far. I finished by recounting how the girls had pulled together and cleaned the kitchen.

"That's good," said Mother Maria looking at her cup of coffee but refraining from taking a sip. "That's what they should do every Sunday after Mass. You're off to a good start, Beth."

I looked down at my notes. I'd covered everything but the identification papers.

After the conversation with Sister Paula, I had looked into what it would take to get IDs for the girls. The bureaucracy sounded like an impossible maze of stamps and *permisos*. I had talked to three people and been given three different descriptions of "standard procedures."

The road conditions would be difficult, too. Some roads were only passable in the dry season, I was told, and up-to-date maps were impossible to get. Military officials wanted to keep them out of the wrong hands, and that meant making them unavailable to everyone. Even if I were lucky enough to get my hands on a map, carrying it might make us suspect if a soldier should find it in my possession during a road check. The fact that I was a foreigner and a woman wouldn't be a problem, the Desk Officer at the Registry of Persons assured me, but didn't I have anyone who would go with me?

Everything I learned should have made me more reluctant to take on the job, but it didn't. The girls needed the IDs to be safe, to take advantage of even the most basic opportunities. And they deserved a chance to go home, to find out more about the past, to settle things.

"There's one more thing I want to talk about today—"

I looked at the phrases I had underlined in my notes. *Dealing with your family history. Understanding the terms of your abandonment.* When I looked up the girls were still smiling about the new plates and curtains that I had promised them. Slow down, I told myself, and I turned over my notes.

"Before you go out on your own I'd like to make sure that each of you gets your identification card. You'll need it whether you're planning to study or work, and these days you need it when you're walking around the city, too."

Mother Maria pressed her lips together and looked down at her lap. When she looked up she met my eyes with a nod.

"Bah," said Luz. "I doubt anyone will even remember that I was born — in the corner of a corn field, and so long ago."

"You'd be surprised, Luz. The records go back over a hundred years. Almost everyone is written down somewhere." I looked out at their faces. "Your birth is more important than you think."

"But Beth, it's not that easy," said Rosa. "Some of us would have to go to the *pueblos*."

"I'll go with you if that's what it takes."

"Watch out," said Katia. "There are dangerous people out there — our parents." Katia laughed nervously at her own joke, while the other girls remained quiet.

"And if we want to see our mothers?" began Vera.

Mother Maria put up a hand in protest. "Getting your papers is one thing, but if you think you are going just to look for your mothers, you'd better think long and hard about it. You have a home and a mother here. Content yourself with that."

"I don't want to." Vera shrunk back. "I was just asking."

My heart pounded. Mother Maria wanted to protect the girls, of course, but she had no right to silence Vera.

"If you really want to look for you mother," I said, "if you feel you need to," I looked from one girl to the other, "I'll go with you."

"Beth is too kind." Mother Maria was flushed and her teeth clenched a bit. She turned to me, "That's not the job I asked of you. The roads in our country are terrible and the *pueblos* are poor. No water or electricity. The girls can't expect you to do that."

Sister Paula held her head down, but her eyes looked straight at me. She agreed with me. I knew it. She thought I was doing the right thing.

"I know it's not my job," I said. "I'm making the offer as a friend."

I turned to the girls. "This is something to think about very carefully, but I promise you this, if you want to make the journey home, you don't have to go alone."

Mother Maria folded her arms across her chest. "Don't imagine that your mothers are out there waiting for you. When they left you here I told them they could come back any time. But they didn't. Now that I've raised you and educated you, yes, they want their daughters to come and take care of them when they're old. Be careful, *mis hijas*. Don't go looking for heartaches."

The girls looked up at her and then down again. Mother Maria stood to leave and they dutifully joined her in prayer. After the Sisters were gone the girls began to disperse quietly, tiptoeing around the fragile bubbles of hope they had sent up and abandoned.

My heart was still pounding. I could help the girls in so many small ways, but this was more important. As I began to put the chairs back in their places I found Felicia by my side.

"I need to make the journey home," she said.

Felicia's Journey

The way I see it now, my journey didn't really begin until I set off with Felicia. I had taken a long trip, of course, from my home to the capital city of one of the poorest countries in the world. I had been lifted into the air then set down again at a prearranged location, but I knew very little about the terrain that had been crossed.

Felicia and I had to make our way by land. We didn't know exactly how to get where we were going. We had to rely on the kindness of strangers. In miles, the distance between La Casa and Vista del Oro wasn't much compared to the distance I had already traveled, but by any other measure it was much further.

I wasn't consciously aware of this when we set out. We were following an ordinary path that people traveled every day. When the next step seemed clear enough, we took it. And I had the feeling there was someone watching over us. Looking back, I still believe that.

*   *   *

The bus depot looked out over the public market. It was just after six and the *mercado* was full of people. Vendors carried fruit and vegetables in baskets on their heads, in sacks over their shoulders, and in pushcarts that they dragged along the ground. The morning smelled of gasoline, dust, and a hint of yesterday's fruit.

It wasn't like me to set off without directions or any kind of a game plan, but Felicia was going to lose her scholarship if she didn't present her birth certificate at the School of Fine Arts by

Monday. We had tried, without success, to find out how to get to Felicia's birthplace. We had to travel to Olancho first — Felicia was sure of that much. From there we would ask for directions until we found someone who could tell them us how to get to Vista del Oro.

We requested two tickets then sat down to wait for them to be issued. Felicia leaned toward me. "If they're taking names they might ask for my ID," she whispered.

"Don't worry," I said. "There must be a waiver of some sort, a form to fill out."

I knew there didn't have to be any such waiver, but Felicia seemed satisfied. She sat beside me, humming a song from a radio that belonged to a passenger further down the line. Her hair was pulled up in a girlish ponytail, and she had laced up her sneakers with brand-new striped shoelaces, the current teenage fad. It was hard to believe that this was the same girl who had shown me her portfolio full of soulful sketches.

In the first sketch, three girls in short hair ate gruel from a bowl. Felicia had captured so much in that ordinary moment. Another showed a turbulent sea with waves whirling and crashing around a small stone. Inside the stone was the shadowy, embryonic image of a child, its arms reaching toward the shore. It was called, simply, *Stone at Sea*. Most interesting was the final work, which showed a man with his face down, shaping what looked like a world in his hands.

"Is that God?" I had asked.

"It was supposed to be a self-portrait," said Felicia, "but I couldn't get myself right. This man kept coming out instead. I call him *The Sculptor*, because that's what I want to be."

I had no idea what kind of reception we would get in Vista del Oro. Felicia's mother had left Felicia at *La Casa* twelve years ago with the promise that she'd be back to take Felicia home. She did visit from time to time, with candy for Felicia, and a story of a new town where they would settle down someday soon. Seven years ago she'd gone up to the North Coast to find work, and Felicia hadn't heard from her since. Felicia thought she still had brothers in Vista del Oro. Everything had happened so fast, that I hadn't even had a chance to ask Felicia about her father.

"Romero. Pellegrino," the ticket man called out.

I took the tickets and was tempted to head straight for the bus, but I didn't want to risk trouble later. "Will they be checking my passport?" I asked.

The man answered without looking up. "The checkpoint is in Olancho. You'll show your ID there when you get off the bus."

"What if I'm on the way to the registry in one of the *pueblos* beyond? Can I present papers on the way back?"

The man gave me a suspicious look that suggested no threat, but promised no special concern, and certainly no kindness. "If you have a passport — what are you worried about?"

"Nothing." I sensed Felicia taking a step away from me. "I'd just like to know what the procedure is, if someone needs to travel to get her papers."

"They'll take care of you in Olancho." The man waved us away and turned to the next passengers in line.

Outside the ticket office, a dozen old yellow school buses sat in a crooked row. The names of rural towns were painted in black script on the front. We found the bus that said Olancho and got on. As we walked toward our seats I felt springiness under my feet. I looked down to find that I was standing on a thin piece of plywood that had been used to patch a hole in the floor. The inside walls of the bus were covered with stenciled pictures — a house in a village, a basket of fruit, the Pope, even Donald Duck — like a body with too many tattoos. The wide rearview mirror across the top of the front windshield was adorned with a border of yellow fringe. The inscription just above it read *Bendice mi camino*. God Bless my path.

A heavyset woman in a faded dress and worn out flip-flops got on the bus and sat next to me. Her hair was pulled back tightly from her square weather-beaten face. She nodded to us briefly as she counted out her bus fare in old one-*lempira* bills, then tucked what was left over into her sleeve.

Soon the bus was full, three to a seat with more people standing in the aisles. Bags and baskets covered every inch of floor space not taken up by passengers. The doors closed and the bus lurched forward, its weight shifting from one side to the other as it made its way out of the bumpy parking lot onto the paved street.

The woman beside me claimed more of the seat. I tried to resist politely with my hip, but with our bags in the way I couldn't find solid footing. I felt myself slide toward Felicia, who had already made herself as small as possible in the space by the window. By shifts and squirms we settled in, until Felicia and I sat shoulder to shoulder, knees up against the seat in front of us, squashed together like twins sharing a womb, the sound of the engine enclosing us in our own private compartment.

"You said your brothers might still be in Vista del Oro," I said now. "Did your mother leave them with relatives?"

"My brothers are older, from a different father. They stayed with their *abuela*."

"Your mother must have married young."

Felicia shook her head no. "She never married their father. It wasn't until my father that she fell in love. The men in town were all farmhands, but my father was a mason, brought in to build a brick house for the big *fincero*."

"What was he like? Do you remember him?"

"No. The house was finished before I was born. He had to move on." Felicia paused. "But he married my mother before he left. He wanted me to have his name. My mother told me the whole story before she went north."

"I bet it's hard, not knowing him."

Felicia tipped her head to one side. "I know my mother, don't I? To know him all I have to do is look at myself and take out what is from my mother. I love my mother, Beth. She's happy all the time and she makes me laugh, but she's not responsible. I'm happy like her, but I don't let people down. I always do my chores, and my schoolwork, too. That's my father, see? People ask where my art comes from. I say I don't know, but it must be from him. Sometimes it is hard."

Felicia drifted off for a moment then unexpectedly came back. "Like I'm drowning, with nothing to hold on to…"

"Like the stone in your painting."

Felicia nodded and her eyes filled. "I'm grown now, I know it's too late, but I do wonder what it would be like to have a father."

"I know what you mean," I said. "I lost my father, too. In a different way. He died when I was twelve."

"How did it happen?"

"He was a doctor. One night he was riding home from the hospital, an emergency call. It was raining and he was tired. There was a car accident. He didn't survive."

Felicia looked up at me, as if she expected to see something she hadn't seen before. "So you're like me, then. You don't have a father either."

"My mother always said we still had him as long as we had memories."

I had done my best to remember, but whole pieces of him had slipped away with time. My mother told us stories, of course, the same ones many times — about his goodness as a husband and father, his kindness to the children he cured, the pancakes he made on Sunday mornings. I sometimes had trouble distinguishing actual memories from these stories, implanted later, because of death. Still, I had one memory that I was sure was my own.

I was riding on my father's shoulders, feeling the sway of his gait under me, holding onto his forehead with my flat palms as we walked through the woods behind our house. I knew that there were prickers below, that the path was rocky, but from above it was easy. I glided along, able to see over the tops of the trees on the sides of the path. When we came to a grassy clearing my father had thrown me into the air, then caught me. I remembered that feeling of free fall, how it rushed in my blood and made me giggle. I would never forget that joy; falling, yet knowing I wouldn't hit the ground.

I straightened up as much I could in the cramped seat and turned to Felicia again. "You were saying that you wished you knew your father…"

Felicia's face looked bright. "I want to find him, Beth."

"But I thought you said he left seventeen years ago."

"I know he won't be in Vista del Oro, but the birth record should tell me his name, where he was born. With that information we could look for him. It's like you said the other day, I have a right to know, to find out about my past."

"It could be difficult after all these years. Are you sure you're ready to do this?"

Felicia's voice faltered a bit. "I thought you'd want to help."

"I do, I just don't want to see you disappointed."

"Why wouldn't he be happy to see me? It's not like I'd be asking for anything. I'm grown now, a good student. I have my scholarship. I could bring my portfolio to show him."

"Let's take one thing at a time," I said lightly. "We can talk about this more after you're settled in at school."

Felicia looked down. "He'd be worried if he knew I was here, riding a bus to Olancho without papers."

There was no point in arguing with Felicia's hopeful logic. "At least this is the last time you'll have to do that."

I felt tired from rising at dawn. I closed my eyes and let the rhythm of the bus lull me in and out of a bumpy sleep. When I opened my eyes several hours later I saw that Felicia had fallen asleep too. According to my watch we had about one more hour to go. The bus began to slow down and I looked out the window, expecting to see a small town, one of a number of local stops we would make before we reached downtown Olancho. But there was no town, just a wooden kiosk with three armed soldiers sitting in the shade of its small roof.

I gently elbowed Felicia awake. "I think this is the checkpoint," I said under my breath.

I felt a hand on my shoulder. It was the woman next to me. "San Juancito," she said. "That's where you change for Vista."

I was puzzled, then realized that the woman had heard our conversation. She was giving us the directions that we needed.

"*Gracias*," I said, while Felicia shook the woman's hand.

A deep voice boomed from the front of the bus, "Please stay seated with your papers ready."

My heart sank as two soldiers boarded the bus. Their matching camouflage, hard hats and guns overwhelmed whatever differences there were in their facial features.

"They're looking for strangers who could be dangerous," whispered the woman next to us. "They'll only check the men."

I kept my eyes down, as the soldiers approached the first row of passengers. I wanted to look up to see if what she said was true, but I didn't dare. The soldiers worked slowly, waiting for people to fish their ID papers out of their pockets.

"You'll have to get off," I heard one of the soldiers say. I watched out the side window as a young man took a place beside the kiosk, his hands together behind his back as if they were handcuffed. Would he be enlisted in the military, as Sister Paula had said?

One of the soldiers checked the row in front of me, just the men, as the woman had said. But the soldier stopped for a second look at me. He touched the heavy canvas of my backpack and looked at my chunky sandals. American goods. "You're a foreigner."

"Yes. I'm from the United States." I handed him my passport, careful not to look at Felicia.

The soldier studied the passport photo and my face as if he wasn't sure it was a match. "You look like you're from here."

"No." I usually enjoyed it when people thought I could be Honduran, but this time it was making things complicated.

"What is your date of birth?" he asked.

I answered, then held my breath while he looked at the picture again. Finally he handed me the passport.

As the soldier moved toward the back of the bus Felicia and I sat still, exchanging glances but saying nothing. After a few moments they got off and before long we heard the bus engine idling.

We were the only passengers to get off in San Juancito. I hadn't anticipated that. It was just after noon, but the town square was quiet as midnight. The dusty heat locked my thirst in the base of my throat, a dry tickle. We couldn't even buy a cold drink because the *pulpería* was closed for *siesta*.

We headed across the square toward the Spanish colonial building that had to be the *alcaldía*, San Junacito's City Hall. Someone there might be able to give us directions.

"I hope we don't have to wait until two-thirty," said Felicia.

As we drew closer we saw that the doors were secured with padlocks. I knocked, then peered in the window. I saw a desk with an open ledger, but no sign of anyone. I was about to knock on the door again, when I heard the sound of low voices and laughter coming from the far side of the building.

There three men sat drinking beer by a fence. They must have seen us go from door to door, but they had offered no help.

Two of them wore straw hats that hid their faces, machetes at their belts. They were laborers of some kind. The third man, the one with the loud laugh, was tall and husky. He wore an army jacket, unbuttoned to reveal his bare chest. He stood up and walked toward the *alcaldía*, beer in hand.

"*Buen día, señoritas,*" he opened his arms as he stumbled over his own feet. He looked disheveled, with the red eyes of a drunk. I saw a gun tucked into the waistband of his pants. Could he be a soldier?

"Let's go," said Felicia, a hand on my arm.

But there was nowhere to go.

I stepped forward. "Good afternoon, *señor*. We're waiting for the office to open."

"Where are you coming from?" asked the soldier.

I wished I didn't have to reply. "Tegucigalpa."

"Two young ladies traveling alone." He looked us both over again and then waved his beer at me. "And you're a *gringa*. They say the *gringas* drink like men."

"We're here on business," I said curtly. "We'll come back later when the office is open." I took Felicia by the arm and started toward the road that led out of town.

The soldier stepped in front of us, blocking our path, then took a step closer to me. "Don't be in a hurry. This is a friendly town." He leered at us, one hand resting on his gun. "We want to know all about you. Please come and sit with us. Have a beer."

My heart was pounding but I looked him in the eye. "No, thank you."

"You're making a mistake waiting for the town clerk, *gringa*. He's a skinny old man." He turned to the other men and raised his bottle. "Tell them who bought the beer, *chicos*? Aren't I the mayor of this town?"

"*Sí, señor,*" said one of the men as he saluted the soldier with his beer. The other man was quiet, his head down.

The soldier kept staring at me, daring me to move away. "Tell me about your business in San Juancito, perhaps I can help you."

I didn't answer and I tried not to look at Felicia. So far he hadn't drawn her into the conversation, and I wanted to keep it that way.

"You won't answer." The soldier ran his fingers through his dark curls then spat in the dirt. "Don't bother. I know why you've come. You university students with your sandals and your back-packs. You think you're going to organize our *pueblos*." He glanced at Felicia. "I suppose the Honduran one, the *catracha,* is your translator."

"No," I said, "you don't understand—"

"Turn around," he barked, waving his gun at us. "Face the wall."

My mind raced. He couldn't shoot us in broad daylight. People would come out of their houses, wouldn't they?

I faced the wall. I could hear the soldier pace back and forth as he spoke.

"You're not the first *gringa* communist we've welcomed here. The other one had a nice ass, too." He called to the men, laughing now. "*Hombres,* it must be a requirement of the party. They check out their asses before they paint them red."

He walked over to Felicia and slapped her on the rear end. "Not bad. I guess they have criteria for the *catrachas,* too."

I turned around. "Leave her alone. You have no right to touch her."

Surprised, he swayed a bit then composed himself. "Oh yes I do. As a soldier of the Honduran army I have the right to know where you are going and to ask for proof of your identity. And I can detain you in the manner that I choose. It's my responsibility to protect the citizens of this town from internationalist communist—"

"I'm not a communist," I cried, "I'm her traveling companion. She's on her way to—" I stopped myself and glanced at Felicia. "She has family in Vista del Oro. They're expecting us."

The soldier hesitated, then called to his friends. "She says they have people in Vista. What do you think?"

"Stop playing," said the quiet one. "They're sure to have people somewhere."

The soldier turned to his other friend but the man shook his head.

"You're looking for trouble with the *gringos,*" he said.

The soldier looked back at us and spat on the ground again. "Wait here. I've got to think about your case," he said, then he disappeared around the back of the building.

We stood still, not sure what to do. He was gone for the moment, but were we still in the range of his gun?

After a few moments the quiet man looked up and shooed us away with both hands. "Hurry. *Andáte,*" he whispered loudly, "before he comes back."

We walked across the square quickly, then broke into a run until we were halfway up the hill that led to the road out of town. From the crossroads we could see all the way back to the town plaza. No one had followed us. It finally felt safe to talk.

Felicia wiped the tears from her cheeks then broke up in nervous laughter. "*Dios*, was I scared."

"We're lucky he let us go." I was still shaking inside, but I put an arm around Felicia. "Let's walk a bit more to see if we can find someone who'll tell us how to get to Vista. We don't want to spend the night here."

Just ahead, on the other side of the road we saw a woman washing clothes in the *pila* outside her home.

Felicia called out to her from her place in the road. "Excuse me, *señora*, does the bus for Vista del Oro pass by here?"

The woman studied Felicia then nodded. "*La Baronesa* passes in the afternoon. It stops up at the fork."

We headed to the fork in the road and waited in thirst and silence for some time. I began to worry about the welcome we would receive in Vista del Oro. Where would we sleep?

"What if *La Baronesa* doesn't come?" asked Felicia.

"It will," I said.

"But it's getting late. What if we don't get there until after dark? What if Vista del Oro is like this town?"

In spite of the soldier in San Juancito, I believed that the world got safer as it got smaller. And if that was true, Vista del Oro had to be one of the safest places on earth.

"We'll find someone who knows your family on the bus," I told Felicia. "They'll help us."

After another half-hour passed we heard the heavy vibrations of an engine. The name *Baronesa* had led me to imagine an air-conditioned Greyhound bus, with windows high off the ground so that the view of the countryside would not be obscured by the layer of dust that hung over the dry road like a fog. The actual *Baronesa,* it turned out, was nothing more than a grand old motorized cart. A tin roof hung over a flat truck bed and wooden slats made up the side rails. The backless benches were full of people who must have been on their way home from buying and selling in markets in larger towns. They carried coarsely woven bags full of food. Heavier items were tied down with rope. A few chickens roamed freely.

As we boarded the bus we were met with nods and curious smiles. We filed into the back row next to a clean-cut teenager with a schoolbag between his feet and a clipboard on his lap. "Can we squeeze in here?" Felicia asked.

The boy smiled and put his clipboard away. "Math homework," he explained as he zipped his bag closed, and slid over. "You're visiting Vista del Oro? Where are you from?"

When he found out that Felicia went to school in Tegucigalpa he was impressed. "I'm going there someday," he said. "If God is willing."

Why was Felicia visiting Vista, he wanted to know.

"I was born there. I've come for my papers," said Felicia.

"Born in Vista? What's your name?"

"Felicia Romero Ortiz. My mother was Magdalena."

The boy's face widened into a grin. "My father's sister! I'm Rafael, your cousin." He offered his hand first to Felicia and then to me.

"And where are you staying?"

"I'm not sure... It's my first visit."

"I'll take you to my mother, then — she's your aunt, Josefina." Felicia accepted quickly.

Thank God, I thought.

The roof of the *Baronesa* provided welcome protection from the hot sun. After a few minutes I felt my energy returning. I breathed in the country air, which felt fresh now, instead of thick with dust. We were heading up toward the mountains in the distance, toward Vista del Oro. We would get there, and we were no longer strangers.

The center of Vista del Oro was a small plaza with a few patches of grass. At one end stood an adobe church with wooden doors, the largest building in the town. Its late afternoon shadow reached all the way across the courtyard.

As Rafael led us past the short row of houses that lined the square he pointed to a low brick building on the other side.

"That's Town Hall, where you'll find your birth certificate, but it's closed now. And here's the *pulperia*."

He ducked inside an open doorway. A few minutes later he came out with three Cokes and offered us a seat on the narrow bench outside the store.

Felicia took a sip of soda. "It's quiet today."

Rafael shrugged. "It's always like this."

"I can't believe I waited this long to come." Felicia faced the square as she spoke. "I'm seventeen and I don't know anything about the place where I was born."

Rafael shook his head and kicked the dirt in front of him. "You're not missing much."

"My mother always said it was a mining town."

"It was a mining camp a long time ago, but the Spaniards left when they couldn't find gold. Our people stayed on and planted corn and beans. Later the visiting priest convinced them to build the church. 'That's when they finally saw gold,' my grandfather used to say, 'when the *padre* held up his chalice.'" Rafael laughed briefly then shook his head. "There are still some who think they'll find gold. Old men mostly, but young people, too. They poke around in the mountains for gold instead of going to school."

Rafael led us past the church and up a hill, then turned down a narrow dirt lane. A boy in sandals ran after a patched rubber ball, while a barefoot boy chased him with a stick. A little girl who couldn't have been more than six carried a baby on her hip, and a toddler with yellow-orange hair sat in the dirt licking a stone.

How unusual to find a blond child here, I thought at first. Then I saw his distended belly and an open sore on his leg. I had read about *kwashiorkor*, but I had never seen an actual case until now. I looked at his fair hair again and saw that it wasn't supposed to be blond at all — the color had been drained out of him by lack of protein.

Our footsteps crunched on the dirt and pebbles as we passed by the open doorways of several wooden shacks. I looked at my feet, mostly, but snatched a few quick glances into the houses. The first had no furniture, just sleeping mats and a wood-burning stove. On a shelf was a small pile of what looked like rags, but must have been the family's clothing. A woman carried a bucket inside, shooed her children out, set down the bucket, then wiped her forehead with her apron. In the next house an old woman slept in a hammock while a younger woman stood by the stove and slapped a tortilla into shape over a pregnant belly.

As we walked, the splash and chop and toil of life inside the houses wafted out into the lane and combined with the voices of the children to create a steady stream of sound.

"We're almost there," said Rafael.

Aunt Josefina's house was larger than the others with a sturdy wooden frame and a small window in front. Rafael knocked on the doorframe. "*Mama,* I've brought guests."

Aunt Josefina turned from the pot she was tending and approached the door, her head tilted in a question. Her hair was pulled back in a tight bun. Her face was scrupulously clean. When Rafael said Felicia's name Aunt Josefina's eyes grew wide for an instant. She embraced Felicia, then hesitated a moment before speaking.

"Perhaps no one told you that your mother has left Vista."

"I know," said Felicia, "I saw her in Tegucigalpa before she went north."

Aunt Josefina squeezed Felicia's hands. "You should visit your grandmother. Seeing your face will do her good."

Aunt Josefina welcomed me with a brief curtsy and a smile as Felicia explained why I was here. "It's an honor to have you as our guest," she said.

She showed us to a well-swept corner where we could place our bags. Then she led us behind the house and set out a basin of cold water for us to wash our faces.

By the time we had washed, Aunt Josefina was heating beans on a skillet. Rafael came in with four fresh eggs and handed them to his mother. Soon we were eating a simple meal of beans, eggs, tortillas and coffee.

After supper Rafael took us for a walk along a footpath that led up to the Patuca Mountains. I walked along behind Felicia and Rafael. It felt good to stretch my muscles after being cramped on the bus for hours. I was soothed by the beauty of the mountains, the colors they presented from a distance in the late afternoon.

Rafael began asking Felicia about Tegucigalpa. He had questions about everything from bus fares to high school schedules to boardinghouses. Felicia, who had spent most of her life at *La Casa,* couldn't answer all his practical questions.

"It's full of people and cars," she said, "and there are so many streets you'd probably need a map at first. If you can imagine the difference between Vista and Olancho, and double it, that's how big the difference is between Olancho and Tegucigalpa."

Rafael sighed as he did the math in his head. "That's what I thought."

The sun's colors sank behind the horizon and left us with just enough time to get home before it was dark.

"We'll cut through town," said Rafael, who led us up a path that led to the plaza where the *Baronesa* had dropped us off, but on the other side. As we approached the church, Rafael waved to two young men who were coming into town carrying machetes.

"Come and meet your sister," he called, and then turned to Felicia. "They're your brothers, Diego and Francisco."

Francisco, the younger of the two, slapped his two hands against his forehead in surprise, then grinned broadly and extended a thin arm. "Welcome home."

The older one, Diego, crossed his arms over his broad chest. "*Buenas*," he said seriously.

Felicia told them why she had come and introduced me. Then they stood there without speaking, a foreigner, a cousin, and two brothers who hardly knew their sister.

Francisco broke the silence. "You look like our mother."

"Has she been back to visit?" asked Felicia.

"Not since she went north." The words seemed to stick in his throat for a moment. "Anyway, at least we have a visit from our *hermanita*," he said brightly, trying the term of endearment that meant little sister.

Diego shifted uncomfortably. "She's a half-sister," he reminded Francisco, then he turned to Felicia. "When you were a baby we called you '*La Chanchita*' — the little pig — because you liked to play in the dirt at our mother's feet while she did the washing."

Felicia blushed. "I don't remember that."

"It doesn't matter." Francisco smiled. "Look at you — you're a city girl now."

Felicia blushed again. "Where are you coming from?"

Francisco held up his chisel with a grin. "Tapping on rocks."

"We were working a farm out that way." Diego pointed to a valley in the distance.

"Three weeks," added Francisco, "*sin pago*."

"Without pay?" Felicia looked surprised. "Why?"

Diego shrugged. "According to the *patrón* all the money he had was in the ground. Once he harvests he'll have cash. We'll go back to collect."

Francisco shook his head. "He was a *sin verguenza*, shameless. He ran us all out of there as if *we* had robbed *him*. My brother worked like a *burro*," he pointed his chin at Diego, "and now his wife and kids are left without tortilla*s*."

Felicia turned to me. "Can I borrow ten *lempiras*?" she asked under her breath.

I handed her a ten-*lempira* note. It was only worth about five dollars, but I guessed it would buy a week's worth of food out here.

Felicia passed it to Diego. "For you and your *señora*."

Diego stood still a moment. I saw the muscles in his face tighten. "I'll pay you back."

When he moved to go, Francisco followed but walked backward for a few steps, facing Felicia. "We'll see you before you leave," he said.

It was still dark the first time the rooster crowed. Confused, I reached for my digital watch and pressed the button that lit the display: 3:50 AM. During the next three hours I was pulled out of sleep at least three times. First the rooster called out alone, then it was accompanied by the sound of birds. Finally, the early morning light broke through. I looked around. The small bed beside me where Felicia had slept was empty, and I could hear Aunt Josefina in the kitchen. I dressed and went outside to wash, joining the others just in time for breakfast.

After breakfast Rafael walked us to the row of municipal offices at the center of town. We arrived at seven-thirty and took a seat on the bench outside the town registrar's office. The office didn't open until eight.

A small line had formed behind us by the time the Town Clerk arrived. At eight-fifteen a tall man with thinning hair walked up to the door, nodding a greeting to the assembled group. "You're first," he noted, pointing to Felicia. "I'll call you presently."

He unlocked the door and went inside. From my place on the bench I could see him take a large ledger from the shelf and place it on his desk. He put on his glasses, opened to a new page, wrote the date at the top, and beckoned Felicia forward.

Felicia rose and went to the desk, and I followed. "I'd like to get a copy of my birth certificate," Felicia began.

"Your stamp, please."

"Stamp?" said Felicia.

"A three *lempira* stamp."

"Can I buy one?"

"We don't take money here. You'll have to go to the cashier's office, one block down on the right. Come back with the stamp and I can help you. Next, please."

When we got to the cashier's office there was already a line. We waited behind a young couple with a new baby. In front of the couple an older woman muttered to herself and wrung her hands nervously around the documents in her hands. The young man in front of her tapped his foot and looked at his watch.

"I'm joining the army," he said.

It took an hour to get the stamp, and when we returned to the registry we saw that those who had gone before us at the cashier's office were lined up ahead of us again. By ten o'clock the sun was hot, and all the seats on the benches were taken.

Finally it was Felicia's turn. The clerk pulled out the book that corresponded to the year she was born. Felicia stood in silence as he scanned the ledger with his index finger.

"I'm sorry, there's no Ortiz Romero listed. Are you sure of the date?"

"Yes, I'm sure it's June 23rd," said Felicia.

"I can't seem to — wait, it's here — Felicia Ortiz."

"But my full name is Ortiz Romero. There must be some mistake."

The clerk shook his head. "To be recognized as Romero, your father would have had to sign here," he pointed to a blank space on the ledger and lowered his voice, "since your mother was not married, that's how it's done."

Felicia stared at the book. "But I've been called a Romero all my life. There must be a way to correct this."

"I'm sorry," said the clerk. "I'm strictly prohibited from changing the record. Even if there is a spelling error I'm required to transcribe it onto the birth certificate."

Felicia stood frozen on the spot, looking down.

The clerk looked at Felicia then cast an eye toward the line.

"Let me prepare this for you today," he said. "That way you'll have the legal document that you need. You can come back with your father. Once he signs, I'll make out a new one with your full name."

I stepped forward and put a hand on Felicia's arm. "Yes, please," I said to the clerk. "That's what we'll do."

The clerk typed out Felicia's name and date of birth, along with her mother's, onto a blank birth certificate. He affixed the stamp, signed his name and then impressed it with the official seal of Vista del Oro. By the time he was finished it was official, a record of the unalterable truth. Felicia took the paper, folded it carefully, and placed it in her purse.

She was quiet on the walk to Aunt Josefina's house.

I squeezed her hand. "Remember, you're a scholarship recipient now."

"Yeah, and the bastard daughter of a woman who lies about everything."

Aunt Josefina placed three large oranges and a small bag of ground coffee into a basket. "Here," she said to Felicia, "you can give this to your grandmother."

With Rafael's help Felicia had already picked out a gift, but she took the basket also, and tucked her own package, wrapped in newspaper, underneath the oranges.

Aunt Josefina led us to the outskirts of town, where we had walked the night before, but this time we turned and followed a rocky path down to a creek. There, among the trees, stood a windowless shack. The door was shut tight, but the roof, pieced together out of tin, was open, only covering half of the housetop. Had the other half been torn off during a storm, I wondered, or had the roof been made out of rusty scraps that had never added up in the first place?

"*Buenos dias, 'buela.*" Aunt Josefina called out as we approached the house.

A hard cackle rose out from the roof. "What's going on? Did God send you around to raise up all the *condenados*? Well, you're wasting time here. The devil doesn't have me yet, I was just taking a nap."

Aunt Josefina sighed. "Please be nice today, Chele."

"If I'm such trouble to you, go away."

"We brought you coffee," said Aunt Josefina, "and I'm going to wash your feet."

The door swung open. By the time we reached the house Chele was back in her hammock, lying back with her calloused feet hanging over the side. Bright eyes protruded from her thin face, as she looked toward the light that shone in through the gap in the roof. Bony shoulders held her faded dress in place like a hanger.

Felicia hesitated at the door, but Aunt Josefina pushed her forward. "You have a visitor, Chele, one you've wanted to see for a long time."

Chele turned in the direction of Aunt Josefina's voice. "Who? Who would come to see me? Come in and show yourselves."

Aunt Josefina smiled at the small victory. "It's Felicia, Magdalena's baby girl. She came all the way from Teguc to see you."

"Where is she?" Chele, groped at the air.

Felicia took a few steps toward the hammock and lifted the basket toward her grandmother. "I have oranges for you, *Abuela*. Shall I peel one?"

"Closer," whispered Aunt Josefina from behind. "She's almost blind."

Felicia stepped up close and leaned over her grandmother.

Chele strained to look at Felicia. Her breathing became labored. "Let me touch your face."

I looked on from the doorway, surprised by Chele's sudden tenderness, and shocked that there could be such a strong resemblance between the old woman and Felicia — the large eyes, the elf-like chin, even the laugh. Chele's was bitter and harsh, but I could hear a familiar cadence underneath. It was like the merry ripple of sound that filled *La Casa* when Felicia was telling a joke or clowning around while doing her chores.

"Everyone calls me Chele, but my full name is Felicia. You were named after me. Did anyone bother to tell you that?"

Aunt Josefina pulled up a chair beside the hammock for Felicia. "Of course we told her. Now I'm going to get some water. When I get back I'll fix some coffee and wash those feet."

When Aunt Josefina left, Chele turned to Felicia, offering her a broken smile. "I bet you're a good girl. Did you come looking for your mother?"

"I came for school papers," said Felicia. "I saw Mother right after she left Vista. She stopped in Teguc on her way north."

"Out of all of them she was my beauty," said Chele. "They said she looked like me, but twice as pretty. And that's what I said about you on the day you were born — like your mother, but twice as pretty. I could tell from the first."

Felicia looked up. "You remember the day I was born?"

"Of course I remember." Chele raised a finger at her. "If they've been telling you I've lost my mind, it's a lie. You were born right there on the ground." Chele fixed her eyes on a spot just a few feet from where Felicia was standing. "Your brothers were watching, and being the third, you came out easy. Then Diego said, 'Mama did it just like the pigs.' And we all laughed and thanked God. Everyone called you *Chanchita* after that."

Felicia frowned. "That's what they told me."

"Don't be fooled. Your brothers loved you," said Chele shaking her head. "How they cried when your mother sent you to Mother Maria."

"But why..." Felicia composed herself and formed the question again. "Why was I the only one who was sent?"

"Ah." Chele shook her head. "Your mother should answer that."

Felicia looked down and waited.

"Magda took another man. The boys were already big enough to help in the fields. They earned their keep. But you were still a baby, and he was jealous of your father."

Felicia nodded, taking in the information. "Did you know my father? The record says he never recognized me."

"Don't you worry about what the record says. He was your father. A mason. Very handsome, too."

"What happened? Why did he leave?"

Chele shook her head. "Your mother was like me, always reaching up for a better man. They didn't stay long, but they improved the bloodlines. Now look at us," she laughed and shook her head, "with an educated city girl."

"I've thought about looking for him," said Felicia.

"Your mother chased him up and down," Chele waved an arm in the air, "it didn't do any good. He said you weren't his, thought you were a full sister to the boys."

"Is that possible?" Felicia asked.

"No. And I'll swear to it." Chele sat up. "Magdalena didn't take one man for life like she should have, and I'll take the blame for that. I was no good example. But she had her men one at a time. That I know. She and the boys were with me when she was in love with your father, and I never smelled another man on her. Never."

Still frozen in my place by the door, I closed my eyes and put my head down. Would Felicia be able to handle all this? All the sad certainties of her life laid out in plain talk. I opened my eyes and shifted my position. The door creaked in response.

"*Quien mas esta?*" Chele asked.

Felicia beckoned to me to come and share her chair by the hammock as she explained my presence to Chele. "Without her I wouldn't have come. I would have lost my scholarship."

Chele reached for my face, feeling it as she had Felicia's. "A foreigner, *muy fino*, and you have been good to my Felicia." She squeezed my hand, then, hearing Aunt Josefina approach, she lay her head back down, "Shhh. She's coming."

Chele kept a scowl on her face for the foot washing, but Aunt Josefina pretended not to notice, as she scrubbed each foot, then rinsed, catching the water in an empty bowl. Afterward she threw the dirty water out the front door. "There, I'm finished. Now you're ready for some hot coffee."

Felicia stepped forward. "*Abuela*, I have a present for you." She took the package from the basket, unwrapped the coarse rubber sandals and handed them to her grandmother. "Some shoes. Let me put them on for you."

"Ha. I've never worn shoes a day in my life."

"Now you can," coaxed Felicia. "They're comfortable, and they'll keep your feet clean so you don't get worms in your feet."

"I was here before the worms. They don't dare come near me."

"Won't you try them?"

Chele cast a scowl in Felicia's direction. "You're just like the others. You want me to wear them so you won't have to be ashamed. Well, I am what I am, with or without shoes."

"That's not why—" Felicia's voice broke and she pulled back her offering. "I'm sorry."

"Bah. Don't listen to me," said Chele, letting go of her scowl. She offered her foot to Felicia. "For you, I'll wear them. Of all my kin, you're the one who has come up in the world. I'm not going to let people say you came from a barefoot pig."

The next morning we took the early bus out of town. "This one will get you there the fastest," explained Rafael. "it goes directly to Olancho then Teguc."

As we rode away, Felicia was quiet.

"At least we don't have to change buses in San Juancito this time," I said.

Felicia gave me a brief half-smile then looked back toward Vista.

"I hope you're not sorry we made the trip," I said.

"I had to get my scholarship."

"Still, I know it was hard."

Felicia squeezed her eyes shut then and put her face in her hands. "All these years I never admitted to myself that I didn't have a father. I should have known my mother's story was a lie. But I didn't."

"I understand how you must feel—"

"No, you don't." Felicia's voice was forceful, almost a shout. She looked toward the window. "You have a father, he's just dead."

I hadn't been intending to equate my loss with Felicia's, but I accepted her rebuke in silence. Somehow my father's spirit seemed closer now. As so many things changed, his memory was a reassuring constant. All that I remembered and all that I didn't was there, part of me.

After a moment I spoke again. "You're going to be a sculptor, Felicia. You've gotten a scholarship because of your talent."

"You're right. My father can deny me, but I have it anyway." Felicia looked at her hands. "The talent he gave me, I mean."

"Maybe you gave it to yourself," I said. "Think about that, okay?"

Felicia sat back in her seat. "From now on I'll sign my work Felicia Ortiz. I won't use Romero anymore."

La Casa de los Niños
February

V

Crack. I felt a tug at the base of my finger. I stopped scrubbing and looked down. It was my ring. The stone had slipped around to the inside of my hand and caught on the ridges of the cement washboard. I rinsed the soapy foam from my fingers then ran to the kitchen to dry my hands and take a closer look.

It was seven-thirty, so most of the girls were in their rooms getting ready for school or work. Rosa, who had breakfast duty, stood over the skillet, mashing beans with the back of a spoon. Katia sat at the table with puffy eyes, waiting for coffee. I grabbed the hand towel by the stove.

"Beth, what happened? Did you hurt your hand?" Rosa asked.

"No, it's my ring. I cracked it on the *pila*."

"*Que lástima.*" Katia's eyes were dark slits. "Our poor *gringa* broke her golden ring. Don't cry, *gringa*. You can buy another one."

"It's not replaceable." I lowered my voice. "It was a gift from my mother."

Katia shrugged. "And she can't get you another? What is she, dead or something?"

"No, she's not dead." Katia just never let up. I managed to hold back cross words, but when I slapped the towel down onto the table it struck right next to her hands.

"Hey, I'm sorry." Katia put up her hands in surrender. "Jewelry is usually passed on after someone dies, right? I'm sure a goldsmith can fix it."

I took off the ring and turned it over in my hand. The stone was cracked and the gold band was bent, but I could still wear it.

Katia got up and came over to me. "Let me look at it for you."

Don't do me any favors, I wanted to say, but looking at Katia trying to be caring I relented with a sigh. I held out the ring and pointed to the green-black oval.

"It's called a bloodstone. If you look closely, you can see tiny red spots."

"*Sangre*, eh?"

I nodded and sat down. The coffee smelled good. I'd finish my washing after breakfast. I looked at the ring again. "When my mother gave it to me she said that as long as I wore it I'd always be safe. This is the first time I've taken it off."

Katia raised an eyebrow. "Would you be afraid if you lost it?"

"No." I slid the ring back on my finger. "No."

I didn't expect to be waited on at breakfast and the girls knew it. But now Rosa brought me some beans, wrapped in a tortilla, and a cup of coffee. I smiled at the gesture of comfort. "Thanks, Rosa."

She went to the hall to call out that breakfast was ready, then came back and sat down beside me. "Can I see?"

I held out my hand and pointed out the spots.

"A bloodstone for protection," Rosa said, as if she were reciting a law of nature that had just now been revealed to her. "No wonder you were upset."

"It wasn't just that." I realized all at once how little the girls knew about me.

"What then?" Rosa asked. "*Cuéntanos.* Tell us."

Katia got her breakfast and sat down, leaning away, but listening.

"Just after she gave it to me she started to cry," I began. "I thought she was feeling sentimental because her baby was growing up."

Vera came in dressed for work. She served herself breakfast quickly, then sat down and fixed her eyes on me with an expectant smile. She'd caught the tail end of the conversation and wanted to hear the rest. Felicia joined the group. Still barefoot, she sat at the edge of one of the chairs to listen as she toweled her hair dry.

During the past weeks I had seen the girls share stories and confidences at this table, and I'd wondered at it. In many ways they were private and defensive about their lives, yet here they would tell anything. Now I felt what it was like to be at the center, to be listened to, to welcome others to the circle with a nod, the telling uninterrupted.

"A few months later, we were at my grandmother's house looking at old pictures. I asked my mother to show me a picture of her when she was a baby. It was a stupid thing to say. I knew my mother had been an orphan. She was five years old when my grandmother took her in, so there wouldn't be any baby pictures. I apologized right away. Then I said something like, 'You don't know what you looked like as a baby, do you?'

"But my mother wasn't upset. 'Yes, I do,' she said. 'I found out what I looked like on the day you were born.' That's when I realized why she wanted me to have her bloodstone ring. As her oldest child, I was the first person of her own blood that she'd ever known."

"But she must know something about what she came from," Rosa said.

"She doesn't remember," I said.

Katia didn't look up. "She remembers."

The probable truth of what Katia said pierced me. Had my mother kept secrets? I hadn't taken that possibility seriously before. I felt my mother's story move in closer, suddenly more a puzzle than a history.

"She did talk about the time before she was adopted two or three times," I said softly.

"What did she say?" asked Felicia.

"Things about the orphanage... She hated the way they cut her hair, short like a boy's."

78

"They did that to us, too," Rosa said. "No one wanted to comb it. 'A man will get caught in your hair.' That's what we were told. Long hair was a sin."

Vera turned to me. "Did she ever say anything about her real mother?"

"My grandmother was her true mother," I corrected. "My mother didn't want to look for the mother who gave birth to her, and my grandmother forbade it."

"She must have wondered," said Rosa quietly.

"Doesn't it bother you?" Katia asked. "Not knowing what you come from?"

"Well, I do know some things," I said. "My mother was happy and loving — so I think she must have been loved herself as a child."

Katia shook her head. "But you could be from whores or robbers."

"And she sang to us," I continued. "Songs that my grandmother didn't know. Someone taught her those songs."

Katia flushed. "Still, there are things in the blood that you can't escape."

"Maybe," I said slowly, "but I think most things are up to us."

"Does anybody know about the other mother?" Vera asked. "Aren't there any clues at all?"

"There was one clue. My grandparents found my mother — first saw her I mean — in a newspaper photo. My grandmother had given up hope of having children of her own, and never wanted to adopt until she saw my mother. That article, if it could be found, told about the orphanage my mother came from and could lead to information about her birth mother."

"And you're not curious?" Vera asked.

"My mother doesn't want to pursue it. I have to respect that."

"What about you? Don't you wonder?"

"Not really... I know there's something good there that has been passed on to me."

"Because of the songs," said Katia.

"Yes. And other things, too. Anyway, I'll probably never know more."

"Because your mother doesn't want you to," said Rosa.

"Yes."

"But you're teaching us that we have a right to ask questions about the past. Don't you have the same rights?" said Vera.

"I guess I would if I felt I needed to know." I put down my empty coffee cup. "But I don't."

After a brief silence Felicia jumped up. "I have to get ready. Studio starts in ten minutes."

The other girls took their dishes to the sink. Breakfast was over.

I rinsed out my coffee cup, set it out to dry, then headed for the small desk in my bedroom. The house would be quiet until lunch, and I wanted to get some work done. Most of the girls were in school or apprenticeships now, but I was responsible for helping them find jobs and living arrangements later in the year. One by one I was reviewing and updating their files which, in most cases, consisted of a one-sentence case history and hard-to-read school reports.

Rosa's file was on top. Her cooking apprenticeship was almost over and she wanted to look for work soon. We had started making a list of small hotels that Rosa could approach when the time came. They were likely to pay better than a neighborhood eatery, and some offered benefits.

Next was Katia. I had been surprised to find that she was one of only three girls to earn an excellent rating for her sewing. She had finished sixth grade, too, but refused to enroll for further study. I had spoken to her, told her that she was well qualified for a job in a sewing factory, all she had to do was apply for a position. But Katia had shrugged off the suggestion. "Why should I sew myself blind for some *rico*?"

I heard a rustling sound in one of the bedrooms. Who was home at this time of day? I went into the hall to find out.

It was Suyapa. She had stripped the beds in her room and turned the mattresses on their sides to air. Her face was red and puffy, and her eyelashes glistened with tears. As she swept the floor, she moved with force, lifting things out of her way without missing a stroke.

"Suyapa, what are you doing?"

"Cleaning. Like you said, I'm good at it. I'll wash the sheets, too. I can have them dry and on the beds by the time my roommates are back."

"But shouldn't you be in school?"

"I'm done with school, Beth."

"But it's only three weeks into the term. Did something go wrong?"

Suyapa shook her head. "I'm not going to be the only stupid *tonto*, yellow, at the bottom of the list for the rest of my life. I'll never make orange if I stay in school."

My heart sank. I hadn't considered that my incentives might somehow cause harm.

"Oh Suyapa, you won't be stuck at the bottom. I promise." I put my hands on Suyapa's broom to stop the sweeping. "Let's talk about this."

"I've already decided. I'm not going back." Suyapa pulled my hands off the broom and swept her way into the hall where the chart hung.

"Look, it's right here. Level two: Orange. Girls enrolled in school must pass ALL classes." Suyapa followed the words on the chart with her finger like a child who has just learned to read. "I know I can't do that. I'm going to get a job. And you can help me. I want to clean house for some *gringos*."

I cringed. I hadn't come all the way to Honduras, armed with ideas about social justice, to run a maid service. I stared at the chart. "I'll talk with Mother Maria. We'll help you find a good job. You can start out living here and going in to work — you'll have to take the early bus," I hesitated, "and then we'll see."

Suyapa heard what was unspoken. She went back to her room and took up her broom again. "Don't worry about me. I'm ready to go. I'm not going to take my bread here at *La Casa* one day more than I have to." She swept with fierce quick strokes. "I don't have to study anymore, and I'm leaving this place."

You can stay as long as you want, I wanted to say. But I held in these words. It was better for Suyapa to choose the moment, to prepare to go.

It was time to go to sleep. I reached to turn off my bedside light then stopped. I just wasn't tired. I opened my book and tried to read, but found myself going over the same paragraph for the third time without taking in a word. I set the book aside, held my ring up to the light, and rubbed my finger over the crack. There were so many things I'd never dared to ask my mother.

I had worked hard to get to know the girls these past weeks. I'd met individually with each of them, to assess their needs and offer support. I'd asked what they knew about details of their abandonment, and if they had living relatives. These questions were the logical first steps of caring, trying to help, yet I couldn't answer these same questions about my own mother. The realization shocked me.

There had always been signs that my mother was different from the rest of the family. She stood out, just a bit, from the dark, laughing Italians, both the Rossis that had adopted her and the Pellegrinos that she'd married into. She had dark hair and eyes like the rest of them, but her skin was a shade fairer. She was the quiet one, the one who freckled.

We had become so close after my father died. Somehow, child that I was, I saw that my mother's loss was somehow greater than my own. I had tried to provide help and comfort. I prepared simple meals for the family in the early days of grief. I found that my arms fit around my mother's shoulders. I could hold her, let her cry like a child.

My psychology professor from sophomore year had described such relationships as unhealthy. Parentification, and the related role confusion, as he called it, was dangerous because it put undue pressure on a child, and made it difficult to establish an autonomous sense of self. But I had been pleased to find the strength inside myself to be the mother, to be of use.

As far as my self went, I wasn't sure. That kind of individualism wasn't what I was about. I was glad that I was the kind of person who could feel someone else's pain. If I lost myself at times, so what? Was my "self" really that important?

Still, I wondered if my mother had secrets. I let images pass through my mind, looking for clues. I saw my mother fold a warm sheet, spreading away the wrinkles. Then I watched from the kitchen table as my mother tasted soup from a pot and frowned because it needed seasoning. I sat by my mother at the piano, listening — first to a Bach minuet, fluid and simple, then to the resolute firmness of a Beethoven sonata. On the final chord my mother let out a breath and closed her eyes, putting her whole soul into it. Was it the song that had moved her, or was it something else? A memory? A longing?

I lay back and pulled the bedcovers up to my neck. I had imagined so many possible lives for my mother. She'd been adopted in 1940, the year after Eleanor Roosevelt brought hundreds of war orphans to the United States. I saw her in a thin coat, standing on the deck of one of those boats. Or maybe she was part Native American. Pammy's dark eyes and high cheekbones suggested that. Was Pammy's face reflecting some unknown ancestor? Had my mother been born of some forbidden love, the shame of some family that decided to give her away and go on without her? And there was the music, a gift that no one could explain.

In the past thoughts like this had made me feel connected to the whole world, a daughter of Earth. But now I wished I could plot myself precisely on the map of possibilities. Exactly which daughter of Earth was I?

It doesn't matter, I tried to tell myself. This is my life. I shouldn't have to find my mother before I can find myself...

Did I have the right to disregard her wishes? I wasn't sure, but the newspaper clipping was a public document, and it couldn't be that hard to find. I thought I had a right to at least take things that far. From there I would just have to see...

I looked at the ring again. When I held it up to the reading lamp in just the right way I could see my own eyes reflected in the stone.

I wished I didn't have to wait until I got back to the States to start the search, but that was silly. After all these years another ten months wouldn't matter, would it? I lay still for a moment, then got out of bed. I put a clean sheet of paper into the typewriter. Of course Jake would do this for me.

After I finished the letter I scrolled to the top to type in the date: February 20th. It was winter at home, I realized, and suddenly felt hungry for cold air, the cleanness of snow. I scrolled back to the bottom of the letter. "I wish we could go for a walk by the lake," I added. "I long for a friend."

VI

Mother Maria sat down and positioned her skirt around her chair. She blessed herself, then looked up, finally acknowledging me.

"It's good that you came to me this morning, Beth. I want to talk to you about one of the girls." She took a sweet roll out of the basket and placed it on my saucer. "You must."

I bit into the sweet roll and chewed slowly. I had to admit meals at the big house were something to look forward to. "Who did you want to talk about?"

"Dina. She and Pedro came to me yesterday. They're to be married this Saturday."

"So soon?"

Mother Maria buttered a roll for herself and took a bite. "We can't have a wedding during Lent, and they didn't want to wait until Easter."

"You'll have the wedding here at *La Casa?*"

"Yes, and the wedding party too. Dina has been an important example to the other girls. A good student, and she comes to Mass every day. Not perfect," she paused, "but I want them all to see how things should be done. After the wedding I've arranged for Dina and Pedro to go up to San Pedro Sula to live. She can finish her training there. I'd like her to get away from the *Residencia de las Señoritas* for a while."

I thought of how Dina held herself above the other girls, how she challenged me at every turn. I had to admit I'd be glad to see her go. "She'll have a fresh start," I said. "A whole new life."

"Yes." Mother Maria eyed me kindly, but seemed to be looking for something too. After a moment she seemed satisfied. "You wanted to see me today?"

"Yes, I'm concerned about one of the other girls."

"Who's in trouble? Is this about Katia?"

"No, it's Suyapa."

Mother Maria's jaw dropped. "Pregnant, that one?"

"She's not pregnant." I let out a sigh. "She's decided to drop out of school. I'm sorry to say it's because she was discouraged by my levels."

Mother Maria paused to wipe the sticky tips of her fingers on her cloth napkin. "Has she made any plans?"

"She says she wants to work as a housekeeper."

"Good." Mother Maria placed her napkin in her lap and took up her coffee. "You can get her a job with some *gringos*."

I hesitated. Mother Maria thought like the girls at times. "I'm not sure I would be comfortable doing that..."

Mother Maria took a sip of coffee and set it down. "I see."

"I hoped we could explore some other options before she settled for housework. Maybe we could find an apprenticeship for her. She might even be able to stay in school with some tutoring."

"A steady job with people who will protect her would be good for a girl like Suyapa." Mother Maria raised an eyebrow at me. "I hope you didn't expect to come here from the United States and turn all my girls into nurses and teachers."

"Of course not." I blushed. "I just thought living in a household of foreigners would be difficult — isolating. Couldn't we find a good Honduran home for her? She could become like family over time."

"The *gringos* can treat her like family, too. And with *gringos* she'll eat at the table and have the weekend off. With Hondurans she'll eat leftovers in the kitchen, and she'll only have Sunday afternoon." Mother Maria leaned toward me. "I'd like you to help Suyapa find a position."

I was ready to protest further, but Mother Maria didn't let me.

"I expect you to make a good faith effort," she added. "Suyapa will be counting on you."

I looked down at my hands and said nothing.

Mother Maria sat up straight and brushed some crumbs off the table. "Leaving school is the right thing for Suyapa, Beth. It's a step forward for her even though it may not look like it. Some of the others should probably move on as well. Like Luz. She's repeating her grade for the third time, isn't she? I want you to speak to her about a job in a seamstress shop. She'd make an excellent assistant."

My jaw dropped. "But Luz can make it..."

"We can't be too soft-hearted, Beth. Luz needs to accept reality. To find her place. She's not sixteen like the others, you know." Mother Maria paused and searched my face. "I'm on Luz's side, Beth, just like you are. But she can't pretend to be a schoolgirl forever."

"She deserves a little more time," I said firmly, looking down at the table, but determined to fight for Luz if I had to.

Mother Maria sensed my resolve. "I promised that you'd be in charge. If you feel there's hope, we'll give her the rest of the year."

I let out a sigh of relief. "Thank you."

"Mercedes, could I ask your advice about something?" I asked, as she was seeing me out.

"Of course, *Señorita* Beth."

"If a girl is willing to work hard — to do any honest work — what kind of a job can she get?"

"Without the elementary certificate? There's just cooking or housework." Mercedes smoothed her hair then retied her apron. "Working for people of means — it's a decent life. Some *patrones* are very generous. The big houses are better, because they have more than one girl working, and the houses of the *gring*—the foreigners, are better still."

I frowned at hearing that for the third time. "What about jobs where she wouldn't have to--uh — live in, where she'd have more independence?"

Mercedes responded briefly through a tight mouth. "If service doesn't suit her, if she thinks she's too good for that, she could try the *mercado*. Some of the vendors hire help. They pay a percentage."

A percentage of sales in the public market didn't sound too steady. "Anything else?"

Mercedes shrugged. "There's a shrimp cannery down the road. It's day work, but an honest living, if she wants her independence so badly. They take a few new girls just about every morning. All she'd have to do is go early to get a place in the front of the line. It's only a mile down the road — the *La Casa* girls wouldn't even have to pay bus fare."

When I got back to the *Residencia de las Senoritas* the girls were cleaning up after breakfast. Rosa, who had been going to church with Alberto's family lately, rushed into the kitchen, a single white rose in her hand.

"I'm getting married," she said.

"I knew it," squealed Vera. "When you said his parents invited you to dinner, I knew he'd ask soon." She took Rosa's hands and spun her around. "When is the wedding?"

"June," said Rosa, breathless and laughing. "It seems like a long time, but there's so much to do. Alberto has to get the house ready, and I need to save some money."

"I'll help you with the dress," said Vera.

I waited behind Luz and Felicia to congratulate Rosa with a hug. There would be two weddings then, but this one didn't surprise me at all.

"We want details, *chica*," said Felicia. "How did he ask?"

"Yes," said Katia. "Who knows if the rest of us will ever get a decent proposal — at least we should hear about one."

Rosa twirled the white rose between her thumb and forefinger. "Okay, let's see. We went to church like always. He gave me this flower as a surprise."

"Only Rosa could be surprised," teased Vera. "He gives her flowers every Sunday."

Rosa blushed. "But he usually gives me a carnation. This was different — a single white rose. I've never seen one like it — it must have been imported. After Mass we walked in the garden by the cemetery, and when we sat down on the bench — we rest there every Sunday before we walk home — he asked."

"How did he say it?" asked Vera.

"He got down on his knees, like a gentleman. Then he said, 'I can't ask your father for your hand, so I'll ask you before God instead. Will you marry me?' And I said yes. We decided to wait until I finish my year with Doña Lula. Then I'll look for a job, something between here and Alberto's house in Bella Vista."

Now Rosa turned to me. "I'll need my baptismal certificate to be married in the church. You'll help me get it, won't you?"

"Of course." I hugged Rosa. I wasn't sure I was ready to make another journey, but I couldn't disappoint Rosa. "Where were you born?"

"Somewhere near Ilama. The priest there brought me to Mother Maria when I was a baby. I don't know exactly where I'm from, but I do know that he baptized me in Ilama before he made the journey to Teguc, so I'm sure the papers will be there."

I nodded as questions about the trip flooded my mind. Where was Ilama? I was going to get clear directions this time, and no jeans and sandals. I'd travel in a professional dress and a pair of low pumps, as crazy as that seemed, and carry a letter of introduction from Mother Maria that I could present to any small town "officials" who wanted to know who I was.

The journey was sudden for Rosa, too. She probably hadn't had time to think of all the ramifications of going to Ilama. Her mother's name would likely be on the baptismal certificate. Would

Rosa want to look for her? Now wasn't the time to ask, but I planned to make sure that Rosa was emotionally prepared for the trip.

"What about your mother? Are you going to look for her?" asked Felicia.

"I don't think so." Rosa set her lower jaw forward. "She dropped me on a doorstep and threw away the milk. I doubt she would want to see me."

"You don't know that," said Felicia. "The people in the *pueblos* are so poor. I didn't realize it myself until I met my grandmother and my brothers. Your mother gave you to a priest. She must have wanted something better for you."

Rosa's chin quivered. "I don't know." She looked at me, and then away.

"There's plenty of time to decide." I put an arm around Rosa and lifted up the hand that held the rose. "Let's put this in some water."

Vera got a plastic drinking cup and went out to the *pila* for water. The outside of the cup was still dripping wet when she handed it to Rosa, who placed the flower in the water and set the cup on the kitchen table.

"You have a wedding party to plan, too," Vera said. "I'm sure Mother Maria will want you to have one."

"I'm not planning to have a party here. Alberto's family will have a party for me in Santa Lucia."

Vera looked disappointed.

"Don't worry, you'll all be invited," said Rosa.

"Anyway," said Vera, "this isn't one of those emergency weddings that Mother Maria has to throw together with a party on top. Rosa's wedding gown can be made months ahead without any problems."

"Without alterations," added Luz with a smirk.

"Without an elastic waistband," Katia guffawed.

My mouth opened and then closed again. How could I have been so stupid? Dina was pregnant and all the girls knew it.

Rosa's Journey

Rosa stood out as the one who was unmarked by her abandonment. She was kind and competent, neither bitter nor overly grateful. She knew how to love, and had found her way into a family. I could see that she was heading for an ordinary life; a caring husband, children, the everyday miracles. How had she pulled it off, I wanted to know?

Was it some great feat of self-awareness and personal growth? I doubted it, not at seventeen. Perhaps prayer had bred gentleness and hope in her. Mother Maria would have said that, credited Rosa's success to daily Mass. I didn't put much faith in rote routines myself, but I did think there was a larger grace, a blessing, at work. Perhaps the blessing came from rainwater, or the waters of her baptism. Or had she been washed in her mother's tears first? Was that what made the difference?

*　　　*　　　*

The trip to Ilama couldn't have been more different from the trip to Vista del Oro. Alberto accompanied us to the bus station, carried our bags, and even boarded the bus to see us to a seat. Alberto's mother, who was a telephone operator in Santa Lucia, had taken it upon herself to speak with the *telefonista* from Ilama and arranged for lodging with a local family. When we arrived in Ilama that afternoon, Sonia Molina was there to escort us to her home.

Of course the Molinas knew why Rosa had come. Alberto's mother had told them about the upcoming marriage, and that Rosa needed proof of her baptism so that she could be married in the Church. The Molinas made baskets for a living. Long palm strips stood along the side wall of the *sala*, some natural, some dyed bright pink and blue. Beside the wall was a table covered with baskets, some complete, some works in progress, and a small stack of straw hats.

In the center of the room the family table was already set for dinner with eight mismatched dishes and cups. Two school-age boys climbed in and out of the chairs while a little girl chased a baby pig under the table. The child squealed with delight when the pig wriggled away from her.

Sonia laughed as she led us toward the back door. "My children — Pablo, Esteban, and Delia."

Just outside the back door, Sonia introduced us to her mother-in-law, who stood by the *horno* making tortillas. She told us to call her "Abuelita." Her face framed by a tight red kerchief, she slapped a tortilla back and forth from one hand to the other then placed it on the hot stone. Behind her a small but well-tended herb garden was marked off with wooden stakes, and in the back corner, beside the latrine, stood a banana tree. Chickens ran freely in the fenced yard. One pecked around the back door, and tried to enter the kitchen, but Abuelita shooed it away with a "*ch ch*" and a stamp of her foot. She wiped her hands on her apron and smiled at us through rotted teeth.

Rosa stepped toward Abuelita and patted her on the shoulder in greeting. I held back the impulse to shake hands and mimicked Rosa's gesture as best I could.

Abuelita lifted Rosa's chin to study her. She nodded approval as she took in Rosa's eyes, coffee-colored in the shape of large almonds, her caramel skin, and her wavy brown ponytail that had become loose on the long bus trip. "Your face is proof you're from Ilama," she said as she smoothed away a stray hair from Rosa's face and placed it behind one ear.

Next she turned to me, assessing me at arm's length. "You're the *gringa*? You're not even blond," she said, not unfriendly, just stating the fact. She looked into my face, then behind and beside me for some clue that would explain. "What's your name? Where were you born?"

"I'm Beth, from the United States."

"What town?" asked Abuelita.

"Providence. Here you'd say *Providencia*."

Abuelita's face lit up. "We have a *Providencia* just down the river. Good people. *Muy buena gente.* They work baskets like we do."

"I've heard about the beautiful baskets," I said. "If we have a chance to go to the market I'd like to get one."

Abuelita frowned. "But not from *Providencia*. The best work in all Honduras is done here, in Ilama."

"That's what we heard. Of course I want one from here." I looked to Rosa for help. "We both do."

Then Sonia was at our sides. "Let me show you where you'll sleep," she said.

We followed her through the house into the bedroom, separated from the *sala* by a blue plastic curtain that hung over the doorway. Two narrow platform beds supported thin pieces of foam with straw mats on top. Neatly folded at the bottom of each bed were a sheet and blanket. There was another cot on the far wall and more sleeping mats laid out on the floor.

"With us," Sonia said, looking at me. "I hope you don't mind."

"No, of course not. We'll be very comfortable."

"These straw mats keep you cool," put in Rosa. "You'll see, Beth, they're more comfortable than mattresses."

There was not much furniture, just a small dresser with a half-spent candle and an open Bible on top, along with a bundle of papers bound together neatly with a rubber band. Next to the papers, in a neat row, sat a pair of rubber gloves, a few bottles of medicine, a bag of herbs, and the glint of what looked like a razor.

Sonia must have seen my curious glance. "We don't have a nurse or a doctor here — just the ones who visit from Santa Barbara. So the women of Ilama, and the *aldeas* too, they call me."

Sonia stood before me in her homemade blue cotton shift, her long braid draped over her right breast like a ribbon. Her face glowed in spite of a few age lines, and her dark hands were clean, with strong sure fingers. She worked with her hands, making baskets for a living. She must have made the sleeping mats, too.

I looked down at my smooth white hands, those of a well-educated American. As a counselor I was supposed to be able to heal with talk, but I was useless in the event of a birth, or even a bad cut.

Rosa took a step closer to look at the instruments. "Were you afraid the first time you delivered a baby? How did you know what to do?"

"My mother taught me. She knew all the old ways. She used herbs and plants — chamomile for cleanliness, aloe for healing. Later I learned some of the modern ways too, at a class at the clinic in Santa Barbara — how to prevent infections with washing and gloves, and when a doctor is needed."

"Is it true that you can't remember what the pain feels like afterward?" Rosa asked.

Sonia laughed. "Your time will come soon enough. You'll see for yourself. But there's nothing in the world like being a mother. All the pain is rewarded when you hold your baby. That's how it was for me, and I think every mother in the world would say the same thing."

Most likely the Molinas ate a simple supper of beans and tortillas every night, except maybe on Sundays. But today, an ordinary Thursday, Sonia had prepared a beef stew with potatoes and carrots and *potaste*, a local vegetable that tasted like a cross between squash and potato.

"*Muy rico*," said José, exhaling with pleasure after the first taste of stew. "The broth is so thick."

Abuelita nodded and took an enthusiastic bite. "Don Geraldo must have given us his best cut."

I looked down at the fatty piece of stew meat that I had pushed aside on my plate. I picked it up in a spoonful of broth and made myself swallow it whole.

After dinner, Sonia poured a second cup of coffee for us, then sat down to work baskets with Abuelita.

I picked up a basket and turned it over in my hands. "I've seen baskets like these in stores." Abuelita took the largest basket off the table and held it up. "How much would this one sell for?"

"About thirty dollars, I'd guess."

Sonia took the basket in her hands and nodded seriously. "And what do they put in it?"

"In that one? Maybe a plant," I began, "or they might keep magazines or newspapers in it. The larger ones could be used as a clothes hamper. Sometimes they're just decorative — not filled with anything."

Abuelita let out a low laugh. "*Decorativo.*"

Rosa had gotten up to look at a small basket that sat on the sill of the front window. "Come and look at this one, Beth."

The round basket, which was small enough to fit in the palm of a hand, was filled with beans, kernels of corn, and dried herbs. The weave was the same as the one used for the baskets on the table, but in miniature it looked delicate, almost like lace. The tiny basket must have required at least as much work as the larger ones, maybe more. The palm strips would have to be split in half, maybe even in half again, and the tiny weave was as precise as fine embroidery.

Rosa picked up the basket. "This one's so pretty. How much will it sell for?"

"That's not for sale," said Sonia. "That's my *abundanza.*"

Rosa put it down. "It's such beautiful work."

Sonia smiled. "You can hold it if you want to. A visitor's touch brings good luck to our house, but you have to bless yourself afterward."

Rosa picked it up again, smiling at Sonia, and blessed herself.

"My mother made it for me," explained Sonia. "It's a custom here in Ilama when a daughter gets married. Her mother gives it to her to protect the family from hunger. It's full of corn and beans and rice. In the old days they would have filled it with seeds of all kinds, and the daughter would use it to plant her first garden. But now that we live in town, we don't plant them, we just keep them on the sill.

"You'll see one in every household, but this one is very fine. My mother was the best weaver in the whole town." Sonia smiled shyly. "I'm not the only one who says it. She was famous for her baskets. There were ladies from Santa Barbara who would come here and ask for her by name..."

Rosa offered the *abundanza* to me. "Go ahead."

I hesitated. Was it okay for me to touch it? Sonia and Abuelita exchanged a glance, but said nothing. I cupped both hands around the *abundanza* as if it were a china egg. Then I placed the basket back on the sill and made the sign of the cross.

Abuelita smiled and licked her lips.

"*Gracias*," said Sonia with a slight bow.

The sun had begun to set and it was getting dark in the house. Sonia and Abuelita moved out to the front steps and let the children play in the street while they got in one more hour of weaving by the last light of the evening. Rosa and I joined them.

They worked quickly and expertly, threading the palm through small openings without looking. Rosa had learned a bit of basket weaving at school and, at Sonia's invitation, had started on a hot plate. She could take it with her, Sonia said, for the home she would share with Alberto.

Would I like to learn how they made baskets, Sonia wanted to know. I had been hoping she would ask. I watched carefully as Sonia held a small round of palm strips over my lap and demonstrated the stitch.

"Through the bottom and over the top," said Sonia. "Then you wrap it around the middle and pull it tight, like a knot."

After I watched Sonia the third time through, I thought I had it. Sonia handed me the woven round the size of a coaster, along with a long palm strip that was to be woven onto it. I made my first stitch, imitating the sharp sure tug that Sonia and Abuelita used at the finish. I envisioned a small round basket the size of a bread loaf with a splash of blue woven into the rim and handle.

"That's right," said Sonia, "pull tight. That's what makes the basket strong and the stitches even."

We worked without talking for a while. I looked up to take in the evening more fully. I thought I heard an airplane idling in the distance, but of course that wasn't likely. It was the metallic humming and chirping of thousands of unnamed insects.

The street wasn't quiet either. The houses were so close together I could hear voices through an open window across the street and a door shutting with a squeak and a clap at the end of the block. Still, it felt peaceful, maybe just because my own world was so far away.

After a while Abuelita broke the silence. "Tonight I'm going to finish this big one. All that's left to do is the rim."

She rested her elbows on the basket for a moment. "Rosa, you're such a pretty rose," she said. "When is the wedding?"

"June," said Rosa. "I'm already saving for it. Alberto knows that I can't bring much, but I want to buy my own pots at least, and make some sheets for the bed."

"He'll forget where the pots came from," said Abuelita. "Make yourself a nice dress instead. You want him to remember you the way you were on your wedding day."

Rosa blushed and grinned. "A dress, too, of course," she said.

Abuelita was quiet for a moment, then she looked up at Rosa again. "When his mother called to make arrangements for you to stay with us, she told us that you're one of Mother Maria's children."

"*Sí*," said Rosa.

"They say she's like a saint."

"She's been very kind to me," said Rosa respectfully.

I felt Rosa's discomfort, and tried to change the subject. "Did you know that Rosa is a professional cook? You should taste the cakes she makes," I said brightly.

Abuelita seemed impressed. Cakes weren't part of the traditional cooking in the countryside. "I've tried cakes, but they never come out."

"The secret's in the batter. You have to beat it until it's very smooth — at least three hundred strokes," said Rosa.

"We'll have to put her to work in the kitchen. She can make a cake for Sunday dinner." Abuelita said it with a light laugh, but she looked intently at Rosa.

"I'll be glad to," said Rosa. "We'll just need flour, sugar, eggs and some baking powder, and if you can get a pineapple I'll bake it into the top. That's my best cake."

Abuelita was satisfied with the cake for a moment, then she went back to her questions. "Is it true that you don't know anything about your mother? No idea where to look for her?"

I bit my lip. I'd asked Rosa if she wanted to try to find her mother, but Rosa hadn't wanted to talk about it. It was too painful.

"I don't even know her name," said Rosa matter-of-factly.

Abuelita clucked and shook her head. "So beautiful. Your mother would want to see you. When were you born?"

"The *padre* brought me to Mother Maria in 1965. I was only a few weeks old."

"Sixty-five," Abuelita strained, searching her memory to find the faces that went with that year.

"It was before the drought. That was seventy-one," offered Sonia. "When was the flood? Do you remember?"

Abuelita shook her head as if she was being asked to speak another language. "It was after Jorge died. But the year, I don't know." She thought a minute more then shook her head. "I can't imagine who she might have been, but you could ask Padre Ramon..."

"You mean he's the same one?" Rosa looked surprised.

"He's the only priest we've had here since before José was born," said Abuelita. "That's at least forty years." She nodded her certainty. "He'll know where to find her."

Rosa went back to her weaving, but the silence was different because of the possibility that hung in the air.

"I promise you, your mother suffered for you all these years," said Abuelita. "She couldn't have lived in town — we would remember her. She must have come from out in the *aldeas*. Life is hard there. The *padre* goes out there to bury a child at least once a month." She lifted her eyes to assess Rosa again. "Go to find her, *mi hija*. Forgive her."

Rosa kept her eyes down on her weaving. "I doubt the *padre* would even remember."

"He'll remember," said Abuelita taking the weaving from Rosa's hand, "pull tighter like this, there, that's nice and strong. And if he doesn't, her name will be on the baptismal certificate. You'll find her. If she was near here when you were born she couldn't have gone far."

I was stunned. Abuelita had made more progress with Rosa in ten minutes than I had in an entire week. And she was probably right about Rosa's mother being nearby. People didn't just pick up and leave a place like this. The young men might leave to get jobs in the city. But a poor woman who couldn't even keep her baby? She wouldn't even be able to buy a bus ticket.

Rosa kept weaving, but her hands were shaking. She looked up and gave me a half-smile. "I'll see."

*   *   *

The *padre*, it turned out, was out of town, and not expected back until Sunday. That meant Rosa couldn't see to her papers until then. Wasn't there someone who could take care of this in his absence, I had asked. But Rosa and the Molinas didn't seem to think waiting two days for the priest was anything more than a mild inconvenience. He'd be here soon, and meanwhile Sonia and José arranged to take us on an outing to the swimming hole at the bend in the river.

"Hooray!" Esteban and Pablo jumped to get their fishing sticks when they heard the news.

Delia clapped her hands at the news and made a popping sound, like a fish kiss, with her lips.

"Maybe we'll be eating fried fish and potatoes for lunch," said Abuelita. "Pack the skillet, Sonia, just in case."

Sonia, who had started to pack tortillas and napkins into a straw bag with straw handles, got the skillet from a low shelf and groaned at its weight. "It barely fits," she said as she found room for it in the bag.

After walking for about a half an hour, we came to the path that led down to the river. The boys ran ahead with their sticks in the air.

The rest of us slowed their pace a bit, enjoying the shade provided by a canopy of trees. When we got to the river, Sonia put the sack of food and some thin towels down under a tree. José followed with a six-pack of cold Cokes we had bought at the *pulpería*. He opened one and offered it to me.

I took a sip and looked around. The swimming hole that Sonia had talked about was the size of a small lake. Branches from low trees reached out over the water, as if they did all their growing at sunset, when they had to stretch their limbs toward the west side of the river to find light. Most of the riverside was covered with a bed of smooth stones, but there was a small sandy area near the shallows that made a perfect beach for the children.

I heard laughter in one of the trees overhead. Pablo and Esteban were climbing up a supple young tree, whose branches were spaced out like steps. When they got to the top, they threw their weight forward just enough to make the tree bend, so that it held them dangling above the river. Then they dropped into the water, their noses plugged, their legs scrambling for a foothold in the air.

"I hope you're going to try dropping from the tree, Beth," Sonia teased. "It's the best way to get in."

Sonia stood behind the tree as she spoke. She had slipped her arms out of her dress and was putting on a slip over her underwear. Once her swimming outfit was in place she took off her dress and hung it over a tree branch to keep it dry. I was the only one who had a bathing suit under my clothes. I'd packed it just in case when I heard that Ilama was by a river.

I smiled. "Maybe later. First I'm going to swim across to the other side. I need the exercise after sitting for so long on the bus yesterday."

I took off my skirt and T-shirt and laid them under a tree. I felt naked in my bathing suit. Everyone else was more covered up in T-shirts, pajamas, slips, but if I left my T-shirt on I wouldn't have anything dry to wear home. I offered to let Rosa have a turn with the bathing suit, since we were about the same size, but she seemed just as happy to sit under the tree with Abuelita, who had brought along her weaving.

I waded out until I was waist deep, then started to swim. There was a large rock in a clearing across the way. I would swim to the rock, rest there a bit, then swim back. I stretched my arms in clean circles and kicked the fatigue out of my legs, savoring the allover embrace of the cool water.

I swam to the rock, then pulled up onto its warm dark surface. I lay on my back and propped myself up on my elbows, my head leaning back. I felt clean, pleasantly awake. I closed my eyes and lifted my face to the sun. The voices from the other side reached across the water as if they were just a few feet away.

The boys had been in the water the whole time I was swimming across, and now I heard them begging Sonia to come in with them.

"Please, Mama, I want to practice my *bombas*, but I can't jump unless you're here."

Sonia waded over to the rock where they were playing.

"*Contigo, Mama,*" Delia begged to be taken along.

I turned on my side and watched them play. The boys took turns seeing who could make the biggest splash. Then Delia climbed onto the rock and jumped into her mother's arms. She came up laughing. "Again, again!"

The Molinas were poor, I knew. Even the *La Casa* kids had more than they did in terms of clothes and toys. But in another way these children had so much, sunshine and fresh air, a loving family...

José was off by himself, across the river. I looked at him again. He was strong and fit from working outdoors; he seemed young for forty. He caught me looking at him and I quickly looked away, but out of the side of my eye I could see his gaze linger a moment, and I could feel it too, like a forbidden caress.

I thought of Jake. Suddenly it felt wrong to be here without him. The swimming hole reminded me of afternoons by the lake. Was he there now? I always imagined him alone, working on the house, waiting for me, and his letters made it sound like that was the case. But he must do other things, too. Surely he met intelligent, artistic women among the other architecture students. Did he ever invite them to the lake to see his work? Was he ever tempted to forget about waiting for me? I had thought of this year away as my right, my chance to be independent. But I didn't want to risk what I had at home. I slid down off the rock and started swimming back. It would be rude to spend too much time off by myself.

By the time I got back to the other side of the river, Sonia and the children were out of the water. Sonia grabbed a towel and pulled all of the children to her at once. Pablo reached for the other towel but Sonia pulled his hand back. "Leave that one for Beth."

I came out and took the towel, wrapped it around myself with a nod of thanks to Sonia, and went to sit by Rosa.

Sonia and the children sat in the sun to dry. Delia giggled wildly when Pablo tickled her then she nestled her wet head against Sonia's neck. She was ready for a nap and had found the ideal spot. The boys squirmed under the thin towel, gradually settling down as the sun took away the chill. Finally they were still, Pablo's hand on Sonia's shoulder, his arms and legs knotted together with his brother's, whose head rested on his mother's lap.

This was the first time I had seen Sonia relax. With the weaving and cooking and washing and waking up in the middle of the night to deliver babies, Sonia probably never had a chance to be still, to be alone with her thoughts. Even now, at rest, she had hands all over her, clinging to her with the weight of their love. Her life was built around duty, hardship, the necessities of survival, but it had its beauty, too. That life had its treasures.

José came toward us, his fishing pole in hand, a grin from ear to ear. "I've caught fish for us." He showed the fish to the children then Sonia, but his gaze lingered for a moment on me in my wet suit. Of course, there I was, an American woman standing practically naked in front of him. I re-wrapped my towel around myself and praised the catch with the others, keeping my eyes firmly fixed on the fish.

"We'll gather the wood, Papa," said Esteban. Then both boys scurried off together.

Sonia set Delia down in Abuelita's lap. "I didn't think he'd catch anything. I'll have to hurry and cut the potatoes. I brought boiled eggs and beans, but we'll save them for breakfast tomorrow." She turned to Abuelita to measure her agreement.

"That's fine," she said. "Catching all those fish on a Friday in Lent too. These visitors brought us luck."

That night we all went to bed when the children did. I hadn't felt so relaxed and ready for sleep in a long time. I'd spent so much time in the water that I could still feel myself floating, then I felt warm arms around me. I was dreaming of Jake. He was everywhere, so real and with me, I was about to cry out, to tell him that I loved him, when a sharp pleasure pierced through my sleep and woke me. I remembered where I was quickly enough to stifle my cry.

I closed my eyes in the dark room, and tried to go back to sleep, back to my dream, but I heard the sound of labored breathing — it was Sonia and José, making love on the dirt floor.

I was facing them, but it was so dark that I couldn't see anything. I closed my eyes. It was best not to move or they would know I was awake. Of course they were used to making love in a roomful of sleeping children. Rosa and I were just two more. That's how they saw it, I hoped. But could José have forgotten that I was a woman in the few hours between the picnic at the lake and now? Was he trying to show me something, send me a message? I hoped not. I held my breath, afraid that if I exhaled he would know that I was awake.

I tried not to listen and held myself still. It was quiet after a while and their breathing became free and relaxed again. When I was sure I was the only one awake I turned and faced the wall. Even if José had noticed me, it didn't mean much. Just that my white skin was exotic, my flat young stomach attractive.

I lay in the dark waiting for sunrise. I believed in what I was doing with my life, being here in Honduras for Rosa and the other girls, trying to help them in whatever small way I could. Still, I felt such longing now. To have what Sonia and José had. My life seemed so far away, and no one had touched me in such a long, long, time. I wished I could have two lives at once, one to give here, and one to live out at home, with Jake. But I couldn't, I had to choose one, and leave the other dangling, unlived.

Saturday morning was quiet. Sonia went to Santa Barbara, and Abuelita and the children were busy with chores. Rosa and I walked around Ilama, stopping at the fruit market to buy a pineapple. Then we went back to the house for lunch and spent a few hours weaving. Later Abuelita and the children took us out to get the other ingredients for the cake. Now we sat on the step after supper, settling down to work again.

"Look at Beth," said Abuelita. "She goes at it like one of us."

"And she just started on Thursday," said Sonia. "If you keep at it, Beth, you can finish that basket before you leave."

"You're right," said Abuelita, as if she was just realizing the magnitude of it. "This *gringa* is very smart. How old are you, dear?"

"Twenty-two."

"Twenty-two and not married yet." Abuelita shook her head. "Poor Beth."

"In my country twenty-two is still considered young." I smiled. "I have plenty of time."

"Twenty-two ..." Abuelita calculated. "Not so much. You'll be fifty by the time your children are grown, even if you marry right away. Don't wait too long if you want to see your grandchildren. And when you're old like me you'll want to rest a bit. You won't always have the energy of a young girl."

I laughed nervously at the well-intentioned advice. At least Rosa was off the hot seat tonight.

"Maybe you'll fall in love here in Honduras," suggested Abuelita, "you'll marry one of us, a *catracho,* and we can see the babies for ourselves."

"Don't tease her," said Sonia, then she turned to me. "Is there anyone that you write to?"

"Yes. But we haven't made any promise yet."

"Letters. That's good," said Abuelita, "but don't leave him alone for too long. You know what they say, cold feet wrap themselves in the first blanket they find."

I was about to respond when a young man came running up the street. "Doña Sonia, they need you in Las Cruces. Maria de los Santos is in labor."

Sonia rose quickly. "I'm not surprised. That's how her sisters are, too. Always early. When did she start?"

"After supper. The pains were coming steadily for about an hour, then I came here, that's another hour."

"Okay. I'm coming." Sonia started into the house and then turned back to Rosa. "Do you want to come? I have some things to bring to her. You could help me carry them."

Rosa looked to me. "Yes, we'll come."

We followed Sonia inside and held open two sacks while Sonia filled them with a few baby clothes, a blanket, some beans, and a bag of cornmeal.

The house in Las Cruces was a one-room shack made of uneven boards with a low roof. The only furniture was a small wooden table in the middle of the room. Maria de los Santos lay moaning on a straw mat on the floor. Her long wavy hair stuck to her shoulders, which glistened with sweat. Her mother sat by her, holding her hand and offering her water from a tin cup.

"Doña Sonia, you're here. Thank God," the mother said. "She's fine so far, but in lots of pain."

Sonia put her medicine kit on the table and set to work.

"Do you have any water?" she asked the mother.

"Just enough for drinking. The stream is down to a trickle, full of tadpoles. But it looks like the rain may come — we have all the pots and bowls and buckets outside."

"Right now everything is dry in the *aldeas*," Sonia explained to us. "They won't have water again until it rains."

"How will you manage the delivery without water?" I asked, incredulous.

"My gloves are sterile; I boiled them at home. I'll wipe the razor with alcohol before I cut the cord. And there's nothing purer than fresh rain. With luck maybe we can wash the baby in that."

I looked from the young girl on the mat to her mother to the pots in a row outside the back door. How many times had I heard the word luck since I'd been here in Ilama?

Sonia had Maria de los Santos sit up and she massaged her with sage oil. She tied her hair back and spread a plastic cloth and a clean cotton sheet over the mat on the dirt floor.

"This way we won't get blood on the mat," said Sonia, "and you'll have more room to stretch and turn." The girl nodded then doubled over in pain as a contraction came.

"Breathe deep now." Sonia lay her hand on Maria's stomach through the contraction. "That was a good one," she said, with a reassuring pat on the shoulder. "The hard ones are the ones that move things along."

After the contraction had loosened its grip and Maria de los Santos was breathing normally again, Sonia introduced us to her.

"They're staying with me," Sonia explained. "They came to ask you for prayers. Now I want you to walk a bit. I think it would help." As Sonia helped Maria de los Santos to her feet she turned to us to explain.

"Here in the *aldeas* there's a belief that the prayers of a woman who's in labor are very powerful. They say that God grants everything that she asks. When her time is closer and the word is out the neighbors will come. You'll see. They'll ask for prayers and stay and say a prayer for the new baby, too. So think about what you are going to ask for," she urged, as Maria de los Santos doubled over in pain again. "It won't be long."

It was close to midnight when the first neighbor arrived. An old woman with a shawl wrapped tight around her shoulders came in, embraced Maria's mother and handed her a small flask of water. "Let me see her. God bless her," she said.

I stood back and watched as the woman knelt beside Maria de los Santos. She blessed herself and moved her lips through a prayer before she opened her eyes and looked at Maria. "I'm asking for my Jorge," she said.

Maria de los Santos nodded. "For Don Jorge, that he may return to good health." She recited the Hail Mary, continuing even through a contraction. When she was finished she lay back again, spent.

The next woman to kneel beside Maria de los Santos was young, maybe as young as Maria herself. She carried a small baby wrapped in a thin blanket. "Touch him, please," she lay the baby next to Maria, "that God's will may be done."

Maria placed a hand on his head and prayed. "God's will is that he will live," she said.

Another hour had passed when Sonia came over to Rosa and touched her on the arm. "It's your turn."

Rosa followed her over to Maria de los Santos and whispered her intention in a low voice. I bowed my head and said the Hail Mary with them this time. The least I could do was offer up a prayer for Rosa — and Maria de los Santos, too.

Rosa came back with a satisfied smile. "I can't wait to see the baby," she whispered.

Sonia turned to me now. "Are you ready for your prayer?"

I thought of Maria de los Santos, just sixteen and already a mother, the poverty around her, and then of my own life — the education, the comforts, the possibilities. "I couldn't ask her to pray for me. Let her rest. I don't need anything."

"But she wants to." Sonia looked cross. "It's her time to help others. There must be something. Money can't buy everything, after all."

I groped for words to undo the harm. "Oh Sonia, it's not that. I just didn't want to trouble her when she's in all that pain. But if you think it's okay, I'd be honored to ask...to pray with her."

Still hurt, Sonia took me by the arm and led me over to Maria de los Santos. I didn't have any idea what to ask for. I didn't believe that God was a genie who granted wishes. On the other hand, I wanted to believe in a God who would listen to Maria de los Santos, who would make her a priestess and let her heal others, who would ease her pain, too.

I knelt down. Maria de los Santos looked tired now, but her face lit up when Sonia explained to her that the North American woman had come to ask her for prayers.

"Does she speak Spanish?" she asked.

When Sonia nodded Maria de los Santos turned to me. "What do you want?"

I looked up and let out a deep sigh. This was harder than I thought. I couldn't speak.

"She doesn't understand," said Maria de los Santos to Sonia. "What does she want?"

She thought it was a language problem, I realized, but it wasn't. I was afraid to ask for something, to choose my own life.

Maria de los Santos looked alarmed, then braced herself as another contraction came rushing in. "I'm going to ask God," she said, struggling for breath, "to give you a good husband and beautiful healthy children. How many," she asked, as she fought the crest of the wave of pain, "three?"

The question seemed urgent and I nodded quickly.

Maria de los Santos pushed and prayed through the contraction then let out a deep breath. "That one was the strongest," she said, "you'll get your wish."

Sonia massaged Maria's thighs as she got ready for the final push. "I can see the head," said Sonia, already smiling at what promised to follow. "This one has lots of hair — and curly, like the mother."

Sonia's hands gently but firmly grasped the child's head and caught the rest of its body as it slid into the world.

Maria de los Santos rolled over on her side and reached out to take the baby into her arms. "A girl," she sobbed with relief, fatigue.

"Let's see her," said Maria's mother, as she set a candle down a few feet away from them. My eyes had adjusted to the darkness, the candle seemed too bright. I had already seen the outline of the baby, now I saw the head, which seemed large, and the thin, bony body. The baby looked hungry already, and her mop of hair made her look like a shriveled old woman. Her skin was pink and smeared with blood. I expected her to have her eyes closed, but she was awake and her eyes were open, her gaze directed at her mother.

"She looks like Grandmother," said Maria de los Santos. "I'm going to call her Carmen, after her."

The baby's mouth grasped for her mother's breast and sucked desperately as Maria de los Santos gathered her into the warmth of her own body. The infant was so small and fragile looking, I wished I could hold her, and I suddenly realized how much I hoped the prayer that Maria de los Santos had said for me would come true.

Rosa hugged herself as she watched. "Look how she knows her mother."

"It's raining," said Sonia. "Baby Carmen has brought us rain."

"What did you wish for?" Rosa asked me, as if we had thrown coins in a well or rubbed a magic lamp.

"A happy life."

Rosa nodded. "I asked to know my mother. I've decided to look for her."

Now we were all enclosed by the sound of rain beating down on the tin roof. Maria's mother stood up and made the sign of the cross and we all joined hands, ready to bathe baby Carmen with prayer and rainwater.

*   *   *

"It's right here. The seventh of May, 1965."

Padre Ramon remembered Rosa immediately. He was the one who had taken her to Mother Maria, and yes, he had baptized her right here in Ilama before he left. Now he held his place in the ledger with one hand while he shuffled through his desk drawer with the other.

Padre Ramon had a round face that settled into a quiet smile when he wasn't talking. He concentrated on his work as he filled out the certificate in careful letters. When he finished he blew on the wet ink and handed the paper to Rosa.

"Here you are. And God bless you."

Rosa took the certificate in her hand and looked at it. I followed her eyes as she reviewed her name and birthday, the same one she had always celebrated at *La Casa*. Then Rosa's face fell and she shook her head. "It's blank." She looked to Padre Ramon for an explanation.

"I know, *mi hija*. I couldn't fill it out. But this will be enough. There'll be no doubt. Especially since it's signed by me, the same priest who baptized you."

"But I want to know her name, I want to look for my mother."

Padre Ramon leaned forward and rested his elbows on his knees, pressing his hands together at the fingertips. "I don't recommend that, Rosa. You're a young woman now, engaged to be wed to a good Christian man. You have your whole life ahead of you. There's nothing to be gained from digging up the past. And what do you expect from your mother after all these years?"

"Nothing. I know she has nothing to give me. I just want to see her. I want her to know that I'm okay, in spite of ... I'm not asking you to take me to her, but I have a right to know her name." Rosa rose and moved toward the book, which still lay open on the desk.

"Sit down," said Padre Ramon. "I'll tell you the whole story, if you're going to insist." He paused to look Rosa in the eye and placed his hand on her shoulder. "It's a painful one."

I moved closer and put an arm around the back of Rosa's chair. I had been afraid of something like this.

"Our people," he began, "they suffer a great deal, Rosa. I've been walking in and out of the *aldeas* for over forty years, and I still don't know how they get the strength to survive. When you were born — when I found you, it was a very difficult time. There had just been a flood — we're always thankful for rain here, but too much water after all the dryness is no good. The riverbed overflows, and the crops wash out. The year you were born it was terrible. People were left with nothing, and they knew it would be a year before they could put a new crop in.

"A few weeks later, after the river was down, I went walking, my usual route. Everyone knew that I walked every day after my morning prayers, down the path by the river. I found you there, Rosa. Alone. In a basket."

Rosa's mouth fell open. "But Mother Maria said my mother gave me to you. She asked you to make sure I was taken care of." When she heard her own words spoken aloud Rosa gave a nod of recognition. "Of course that's the lie she would make up."

"She didn't lie, Rosa. It was I. I wanted her to have something to tell you."

"But you gave me false hopes," Rosa cried out.

"I didn't mean to. I thought if you knew that your mother wanted a better life for you, with faith in God and Mother Maria's help, you could make a future for yourself."

"So my mother left me by the river to die," accused Rosa. "She threw me out like a piece of trash."

"You mustn't think that, Rosa. Try to understand. Our people have so many superstitions. Some of them believe that babies who are set out that way will survive by some miracle, or, through death, be lifted up and cared for by God. It's a practice that goes back through the centuries.

"What your mother did was wrong, Rosa. But I know she did it with pain and love. She didn't throw you out. You should have seen how she set you in that basket. She was too poor to have any clothes for you, but you were carefully wrapped in a blanket, to keep you warm until someone found you. And she picked a common rose, the ones you see all along the paths here, and set it in the basket with you. I doubt she could read or write. That was her way of saying that your name was Rosa.

"After I found you I hoped she'd regret it and come looking for you. But no one knew about you, or if they did they wouldn't speak out. So I took you to Mother Maria. That's all I know, Rosa. I'm sorry to say it but I don't think there is any way you can ever find your mother." Padre Ramon gave her his handkerchief. "Are you going to be all right?" he asked, looking at me.

"*Sí*," said Rosa. Her chin quivered as she wiped her eyes.

I put my arms around her. "Oh Rosa, I'm so sorry."

Rosa was quiet all morning. I stayed close, working on my basket, raising my head to say something now and then — about the weather, the bus ride home tomorrow, anything, just to remind Rosa that she wasn't alone.

Around eleven Rosa got up to start making the cake. I could tell it was an effort to lift herself from the chair.

"Rosa, if you don't feel up to it, it's okay. I'm sure they'll understand."

"No, I want to do it, Beth."

Rosa measured out the dry ingredients into the large bowl. She cracked each egg sharply and dropped them into a well in the center. She turned the batter vigorously until it was all wet, then began to stir with rhythmic full strokes, losing herself in the count. I was sure she'd gone well past three hundred. "This will be the smoothest cake I've every made," said Rosa wryly.

I sighed. Rosa was right. It was better to stay busy. Soon she'd be home with Alberto to comfort her. And the wedding plans would sweep her up and help her to move past this.

While Rosa prepared the pan and cut the pineapple I went to find Sonia, who hadn't been around all morning. I wanted to tell her what had happened so that no one — especially Abuelita — would ask embarrassing questions.

That night we worked on the front step as usual. After raving one more time about Rosa's cake the group was quiet. Everyone was thinking about Rosa's disappointment, of course. Sonia was in and out, busy with something, and very distracted.

I was disappointed in Sonia. Didn't she realize that Rosa had grown fond of her? A few words of comfort from her would mean a lot. Of course, Sonia had a lot to do just taking care of her own family. Rosa was just a temporary boarder, after all.

It was almost dark and time to go in. Abuelita got up to put the children to bed and Rosa and I went inside to go to sleep. Our bags were already by the door.

Sonia woke us at six. She had prepared a breakfast of sweet rice and milk, beans, eggs and coffee.

"It's a long ride," she said. "I don't want you to be hungry."

By the time we were ready to leave, Abuelita, the children, and José had gathered in the front room. They were all going to see us to the bus.

"Before you go we have something for you," said Sonia, brushing the hair out of her eyes and smiling. Abuelita handed Sonia a small package, wrapped in tissue paper, from behind her back.

"Rosa, we'd like you to have this," Sonia pronounced with an official air, as if she were giving Rosa the keys to Ilama.

Rosa pulled away the tissue paper to find a miniature basket filled with dried corn and beans and rice. She held it up. "My own *abundanza*."

"We don't know who your mother was," said Sonia, "but you're a daughter of Ilama. We couldn't let you get married without this."

Abuelita stepped forward, hugged Rosa and pressed a Coke bottle filled with water and fresh-cut herbs into Rosa's hands.

"These will grow roots. For the garden of your new home. The herbs from Ilama are better than any other place in Honduras. They have more flavor and they're stronger. You'll have the best herb garden. The one you deserve."

"And you must come back to visit," said Sonia. "Not as a boarder. As family."

Rosa hugged Sonia again and looked down at the gifts in her hands. "Thank you," she said. "I will." She looked over at me and we started to head for the door.

"Wait, I have something for Beth, too," said Sonia. She went into the back room and came out with the small basket that I had started. She looked embarrassed. "I finished it for you. I didn't think you'd be able to get the palm in Tegucigalpa ... I did the rim and the handle in blue like you said."

"Thank you so much," I took the basket from her, "for everything."

"But no *abundanza* for you," teased Abuelita. "To earn one you have to marry a son of Ilama."

"Don't pay attention to her," said Sonia laughing as she took my hand in hers. "Goodbye," she said, as if she knew better than to pretend that I might be back this way again. "And remember our little town when you're back in the United States."

I walked toward the bus arm in arm with Rosa, who cupped her *abundanza* in her hand as if it were a newly hatched chick. I carried my empty basket by the handle, letting it brush against my skirt. I breathed in deep and out again. For a moment, I could imagine staying here. I'd weave baskets, have children, then die here. Would that be less of a life than the one I was likely to have?

Probably not, but this wasn't where I belonged. I had to move on. At least I had the basket to take with me. I would have to decide what to put in it.

La Casa de los Niños
July

VII

I was at my desk working when I heard a stir of excitement from out in the kitchen.

"Oo—oo, a letter from the *novio*," someone said.

The girls got excited when the mail came, even though it was almost always for me. The letters had been fewer lately. My mother and sisters had written frequently at first. But now they had worked out a daily life that didn't include me, and, though I was sure I was missed, the collect calls that I made from the big house once a month were enough for them.

My friends wrote less often as well, and when they did write the letters were quick notes, more like reports than conversations, about working in places like New York and Washington. They wrote about briefing papers and important memos that forced them to stay late at the office and order takeout. How could I tell them about my little victories? That Katia had agreed to take a job in a sewing workshop, and managed to get to work and home again without getting into a fight with her boss for three days in a row. That Luz had smiled when she said "good morning" today.

Still, I felt that what I was doing was important. I helped the girls talk out their differences, to see that they had a responsibility to the group as a whole. Simple give and take, forgiveness, even humor — things normally learned by osmosis in a family — had to be spelled out and rehearsed here.

The two weddings had come and gone. Dina's had been a proper *La Casa* affair with Mother Maria playing the role of mother of the bride. Then in June it was Rosa's turn. The girls had been thrilled to be invited to Alberto's family home in Santa Lucia, to what they called a "real wedding." Sister Paula and I had been asked to sit in the front row with Mother Maria, where Rosa's family would normally be. We had sobbed like idiots when Rosa walked down the aisle alone.

"Who gives this bride?" said the priest.

"We receive her as a daughter," Alberto's parents had replied.

Through all this Jake's letters had been a constant. He'd report on his progress on the house and ask about the girls in a way that made me know he took in all the details of my life, read my letters more than once.

One of the girls slid the letter under my door.

"Gracias," I called out. I picked up the letter and sat on the bed to open it.

Inside the envelope, along with a brief note from Jake, was a small white envelope that was sealed and taped.

"Finally tracked down that article," Jake had written underneath the seal.

I hadn't thought about the photo for a while. After I'd written about it in the letter to Jake I'd gotten so caught up with the girls, helping them through one crisis, then the next, that I'd almost forgotten about it. I carefully lifted the seal. Jake had photocopied the article, then folded it around the picture, which he had pasted onto a blank index card. The article was brief, but it did include an address for the St. Bonaventure Home, though I doubted it was still operating, and the name of the religious order that had run the orphanage. Leads, if I wanted them.

I turned to the photo. The child in the photo had bright eyes, and from the way the smiling mouth was set it was clear she was singing. She looked strikingly like I had as a child. I should have suspected that, but it came as a surprise, a shock even, like I was seeing a sister that I'd never met, or a child that I'd somehow forgotten I had.

The caption read, "Five-year-old Frieda sings for visitors at St. Bonaventure's Home for Children."

The smile on the face of the little girl seemed genuine, but there was something else, too. It was as if the girl was looking off into the distance to someone she knew, her eyes asking, "If I sing long enough, will it save me?"

It had. My grandmother had answered the question, taken her home. I thought of the flower girl I'd seen on that first day. Every time I went through the *Parque Central* I looked for her, but I hadn't seen her again. Somehow the photo, from its place in the past, made me feel closer to my mother than I'd felt in a while. I'd resisted the urge to stay home because of her disapproval; I hadn't let her fears make me shy away from doing what I thought was right. I thought I'd broken away, gone out on my own. That seemed funny now. I came here for her, I realized. I wanted to save her again.

Now I felt the bond stronger than ever, the love of child for mother, and mother for child all at once. I studied the photo, seeing the many faces of my mother, and shadows of myself too. I hoped for a clue about what to do next, but the photo only spoke of love and need. It made me so lonely I broke into a sob.

The first of August, Mother Maria's birthday, was three days away, and everyone was looking forward to the *fiesta*. I pulled my old white sock onto my hand and smoothed out the ribbing until it reached my elbow. I made a fist, then frowned. A sock puppet wouldn't work. It clung to my knuckles, a bony, thin-faced puppy, like the neighborhood dogs that scavenge for food in the trash heap.

I took a scrap of white felt that I'd found in the sewing workshop, folded it in half, and placed my flat palm on top. It was just big enough. I drew a line around my hand, then added short stubby paws on each side. I'd use black felt for the ears, more black felt for spots, and shiny brown buttons for the eyes. I imagined myself dressed as a clown, with the dog as a sidekick. The children would love it. If only the rest of the party were so easy to put together. The girls had promised to dress up as clowns and lead the games, but would they?

There was no reason to think they wouldn't. The *fiesta* on Mother Maria's birthday was a *La Casa* tradition. In the past, hired clowns had passed out balloons and organized games for the children, but this year I had convinced the girls to show Mother Maria how much they appreciated her by running the show themselves. There was nothing to worry about, I supposed; the girls had been talking about the *fiesta* all week.

I worked for an hour or so, fastening the two sides of the mitt together with small overlapping stitches, sewing on the buttons and ears, and embroidering freckles on the puppy's cheeks.

At about three-thirty Suyapa came in. Now that she was working at the cannery she was the first one home every day. The cannery workers started at six and kept working until all the shrimp from the previous day's catch were peeled, usually mid-afternoon.

Suyapa passed through the kitchen without a word and headed to her room to change her clothes. Some of the girls had teased her about her fishy odor, and her roommates complained that everything she owned smelled like shrimp.

"I'm going to hang my clothes outside," said Suyapa when she reappeared a few minutes later.

"Good idea," I said, although I was sure that, after a nine-hour shift, the fishy smell had been absorbed into Suyapa's hair and pores as well.

Suyapa came back with a bowl of water from the *pila*. She dipped her hairbrush in the bowl of water and passed it through her thick hair. "There's not enough water in the *pila* to wash." She dipped the brush in the water again. "What are you doing, Beth?"

"Making a puppet." I put my hand inside the mitt and demonstrated how the dog waved and clapped his hands.

Suyapa giggled. "What's your name?" she said to the puppet.

"He doesn't have one yet," I said. "What should I call him?"

"If he were mine, I'd call him Salto."

"*Salto*. Jump. That's good." I slipped off the mitt to look at the dog again. "Why did you pick that name?"

Suyapa put the mitt on her own hand. "Because he can jump." Suyapa's eyes grew wide as she made Salto jump off the table onto the floor. "No one can catch him. When they chase him he laughs and jumps again. He can jump up, too." Suyapa jumped Salto back to table height again. "He can even jump out of his own skin. But don't worry, Saltito, you smell good today."

Suyapa put her face to Salto's and tickled his nose. Then she tossed him aside and put her elbows on the table, propping up her head, and let out a thick sigh.

"How are things at work?" I asked. "Have they paid out the back wages yet?"

Suyapa shrugged. "They're saying Friday, now."

"They said they'd be paying at the end of each day when you started. It's been almost a month now, hasn't it?"

Suyapa confirmed the obvious with a nod. "I've just about earned my green, you know."

"I didn't forget."

Suyapa sighed. "But I can't go to the *fiesta*. I have to work."

"On Saturday? Says who?"

"*La jefa*, my supervisor. There's a big delivery that day. There'll be work for everyone, no one can be excused."

"But that's not fair." How could a day laborer with no guarantees be forced to work?

"Those who don't show on Saturday can't come back on Monday. That's what she said. They need us to peel that big catch. The shrimp have to be canned or they'll spoil." Suyapa's eyes filled. "It's the first time I've ever missed Mother Maria's birthday."

"Maybe I could talk with your supervisor. I'll tell her that we need your help."

"She won't care," said Suyapa looking away.

"Would you let me try? I could come with you tomorrow morning."

"If you want, but it won't help."

The next morning I followed Suyapa into the small stucco building. A long low counter lined the back wall, a scale and cash register at one end. A woman in an orange smock dragged a damp mop across the floor. A thick mask of antiseptic hung in the air, but the fish odor came through. I could barely stand to inhale.

"You must be the first one to work today," I said, trying to conserve breath.

Suyapa shook her head. "This is the room where they weigh the catch and attend the buyers. We work out back."

Suyapa walked around the counter, opened the back door, and looked down. "The supervisor isn't here yet, but I'd better get in line."

I looked out and saw a long row of tables. I hadn't realized that Suyapa worked outside. Suyapa hurried down the hill to take her place in line. Four or five women were already ahead of her.

By six o'clock another twenty or thirty women had joined the line. A stern-looking woman came out and handed out orange smocks and plastic hairnets to the first fifteen or so. The women who were chosen went straight to the tables. The others slowly dispersed, shrugging and shaking heads.

The orange smocks and plastic caps made it hard to tell the women apart. I stood by the screen door, carefully tracking Suyapa as she fetched a bucket, filled it with shrimp, and dumped it out on the table. She peeled shrimp with the others, tossing the shells into the center of the table and putting the cleaned shrimp in the bucket. I knew they got paid by the bucket. Suyapa was slower than the others, but not by much.

They would stand there peeling shrimp all day without a break.

The supervisor came up the hill into the shop. "And you, what do you want?"

"Oh, excuse me." I felt my face redden. I hurried around to the other side of the counter and extended my hand. "My name is

Beth Pellegrino. I work at *La Casa de los Niños*, where Suyapa lives and I—"

The supervisor waved me away. "No visitors on the line. Come back at the end of the day."

"Actually I'm not here to see Suyapa. I want to talk with you."

The woman placed her hands on her hips and looked me in the eye. "About what?"

"Suyapa told me that she has to work on Saturday, but—"

"Suyapa said she would work. It's too late to change it now."

"But that's an important day at *La Casa*. We need Suyapa's help." I saw that the supervisor's face hadn't changed. "At home," I finished softly.

"The peeling on Saturday is between me and my workers." The supervisor opened the back door and looked out. "I'm needed to check the buckets." She stepped outside and slammed the door behind her, the force so strong that the door flapped open a few times before it settled into place.

Through the open door I looked at the row of women, their capped heads bent over their work, but I couldn't tell which one was Suyapa anymore.

VIII

All the girls got up early on Mother Maria's birthday. When I went into the *sala* I found Katia standing on a chair, ready to make a pronouncement. She wore a pair of men's trousers, a frayed button-down shirt, and a garish red and yellow striped tie. Her face painted like a clown, she held one hand in the air.

"Farts, farts, farts, farts. That is my mission. All the children of *La Casa* will know that word by the end of the day."

With that Katia tumbled from the chair. She landed on her bottom and made a loud raspberry sound with her lips. "Now everyone, repeat after me, *pedo.*"

Everyone who had gathered in the *sala* was laughing. Katia stood up and brushed herself off. "Don't worry, Beth. I'm kidding."

I looked around the room. Everyone was getting ready. Rosa sat at the table blowing up balloons. She looked like a traditional clown, with a round nose and a pair of Alberto's striped pajamas. Vera looked like an oversized baby doll with her high ponytails and a big cardboard lollipop. Luz's painted face was sad, with a large tear on one cheek. Her outfit was made of scraps of brightly colored woven fabric — mismatched stripes, bold flowers, and the tail feathers of a Quetzal. She looked more like a crazy woman than a clown. And her laugh only made it worse.

Suyapa came through the kitchen dressed for work and headed for the door. I could see she was holding back tears.

"Suyapa, don't go." I groped for words that Suyapa could understand. "You can still be green, I promise."

Suyapa looked tentatively at me. "You're giving me green because you think I can't earn my colors like the others."

I put myself between Suyapa and the door. "That's not true. You've already earned it, you said so yourself." I put my hands on Suyapa's shoulders and looked her in the eye. "I'm the one who was wrong. Can you try to understand that? I didn't understand the working conditions when I sent you to that job." I threw up my hands. "All that work, standing in the heat, and without pay... If they had levels for counselors I would be the lightest shade of yellow."

Suyapa grinned at that and took a step back. She looked lost, but at least she wasn't moving toward the door.

"I'll help you get a better job," I said, "housekeeping — like you wanted in the first place."

Suyapa looked to the other girls, her brow furrowed.

"With *gringos*," I added, closing my eyes and stepping aside so that Suyapa could go out or stay as she wished.

Vera stepped up from behind and lifted Salto up to Suyapa's cheek. "Nnn-nnn-nnn," he whined. *"Come to the fiesta, por favor."*

Suyapa's frown broke up into a nervous smile. "You promise this won't interfere with me reaching level green?"

"Not at all," I said.

Felicia took Suyapa by the arm. "Come and sit down and I'll paint your face. And then I'll do Beth."

I looked out the door toward "the children's village," a cluster of houses just down the path from the *Residencia de las Señoritas*. Children were lined up at the fence in front of each house, and their *encargadas* stood at the gates, hands on the latches, waiting.

Red balloons along the fence marked the way to the *fiesta*. I had imagined balloons flying in the air, beckoning the children forward. But we'd had to tie the balloons directly to the posts, without any slack, to keep them from settling on the ground. Helium was expensive, and without it the balloons were sad, stunted versions of what I'd had in mind. The dry rocky field was nothing like the fairgrounds that I had dreamed of, either. I laughed at myself now. Had I expected striped tents and plush green grass to magically appear overnight?

All that didn't matter. The children were so excited that the mere sight of my head peeking out from behind the door produced squeals and cries that rolled together and went up like a roar.

I turned to the girls. "Ready?"

The girls giggled and pushed each other toward the door. Finally I got behind them and shoved them out gently, one by one.

When the *encargadas* opened the gates the children took off as if from the starting line of a race, but once on the field they hung back, then formed a line, probably out of habit more than anything else. I looked at the row of dusty worn shoes, and reminded myself that it was a victory that none of these children were barefoot.

A girl with cropped hair and striped shorts jumped forward and waved her arms in large circles. "Hey clowns, look at me," she said, then retreated back to the line.

Among the last to arrive on the field was a little boy of about three, who wore nothing but a pair of sandals and a saggy diaper. At the sight of the clowns he turned around and hid his face in the skirt of the girl next to him.

Luz stepped forward and put an arm around him. "Come here, little one," she said, her shrill voice too loud, her sad face too close. The boy drew back and started to scream.

The girl in the striped shorts crossed her arms and sulked. "They don't know how. They're not real clowns."

Luz shrugged her shoulders and turned to me. "They don't like us. They don't want to play."

"Bah," said Katia, taking Luz by the arm, "I'm not going to hang around waiting to wipe their butts. Let's go get a *fresco.*"

I had thought the *fiesta* would be fun for the girls. I had assumed that they would know how to play. I stretched out a hand toward Katia. "Wait, *por favor*," I mouthed silently.

Katia stood still, her hands on her hips. The other clowns began to withdraw into a huddle.

I lifted Salto from my side. "Arf. Good morning, boys and girls!" Salto earned a few tentative smiles. But now what?

"My name is Salto. And today I am going to teach you how to jump."

"But Salto," I said, taking the tone of a teacher. "Maybe the boys and girls don't like to jump, and anyway, you don't have any feet."

"Thank you very much," said Salto saucily. "Boys and girls, it looks like I have my first volunteer."

"Not me, Salto." My teeth chattered with exaggerated fear. "I'm afraid of heights. I don't know how to jump."

"It's easy, just do this." Salto jumped from my side up to my shoulder.

I put on a startled expression. "Now Salto, don't do that. You scared me."

"What do you think, children?" said Salto. "Should I jump again?"

The children began to giggle. "Yes," cried a little boy as he clung to the arm of an older child.

"Sorry, Beth," said Salto, as he leapt to the other shoulder.

I gave a startled jump. "Salto, stop it."

"See that, I taught you to jump," replied Salto.

I gave Salto an exasperated look, and admonished him with my finger. "No more jumping."

"Ha ha ha. You can't catch me," cried Salto. The children giggled at his naughtiness.

This time Salto jumped onto Luz's shoulder. "You. Jump."

Luz collapsed into uncontrollable giggles.

"Me, Beth. I'll jump," said Katia.

Salto jumped at Katia, but instead of landing on her shoulder I surprised her by landing him on her head. She started to laugh and jump around like a real clown.

Once the clowns were all jumping, Salto turned to the children, setting off a new wave of giggles. Salto jumped among them until they were all jumping and laughing.

"What's this nonsense?" I pretended to be cross. "You're supposed to be playing games and having fun. Now stop all this jumping."

I threw up my arms in defeat and extracted myself from the crowd. As I stepped back, the clowns hesitated. For a moment it seemed that the children and the clowns would retreat to their original positions, but Katia stepped into the center.

"Let's make a circle," she said.

I stood back to watch as the girls organized the game of Wonder Ball that we had rehearsed. Things were more clumsy than we planned, but the game was working, at least for now. I watched for a while. It was good to see the children out in the fresh air, playing freely in the fields. That reminded me of the *Camino Viejo*. I decided to head that way to make sure that none of the smaller children had wandered back there. There were some steep drops along the path, and the compost pit was back there, too. I didn't want anyone to fall.

I headed toward the old road to find Suyapa one step ahead of me, leading a small girl in pigtails back to the *fiesta*. In her clown makeup Suyapa's thick features and round face looked comfortable for once, and her smile was freer than I had ever seen it.

"The clown says 'no, no, no,' that's dangerous, little one," said Suyapa, in a high melodic voice that belonged to the clown within her. "Let's go join the circle."

Suyapa took the girl's hand and led her back. The girl followed, looking up into Suyapa's face every few steps.

Another girl skipped toward them, arms open to embrace Suyapa, but the first girl stood in front of Suyapa and put her hands out. "No, the *payasa* is mine."

Suyapa smiled and put her arm around each girl. "Look, I have one arm for each of you. And my fingers and toes are for the others."

I watched a chubby boy with dimples approach Felicia's easel with its large clean sheet of paper and three paint colors — blue, red and yellow.

"Can I try?"

"This whole page is for you," said Felicia. "Painters call it their canvas."

The boy took the brush from the red cup and contemplated the thick wet paint before he touched it to the canvas. He painted a red dot on the lower left corner of the page. Then he looked to Felicia. His face spread into a grin as he forged a path with dots and lines toward the center of the easel. "It's a ball, bouncing all around," he said.

"It feels good, doesn't it?" said Felicia.

Felicia looked up and noticed me standing there. "See our first work of art?"

I smiled. "It's beautiful."

Suyapa led another little girl over to the easel. Once she handed the girl over to Felicia, she turned to me. "Can I have a turn being Salto for a while?"

I moved in and out of the games. Katia was entertaining the children with her slapstick antics. She hadn't stopped all morning. When she saw me watching she stood straight up and shouted, "Bombs away," then did a messy cartwheel, landing on her bottom in the dirt. The children giggled and let out an echo of "boom, boom, boom." Meanwhile Suyapa had the children singing and kissing Salto on the nose.

The sun was beating down. It was after eleven, time to pass out the punch. I went to the kitchen where I found Rosa pouring punch into small paper cups and setting them on a piece of cardboard that she was going to use as a tray. Then Suyapa came by to return Salto and offered to help Rosa.

I decided to head up toward the big house where Mercedes and Carlos were leaning out a window on the second floor, lowering a donkey with large dopey eyes over the patio below. It was saddled in red, with two colorful drums full of candy on either side of the saddle. In a short while Mother Maria would emerge to preside over the breaking of the *piñata*.

As I passed Sister Paula's house I saw Theo crouching in the doorway, his one leg bent at the knee for balance and the rest of his body leaning over his skateboard. He ran the skateboard back and forth along the cement front steps in a loud rhythmic buzzing. "*Venga, payasa*," he called, then ran the skateboard again.

I winced at the desperate sound in his voice. How long had he been calling out to the clowns? With all the excitement on the field, I hadn't noticed him until now. Of course Sister Paula's children had been kept in today — it would be too hard to supervise them at an event like this.

I put Salto on my hand. "Arf, arf," I called, then skipped over toward Theo.

Theo grinned, then he scrambled onto his skateboard and scooted into the house. "The *payasa* is coming," he called to those inside.

I stepped over a T-shirt in the doorway. No doubt Theo had cast it off because of the heat. Inside the *sala* the wooden shutters were closed. The room was dark, but cool.

Theo rolled down the hallway. "Hurry, she's here," he shouted.

I watched him push off the far wall at the back of the house and come racing back toward me. I'd heard he'd been sneaking off during the day more and more lately, and it showed. The skin on his face and arms were reddish brown, the burnt color of a child who lives on the street. His bare chest and shoulders were much lighter, showing where the T-shirts he wore covered him. I tried not to look at the stump of his leg that protruded out of the red shorts, but I saw the scar, like a seam that was about to burst.

Lola came out of one of the bedrooms, skipping behind a balloon that was tied to her arm. I opened my arms, inviting an embrace. I'd grown fond of Lola, who was so often at Sister Paula's side. But instead of the usual shy smile and hug, Lola's eyes opened wide, and her jaw dropped. Then she turned and ran to the back of the house.

She doesn't recognize me behind the clown face, I thought — had I scared her? I stepped back, unsure.

A moment later Lola came out. Tiny as she was she'd taken on the task of pulling a wheelchair out of the back room. She stopped every few seconds to reassure the child in the chair, then with great effort, turned the chair, which was larger than she was, so that the girl in it faced the clown. Once the girl was in place, Lola turned toward me with a broad grin and clapped her hands in front of her.

In the chair a small girl was strapped in at the waist and again at the chest. She waved her arms about, unable to keep her knobby elbows from banging the side of the chair. Her head was bent back, rigid, and her mouth looked like it was propped open. Her eyes darted around wildly. I stood in front of her, but out of her field of vision because of the way her head was frozen in place.

Not far behind Lola and the wheelchair was Sister Paula, who came to greet me. "We were having our own *fiesta*, but we are so glad that one of the real clowns came to see us."

"Your own *fiesta*. That's wonderful." I moved around the chair and positioned myself so that the girl could see me. "I see you have a balloon," I said, pointing to the red balloon that was attached to the wheelchair.

The girl smiled wide, showing her gums and oversized teeth, and causing bubbly drool to run out of her mouth. She waved her arms with glee, eyes fixed on me, and spit out a few words. "Pa...pa...pa."

I was glad my smile was painted on. A thick wad of pity rose up in my throat, but I froze in place.

Sister Paula smiled, one hand on the girl's shoulder and the other reaching out to me. "This is Celina. She's saying *payasa*." She gave my hand a squeeze.

Now all the children gathered around the chair. Their excitement made me nervous. Would Salto's jumping game work with these children? Nothing simpler came to mind so I tried the routine from the morning again.

Salto jumped to Celina, who was delighted, then from child to child. When about half of the children had had a turn, the mitt slipped off my hand and down to the ground. I reached for it but Theo, already crouched near the ground, grabbed Salto and put him on his hand.

"Can I play with him? *Por favor.*"

I looked at Theo's large head, his pleading eyes, his jaw marked with acne and a hint of a beard. "*Sí.*"

In a moment Theo was scooting around the room with Salto, making the puppet jump all over the children.

"Now you be good." Theo shook a pointed finger at Salto. "Don't scare the children. No more jumping."

Then he hid his face behind Salto and spoke for the dog. "Okay. I promise not to jump. Ha ha ha." Then Salto jumped again.

Sister Paula came to stand beside me. "You certainly found a way to channel Theo's energy."

Theo's Salto was mischievous. His jumps were bolder, and his promises not to jump were more sincere. The children were all laughing.

Then Theo crawled up on a chair with Salto. "Salto is escaping through the window," he shouted.

I laughed at first, then I saw that Theo was growing more angry and excited. He began shouting "no" and banging Salto's head against the wall, until the puppet fell to the floor.

The children focused on Salto, with cries of alarm and tears at the sight of Salto sliding to the floor. "Don't kill him," one child cried out. Theo looked confused.

Sister Paula stepped in. "We'll save our poor Salto," she said theatrically.

The children quieted a bit, reassured that it was still a game, but I heard a slight shake in Sister Paula's voice.

Sister Paula put her arms firmly around Theo's shoulders, in an embrace that bordered on a shoulder hold.

"Let's help our dear doggie," she said to Theo, as she held him tight, trying to squeeze the goodness in him to the surface.

Theo strained against Paula's embrace, grunting and pushing. Then, for no apparent reason, the fire of his rage went out. His body relaxed, and following Sister Paula's lead, he crawled over to Salto.

Theo picked up Salto and held him up in the air, then scooted over to me. "Don't cry, *payasa*."

Theo tried to put an arm around me. I stiffened at first, but the child who placed the puppet in my hand was sweet, not the same boy who'd been enraged a few moments earlier....

"Your doggie is okay," he said.

"Thank you, Theo." I hugged him. "You're a good boy."

I glanced over at Sister Paula, who was looking down at the floor, still catching her breath from the effort of restraining Theo.

Suyapa arrived with punch for the children. "I saw you come in," she said, then she served the punch, stopping to help Celina drink.

I took a cup of punch over to Sister Paula.

"You've done a wonderful thing, Beth," said Sister Paula. "The *fiesta* has always been about candy and clowns. But this year — seeing *La Casa* kids take care of each other ... even mine. We've never been remembered before."

I heard cries from outside inviting the children to gather for the *piñata*.

"I wish we could do more," I said. "A party like this is wonderful, but all the realities are still there at the end of the day."

"It means more than you think, Beth. To have all the hurts pushed into the background for a while. They can sing and play, have their own balloon. Even a boy like Theo can pour out love and laughter instead of..." Sister Paula stopped herself and shook her head. "The love is more real than the anger, you know."

I sat quiet a moment. I didn't want to challenge Sister Paula, but the rage was equally real, it seemed to me.

"Still, I find it hard to accept," I said, "that all we can offer them is a moment of comfort. Something they might not even remember."

Sister Paula hugged her arms around herself. "We have to believe that the moments of comfort are important, don't we?" Then she straightened up, sure of herself. "God was here today. The children will always know that, even if they forget the details — me, you, Salto."

Suyapa finished serving the children and came to my side. "It's time for the *Piñata*."

I said goodbye to the children and had Salto give each of them a kiss. After he kissed Sister Paula I made him bark and howl. "I love your children, I don't want the *fiesta* to end. Please, please, Sister, let me live with you here forever."

Sister Paula laughed, then smiled at me gratefully. "I don't know, Salto, I'll have to ask the children."

Before she could utter a word the children had surrounded me, petting Salto and shouting, "Sí."

I stood on the sidelines and watched the spectacle of the *piñata*. Mother Maria held the baton, and ordered the clowns to line the children up from smallest to largest. They were all giggles and best behavior with Mother Maria there. And the *encargadas* helped, too. While the smaller children took turns swinging at the *piñata* the others laughed and squirmed in their places. Some of the older children practiced their swings and called out "*apúrase*": "hurry."

After each child had a turn, Mother Maria announced that the second round would go from tallest to smallest. The tall boys moved quickly through their ranks, the *piñata* flying at every turn. It didn't break, but the crowd grew excited at every crack or tear, and let out a cheer when one boy struck the *piñata* so hard that the donkey's saddle caved in and one drum was dented.

The next boy stepped forward to take his turn. He let out a battle cry and ran toward the *piñata*. The sack broke, and a trickle of candy fell to the ground, leading to a wild rush of children who fell over each other, grappling on the cement for the few pieces of candy. Mother Maria asked Carlos to strike the sack a few more times. Then came a downpour of candy, and the children ran forward again, those with pockets at a great advantage over those who filled their hands and then looked up, dismayed at the obstacle presented by their own success.

After the *piñata* the children headed back to their *casitas* for lunch. On the way to the house I saw Suyapa dividing up a bag of candy among the last of them, the youngest children who'd been too small or too slow to get any on their own. Suyapa looked up and smiled.

I loved seeing Suyapa like this. This clown was so different from the girl who knew herself to be slow and ugly and dumb.

I waited and walked alongside Suyapa. We dropped the children off then headed for the *Residencia de las Señoritas*.

"Suyapa, I've been thinking. I don't want to put up your notice about housekeeping just yet."

Suyapa's face fell. "But you promised..."

"I know, but you have talents I didn't know about. I think we might be able to find something better."

"Like what?"

"Like working with children."

Suyapa shook her head. "They'll say I'm slow—"

"Well, you're not." I was stern. "Please don't say that again. When it comes to safety and patience, and comfort, you're just right. You have some things to learn. But I think I can arrange that with Mother Maria." I paused and looked at Suyapa, "Would you like help out at the kindergarten here at *La Casa*? You'd have to volunteer at first, but later, after you're trained, they might be able to pay you, or you could try for a job in a kindergarten or child care center on the outside."

Suyapa eyed me carefully. "What if I try and it doesn't work out? Will you still get me with *gringos*?"

"Yes. If it doesn't work out for you I'll help you get a job as a nanny, or a housekeeper. For *gringos* or whatever kind of people you want."

Suyapa gave an excited jump. "I want to try. It's like I can be a teacher even though I'm dumb—"

Suyapa paused and looked at me. "I know you don't like me to say that. I wasn't insulting myself, I just meant that I can be like me."

I smiled. "You can be like you were today."

Luz's Journey

Luz saw darkness in everything, and I was desperate to make her see light, to embrace hope in some small way. If I helped her at all though, it was a total accident, because I was as busy denying obvious truths as she was.

Walking with Luz to Juntapeque, I saw the world through her eyes, if only for a moment. I won't say she saw the world through mine — though I wanted it to be that easy at the time. She saw the same things she always saw, but having me there was some sort of comfort, a relief. Instead of looking at the things she feared, she could watch me. Seeing her demons reflected in my eyes was a break from looking at them straight on.

*   *   *

The first tap-tap of rain sounded on the tin roof. I got up and closed the shutters, expecting those few drops to turn into a blanket of water in minutes. I liked the wet season, the way patches of green grass sprang up, the pulse of thick rain. After a few moments I got up again, opened one shutter, and looked out. The trickle had stopped, just like the night before. It was October already. Were the rains ending? Without the four seasons of New England as anchors, I had trouble keeping track of time. Hours and minutes passed slowly here, but there was a distorting acceleration that made the days and weeks fly. In just three months I was supposed to go home. A part of me couldn't wait, but I felt a sense of loss, too. The comforting rains were almost gone. Would they ever be a part of my life again?

I went to the *sala* to see if there was any coffee left over from dinner. The side of the pot was barely warm, but I decided to have a cup anyway. As I poured coffee into a plastic tumbler, Luz came in.

"*Hola*, Beth. Did you see that the rains have stopped?" Luz looked me in the eye as if to challenge me. "Now you can plan your vacation to the beaches on the North Coast."

I could see through Luz's remark. "I'm not planning to go to the beach, Luz, and I haven't forgotten about our trip. As soon as the roads are dry we can go. Maybe in a week or two."

Luz poured some coffee for herself. "I don't know if I want to make the trip anymore."

"I thought you said you wanted to go to Juntapeque?"

Luz shrugged. "To look for a bunch of half-starved Indians? I don't even know where my relations are buried."

I felt sure that Luz's depression was connected to the loss of her parents and her longing for her *tierra*. Getting her to the farm, closer to the memories, good and bad, might help her find the strength to move forward.

I followed Luz to the table. "You wanted to see the farm."

"You've already ridden enough rickety buses." Luz looked down. "You don't have to take me."

"But I'm looking forward to the trip. I thought we might stop and visit the Mayan ruins at Copan on the way."

Luz swirled her lukewarm coffee in her cup and stared down into it.

"It's your heritage, Luz. People come from all over the world to learn about your ancestors."

"You'd really take me there?"

"Sure. It's right on our way."

"You're not afraid to go to the land of the witches that torment me?" said Luz with a tentative laugh.

"You know I don't believe in them, Luz."

"That doesn't make them go away," she said.

I splurged and bought two tickets on the *Cama-Bus*, a tourist line that boasted hot meals and seats that reclined into beds. It only cost twelve American dollars each — not a lot — and it promised to be safer and a lot more comfortable than the commuter bus.

Luz was impressed with the warm wet hand towels and pillow service, and she was excited about staying in a hotel for the first time. She hadn't mentioned the farm, though, or anything else about our destination since we left *La Casa*.

"How are you feeling about making the journey home?" I asked as dinner was served.

Luz held up a piece of ham on a toothpick. "Look how they rolled up the meat, and the strawberries are sliced like a fan. This is first class."

I didn't press the issue. There would be plenty of time to talk later. It was nice to get away from *La Casa* for a few days, and the side-trip to Copan made me feel like I was on vacation. I had been dubious about the bus company's claim that every seat was as comfortable as a bed, but my seat was wide and reclined almost completely. After dinner I settled back with my pillow and listened to the conversation of the American travelers seated behind me.

"I led a dig at Tikal about ten years ago, but this is my first visit to Copan," said a low voice.

"What was Tikal like?" asked an eager young woman. "Did you find anything?"

"We worked the ruins of a life-size *stela*. It's like putting together a puzzle made of small boulders. We rearranged stones in the heat for three weeks. Finally we felt confident that we had reconstructed it properly. It was a representation of the Corn God — the iconography perfectly matched images that had been found further north in Mexico."

"Wow. I hope we find something like that here. I'm doing my dissertation on the symbol of corn in the fertility rites of the Maya. It would be amazing if I could include some primary research."

The older man chuckled. "You can't study the Mayans without finding corn. You're sure to see something you can use at Copan.

Every rock you stumble on is likely to be part of a ruin, if you can imagine that."

They went on to discuss work schedules and accommodations and I let the familiar cadence of their American English lull me to sleep.

I woke as the first whisper of morning light marked the hills and small cornfields on the horizon. We were just approaching the town of *Copan Ruinas*. As we entered the little town the sky exploded with all the colors of fire — orange blazes and the warm blues and purples of the most intense heat.

Luz was sitting up straight beside me. Had she been awake all night? "There's a battle in the sky," she said.

A few hours later we found ourselves seated at a table on a clean-swept open patio, with pots of tropical flowers set up around us. We'd checked in and gotten a few hours of rest and now we were having breakfast. It was nine-thirty, a late breakfast by Honduran standards, but the tables were full. Other than a Honduran family seated in the far corner most of the guests seemed to be American. Some were obviously tourists. Their sun hats and cameras lay on the tables as they poured over guidebooks and bus schedules. The others were dressed in jeans and carrying tools and water bottles. More archaeologists.

The tourists ordered *café americano* and "eggs American-style." The archaeologists called for more coffee and tapped their knees impatiently as they ate Honduran sweet breads.

Luz was quiet and ate her breakfast self-consciously. "All *gringos*," she said in a small voice.

I wished I could do something to make Luz feel like less of an outsider. If this place belonged to anybody, it belonged to Luz. The tourists would get a glimpse of another civilization, digest it, and move on to the grander sights of Palenque or Tikal. The archaeologists would put together their puzzles, pick through the ruins methodically — hot, tired, even bored at times. But Luz was coming home. She had to try to recognize something in this rubble, to find a trace of her own life.

*   *   *

"Be careful," I said, a hand at Luz's elbow. "This path is rocky." We had to walk the last mile to the center of Copan. No one wanted tour buses crunching on the ancient stones.

We walked by a mound of rocks. I circled around it, then picked up a stone, and turned it over. A small crescent was carved in the stone. An eyebrow, maybe, or the rolled-over husk of a half-peeled ear of corn. I replaced the stone carefully and continued down the path to the ruins.

In a few moments we reached a wall where a number of American tourists were gathered. I looked to the top of the wall and slowly deciphered a beak, an eye, and a long plumed tail that matched the ones I'd seen in the guidebook. "Those must be the macaws that mark the ball court," I said.

"Good morning, *señoritas*." A young man who wore a badge that said "Tour Guide" extended his hand to me, then to Luz. He smiled through a full set of white teeth, his bronze skin tight and smooth against the bones of his face. "I'm Frederico. I study archaeology at the university. Would you like me to tell you about the ruins?" He bowed his head slightly. "I can do the tour in English if you like."

Before we could reply, an older man in a hand-woven tunic of bright red and black stepped in front of the guide, hands on his hips. He squinted in the sun, his right eye half-closed. I could see through the slit that the pupil was obscured by a bluish white film.

The man looked at Luz off center, with his good eye. "Perhaps you would rather hear the story from one of your own people."

I looked to Luz to decide.

Luz pointed to the older man. "With him."

He extended a hand to Luz. "I'm Reinaldo, at your service."

Luz let him take her hand and smiled coyly, as if she'd been asked to dance.

Reinaldo looked into Luz's face. "You were born here. Juntapeque, maybe?"

Luz's mouth fell open. "*Sí.*"

Reinaldo nodded. "You're a good daughter, but you haven't been home in a long time."

Luz flashed a look at me, then back to Reinaldo. "How do you know all this?"

He moved closer to Luz and pointed to his cloudy eye. "See this? Most of the time it's blind, like a dead man's eye, but sometimes it shows me things that others can't see."

Luz stepped back. "Are you a witch?"

Reinaldo laughed. "Those who don't like what I see call me that. But you have nothing to worry about. In you I see a Mayan queen. You have nothing to fear."

Reinaldo extended his hand again, and Luz took it without reservation. Reinaldo was a little too slick for my taste, but it couldn't hurt Luz to be told she was a queen.

Reinaldo led us along the wall until we stood in front of the open court. It was early still, but I could already see the heat of the day forming waves in the air. "The Mayans are the most intelligent people who ever lived," he began.

"Ha," said Luz. "Tell that to my teachers."

"Tell your teachers that we Mayans were the first to read and write. Our story is all over these walls and buildings. The ancestors knew how to do complex calculations and they studied the skies. They could predict the movements of the planets when the Europeans still thought the world was flat."

Reinaldo offered his hand, first to Luz and then to me, so that we could step up onto the stone courtyard. "We will begin our tour in the ceremonial ball court."

He looked from one end of the courtyard to the other, nodding approvingly at what he saw. "You're in luck. The Ball Game is underway. See the Hero twins?" He pointed to the far end of the empty courtyard. "They're ready to reenact their struggle. That ball there is the sun. The twins want to reach it, but they are caught in the Place of Fright."

Luz moved out of the line of combat and stood over by the stone wall. I took a place beside her, but Luz turned her back to me so she could face Reinaldo.

"They'll battle with the Gods of Darkness," Reinaldo said. "It's the journey of every Mayan. They'll fight their way through the blackness of the underworld — it is full of vile things, human rot, dried blood, every kind of decay and pestilence."

"What happens there?" asked Luz. "What kind of vile things?"

"All that you can imagine. Violence by sword and club." Reinaldo looked at Luz carefully before continuing. "And other human cruelties, too. Men with severed limbs. Women forced to abandon their own flesh. People work their own sacred land as slaves. Every kind of violation and betrayal. All these are part of the struggle."

"What happens to the mythical twins?" I asked.

Reinaldo turned to me. "They are only mythical if you are afraid to admit that their struggle is real."

Then he spoke to Luz again. "The twins succeed in their fight. They are reborn and rise to the place of the sun. Of course our people continue the struggle. In that sense the battle never ends."

"See, Beth, that's the difference between us." Luz stood close to Reinaldo now. "Your people know how to get rich and rule the world. Mine know how to suffer. No wonder you don't believe in evil spirits."

I felt the sting of Luz's bitterness. I didn't like Reinaldo filling Luz's head with these grim Mayan stories... But when I considered the hardship of their everyday lives, what other story could they have? Certainly not the ones I had been raised on, where life is a plan that you carry out, where suffering is the exception rather than the rule, where hard work always pays off in the end. How could they believe that when the rain and wind could come and wipe away everything in seconds?

When I looked up Luz and Reinaldo had already moved on, out of the Ball Court and across the field. Even from behind I could tell that Reinaldo was telling a story by the way he drew pictures in the air with his hands, arms, and occasionally a fist. Luz looked into his face as they walked.

I finally caught up.

"Next we'll visit the temple," I heard Reinaldo say.

"I should say temples," Reinaldo explained when we got to the site. "There are other temples below this one."

I listened as Reinaldo described layers of temples that dated back almost one thousand years. The experts felt they had found the first and oldest. It was currently under reconstruction.

"But how can they know that for sure?" asked Luz.

"They've been sure about every layer so far." Reinaldo chuckled.

"Do you think this one is it?" Luz wanted to know. "The oldest?"

Reinaldo led them across the field to a large mound of rock covered with brush. It was almost as tall as Reinaldo himself and had an opening on one side.

"I've found one that's deeper," he whispered. "One that a Mayan queen should see."

"I don't think we can go into an unexplored cave," I said. "It could be dangerous."

Reinaldo ignored me. "This is the entrance," he said to Luz. "The cave is partially excavated. We'll go down to the deepest level. It's only dangerous if you're not sure you want to do it."

Luz looked confused at first, but then it was as if the other Luz, the wanderer, the girl who sought darkness, had been called up. "I have to go down," she said flatly.

I moved closer and touched Luz's arm. I felt Luz's thin bones, her frailty. Luz was shaking. I had no choice but to go with her. I took a sip of water to prepare for the descent into the dry earth. I watched as Luz followed Reinaldo through the crevice that opened into the cave.

I followed Luz, squeezing myself between the rocks, and found myself in a large cave. Some excavating equipment stood nearby — a small digging machine and a few hand tools — comforting evidence of an expert presence.

"The archaeologists aren't working now," said Reinaldo, "but we still have to be careful that no one notices us as we enter."

I turned to him with a look of surprise. Weren't we already inside?

Reinaldo explained in a low whisper, "This is just the first chamber. We'll enter the temple through a tunnel at the back. The archaeologists haven't explored it yet. They will, of course, after they do all their tests and measurements."

They were testing whether the tunnel was stable, I supposed, making sure it wouldn't cave in before they ventured inside.

Reinaldo beckoned us toward a large rock along the far wall.

He put Luz ahead of him, directing her to slide behind the rock sideways. He took my arm and positioned me beside the spot where Luz had just entered. "Quickly," he said.

As I slid between two slabs of cool rock Reinaldo's hand pressed me on a little faster than I wanted to go. I looked back toward the light that crept in around Reinaldo's silhouette as I moved sideways into the tunnel. After three or four feet the path opened up and we could turn and walk upright, with one hand on each of the side walls.

I felt Reinaldo's presence behind me. The tunnel was getting steeper, and some of the rocks felt loose underfoot. How much further down would we have to go?

We came to a rock that hung down from above, blocking our path. Luz stopped abruptly. "My God. It's so steep here. I'm going to fall."

"Don't worry, *hija*," said Reinaldo, "just crouch down and crawl, a little bit at a time. You're almost there."

I crawled under the rock overhang with small steps. I understood why Luz had cried out. The path was so steep, a near vertical drop. There was no choice but to keep going. After what seemed like a ten-foot descent I felt my feet rest on a wide flat ledge, and the cave opened above my head. Luz was beside me on the ledge, panting from the exertion. I sat up and caught my breath, relieved to feel space around me again.

Reinaldo slid down and perched himself between us. "Here we are. What do you think?"

"It's too dark to see anything," cried Luz.

Reinaldo laughed. "Don't worry. You'll see."

A small match flickered in Reinaldo's hand. He lit a candle that he must have carried with him. He tossed the match to the ground below, and held up the candle.

Now I saw that the ledge we sat on fed into a chamber with smooth walls and a floor of packed earth. The cave had a high round ceiling and was a little larger than an elevator. Normally I would have felt claustrophobic in a space this size, but after the passageway we had just been through, the cave felt safe, inviting.

"Can we go in?" asked Luz.

"Of course," said Reinaldo. "If you want to know the Goddess you must stand before the altar."

Luz jumped down into the cave. It was at least a six-foot drop. "Come on, Beth."

I jumped down, landing on my feet a little too hard. I looked around, taking quiet steps, as if I were in church.

At the far side of the cave there was a statue, similar to the *stelae* above, but smaller, more roughly hewn. Beside it was a stone bowl, round and shallow, like an offering plate.

The bottom of the bowl was carved with circles within circles. A tree trunk, maybe? The wall behind the altar was marked with the same large circle with smaller circles inside. Just above there were two large single circles. These had dark centers. Together the three circles formed a triangle that pointed down to the bowl.

Luz touched the edge of the bowl. "Is this the altar?"

Reinaldo nodded. "Lay your hand there. Feel the stone."

I traced the largest circle with my finger. "Are these just designs or do they symbolize something?"

"Nothing here is just a design."

"What do the circles mean?" asked Luz.

"I was puzzled at first. But after being here with her," Reinaldo gestured to the statue, "I think I know."

The body of the statue was an ear of corn with the husk torn open at the center, but at the top of the ear was the head of a woman, with her face up to the sky, her mouth open. The husks that had been torn away were positioned like arms lifted toward the sky. One arm held an ear of corn, and the other cradled a crudely carved infant.

"The Goddess of Fertility has many names," began Reinaldo. "One of them was Ro, the first female to give birth to her own kind. This *stela* tells the story of Ro's origin, her own birth."

"But if she was the first to give birth, how can there be a story about how she was born?" asked Luz.

"That's exactly what puzzled the ancient Mayans. Ro's story was the answer."

Reinaldo held the candle in the direction of the statue. "In the beginning the Goddess was as a complete being. She had dominion over the fields and the skies — no suffering, no hunger, no pain." He looked to me, "Like your garden of Eden perhaps.

"But then she conceived a child — it was an unnatural thing, and the Great Ruler, the most powerful God of all, was very angry. He vowed that he would destroy her."

Luz moved closer to the statue. "Did he?"

"No. Ro was able to outsmart him. She survived by giving birth to herself and destroying herself at the same time."

Reinaldo pointed to the statue, casting a long shadow across it with his finger. "Look here. Ro is tearing open her own womb. She is corn and she governs the crops, but she is also a human being, crying out in pain. You can see her head at the top."

"What happened next?" asked Luz.

"She gave birth, then she tore herself in half in an attempt to kill herself. She almost succeeded, but her penis stayed whole and continued to live, so Ro wrapped it in her own flesh and buried it alive beneath the cornfield. It is said that this act ensured the supply of seed for the Mayan crops for eternity.

"After she gave life to the child and the crops she dragged herself to her grave. We don't know where it was, but it doesn't really matter — because the child was her incarnation in every way. From birth that child knew the pain of both mother and child, and the power of the Gods. So Ro survived, but only through her own self-destruction."

"But what about the Ruler God, wasn't he still angry?" Luz asked.

"Yes, but he felt that she deserved leniency for her pain, so he reduced her punishment. Ro, the child, would live and reproduce, but never again like the first time. And men and women have lived that way since then."

"So you think this is a temple to Ro," I looked from the *stelae* to the altar. "Is this where they would have made offerings?"

"Yes. The circles within circles symbolize the endless chain of birth. And Ro is there again in the drawing on the wall behind the altar. Those two large circles above it are the breasts of the Goddess."

"But she doesn't have a face," I said.

"Probably the small triangle between the breasts is the head. The Mayans showed what was most important in a drawing by making it larger — the womb, the breasts; for the female these are the essentials. The head and face are not as important."

The head that cooked up a scheme to save all future generations wasn't important, I mused. Reinaldo's story had its shortcomings. Still, there was so much power, so many layers of meaning. He couldn't be making it up....

"Were there human sacrifices right here?" Luz placed her hand on the altar and braced herself. "Babies, animals, burnt for the Gods?"

"Nothing like that, *hija*. At least not here. The offering plate shows no evidence of burning, and it looks too small even for a small animal. Our people probably made their offerings of simpler things, like food or seed. Flower petals were common prayer offerings, too, and they are still used today. Each color has a different meaning. My mother always offered red petals for health, and yellow for a good corn harvest. If you go further north you'll even find these offerings made right in the Catholic church."

"I can't believe that," said Luz.

"Believe it. Right beside the wax candles of the church, our people are keeping their ancient traditions."

Luz shook her head in awe. "And no one has entered this temple?"

"Who knows. Other explorers like me maybe, but it hasn't been used by a community in hundreds of years, I would guess. Remember, they would have tended the altars above us." Reinaldo pointed up, reminding me how deep into the earth we had crawled.

Reinaldo blew out the candle, then jumped down into the cave.

My sense of comfort inside the temple was shattered by the darkness and his sudden movement. "Isn't it about time for us to go?"

Luz's voice rose thinly, "How will we get back up to the tunnel?"

"We're not going through that tunnel again." Reinaldo's face was close. I couldn't see him in the darkness, but I could smell his sour breath. "The exit is this way."

My throat tightened. "Why can't we go back the way we came?"

"It's too difficult, too steep. We can't even get back up to the ledge."

"We could have if you had stayed up there to give us a hand." I regretted my words immediately.

"Don't question me." I could feel Reinaldo pointing a finger at me in the darkness, "You wanted to come here, now I'm telling you there is only one way out."

As I opened my mouth to protest I felt Luz's hand pressing against her arm. "He's right, Beth. Let's do what he says."

Reinaldo took a few steps. It sounded like he was moving toward the altar. "We'll enter here. The tunnel is smaller than the other one but not as steep..."

"How long is it?" I asked.

"It's as long as it is. That's all we know about the journey, *gringa*."

Near tears now, I swallowed hard. "Can we at least light another match to get started? I can't do it if I can't see anything."

"You don't need light. Your own fear is the greatest danger here. It can strangle you, cause you to misstep — otherwise the path is clear." Reinaldo shifted his weight and sighed. "We'll come out just beyond the Ball Court. If you do what I say, you'll be delivered safely."

I nodded my consent in the darkness. I felt Reinaldo's hand on my arm, guiding me toward the tunnel.

"It's big enough to crawl through," continued Reinaldo, "and there are rocks all along the way that will help you to move forward. Rely on your knees and feet to push yourself through. Forget how large you are. You must become like the snakes that crawl through these tunnels every day."

"Snakes?" I said. "Do they bite?"

"They tickle a little here and there, but they don't usually bite. And poisonous snakes are rare. Remember your worries are futile — the pathway is what it is. We have chosen it and now we must pass through it."

I reached out for Luz. "Are you ready?"

"Reinaldo is telling us that it is time to go in," said Luz steadily.

"There we go," said Reinaldo, "that's the courage of a Mayan. I'll lead but you must stay close behind. I'll try to tell you what's coming ahead."

Reinaldo entered the tunnel. Luz and I clung to each other for a moment.

"I'll go next," said Luz.

I let go of Luz and watched her enter the tunnel. As soon as her feet were inside I put my head in to follow her. The air was thick with the dust that had been let loose when Reinaldo and Luz scraped their feet against the dry earth. I crawled a little way, surprised at the effort it took to push myself forward. Once my feet were inside I remembered what Reinaldo had said — I used my feet and knees to propel myself up the incline. I turned back toward the entrance, trying to use my eyes out of habit, but I saw nothing. When I faced forward I could feel the presence of Luz's foot in front of me.

The passageway became even narrower but the incline was not very steep. How long was the tunnel? I imagined the geometry of it — the steeper path would get to the surface more quickly, of course. Would an incline that was half as steep be twice as long? Maybe. And there would be natural dips and valleys under the surface, too — the imperfections of the real world could only make the path longer.

I tried to take a deep breath, to focus on the light that awaited me at the top. But the air in the tunnel was so thick it gagged me. I felt my throat close in panic. Would I let myself stop breathing? Could I contain the screams that I felt rising in my blood? And if I gave in and cried out, would I be able to stop?

I closed my eyes to the darkness around me and put my head down. That was the only way out. I forgot about time and distance and moved upward. I was sweating from the effort and began to accept refreshment from the cool rocks.

After a while the rocks and dirt began to feel moist; we were getting closer to the surface. I heard muffled words. I lifted my chin and opened my eyes. A hole of light opened ahead of me. Luz was out of the tunnel.

I felt a surge of strength. "Oh, thank God, I'm almost there."

When I got to the top Reinaldo and Luz were there, pulling me out, one at each arm. I felt the space around me and took it in like breath.

Luz beamed and embraced me, and I couldn't help but smile myself.

Reinaldo approached me with a solemn nod. "That's our struggle. You liked it in the end, didn't you?"

I brushed myself off. "I don't know if I liked it, but I'm ready for the rest of our journey. It couldn't be harder than that, right?"

Reinaldo put his hand on my shoulder. "From now on you're a *tahi-pi*, you know."

"What's that?"

Reinaldo looked at me with his good eye. "The word means sister, but the ancestors used it to honor strangers who chose to walk with us, even though our road is one of suffering."

I blushed. "I hardly deserve the honor, the way I argued with you down there."

"You're right, you were a coward. But it's not for that. It's because you walk with Luz. You've brought her home."

The sun was too bright now, and my eyes filled. I want to do more than bring her home to this, I thought. I want to help her find a place where she doesn't have to suffer. I want to save her.

*   *   *

"I knew we wouldn't find anything." Luz hung her head and let her hair fall forward, casting a shadow over her face.

I breathed out my own disappointment. "We've only been here for an hour. We'll find your relatives, and the farm too. Let's rest a bit, and then ask a few more people."

"There's no one left to ask. Let's just go home."

Luz was right. We had already gone around the town square twice and up and down the two dirt roads that made up the town. No one knew anything about Luz's parents.

I led Luz into the small dark church to get out of the sun. We sat down in the last pew. "What about aunts and uncles, or your parents' friends?" I spoke in a low voice. "What were their names?"

Luz shook her head. "I just remember being with my parents out on the farm. I don't remember anyone else."

A woman entered the church by the side door at the front. She walked to the middle of the church, genuflected, and made the sign of the cross. Then she went to the right side of the altar, to tend the votive candles. Luz and I got on our knees and bowed

151

our heads. I watched out of the corner of my eye as the woman checked the cup that held matches and took the money that had been laid in the small offering dish and put it in her pocket. She bent over one of the candles, straightening the wick so it wouldn't go out. She stood back and looked over the candles once more, then left.

I sat back up in the pew. "We may not be able to find your relatives, but we can visit the farm."

"The farm." Luz shook her head. "There are probably a bunch of strangers living there now."

"I'm sure they'd let you look around."

Luz looked out the back door. "See that tree with the twisted trunk? The farm is out that way. I used to take that path into town with my mother, to sell tomatoes and eggs." Luz laughed, mocking herself. "Imagine me, Beth, a little girl with a basket of eggs on her head. And I never dropped them. My mother trusted me and I never let her down."

"Let's go then. We can get a quick lunch at the *comedora,* and then head out." I shook my canteen. "I'll refill this, too. It can't be that far if you walked it when you were a little girl. Do you remember the way?"

"Of course I remember."

Just beyond the twisted tree was a well-worn path, with high grass on both sides and enough trees to break up the bright sun here and there. The gentle uphill slope made the walk invigorating. I smiled to myself. Everything felt right, walking home to the farm with Luz.

After about a half a mile we reached a high clearing where the path continued, surrounded by cultivated hillsides. Patches of corn, coffee, and beans were set against one another in clean lines, like a patchwork quilt, in shades of green and brown. In a nearby field a woman bent over a row of plants, tearing leafy sustenance out of the seam, then mending the earth together with her hand.

The cultivated area was bordered with a thick forest. From the crest of the hill the treetops looked like a flat of fresh green broccoli. We walked for an hour or so, passing only a man with a machete and a woman carrying a basket of vegetables on her head. Finally we reached the edge of the forest.

"Are we almost there?" I asked.

"That way," said Luz, pointing to the forest with her chin.

The path through the forest was hard to make out among the gnarly trunks and brush. We walked more slowly, in silent concentration. After a while I reached for my canteen, but decided against drinking — it would be better to save what was left.

Was the sun starting to wane, or was it just the shade of the forest? I looked at my watch. It was already four o'clock.

"Luz, are you sure we're getting close? We can't go much farther and get back by sundown."

"It's not much farther." Luz put her hands on her hips and looked to either side. "Don't worry, it'll be downhill all the way back. My mother always said it took twice as long to get to the farm as to go into town."

I frowned. I didn't want to have to turn back, not when we were this close. As long as we were out of the woods by nightfall we'd be okay. We could follow the path through the fields in the moonlight easily enough, and still make it back to town in time to find *hospedaje* somewhere.

We walked without talking. The path was overgrown, and Luz seemed to have trouble remembering which way to go. She backtracked twice before she decided to forget the trail and just head straight for the farm.

"We'll cut our own path," she said. "It's probably faster."

A patch of sun penetrated the forest. We walked through low brush for a while, dry sticks scratching our legs, too many rocks for us to set our feet down flat. Progress was slow, and we were both tired. I looked at my long shadow. It was getting late.

We came to a large tree with a patch of bare ground around its base where the sun could never reach. Luz collapsed into a sitting position, leaning back against the tree's massive trunk.

"I need water." She reached for it without raising her head.

"Go easy. There's not much left," I said.

Luz avoided my eyes.

"Are you okay, Luz?"

Luz gulped the water and returned the empty canteen.

"This was the spot." she pointed to the woods around her. "The farm's not here."

I saw no evidence of a clearing. The trees had to have been there for at least fifty years. "There should be something left — at least the abandoned remains. Are you sure it was here?"

Luz let out a hysterical moan. "I don't know, Beth. I don't even know where we are, Guatemala? Honduras? Is it *Lunes? Martes?* What's my name? I don't know. And it's not written down anywhere, that's for sure."

Luz's meaning took hold of me slowly. "But you said you remembered the way."

"Ah." Luz threw her head back. "It's confusing. What I remember is confusing."

I put a hand on Luz's shoulder. "We're going to have to head back, Luz. If you can lead us back the way we came, we can still get to the clearing before dark."

Luz slumped back against the tree. "Couldn't you see that's what I was trying to do? We're lost, Beth. *Perdidos.*" She closed her eyes and let her arms hang limp.

I tugged at Luz's arm. "We're not lost, Luz. I'll help you remember."

Luz opened one eye, "Remember what?"

"The path. The way down to the market. The one you took when you were a little girl."

"The market, ha." Luz's laugh would have been demonic if she hadn't seemed so scared. "I made all that up, Beth. Pure lies. The farm burned. I watched it with my own eyes."

I almost fell down from shock, but caught myself against the tree. "But we came all this way. You dragged me to the middle of nowhere for no reason. And now we're lost?"

I took Luz's head and lifted it up to my own face, speaking loud and close. "Open your eyes, Luz. Do you understand how dangerous this is? We're in the middle of nowhere. You can't walk back to your room when you decide the game is over."

Luz opened her eyes to reveal a vacant stare. "I was born somewhere in these woods. I might as well die here, too."

I took Luz by the shoulders. "You want to kill yourself? Go ahead and do it. Do you think I won't leave you here and find my way out? I will. You had no right to lie to me."

I let go of Luz with force.

"Don't push me," shouted Luz, sitting up and swinging her arm at me. "You said you wanted to come with me. It was your idea to try to find the farm. Hasn't anyone told you that I'm part crazy? I've lied about everything. You think I don't know where my parents are? My father lives out by Zanmorano with that witch, and my mother is alive and crazy right in Teguc. You can find her in the marketplace any day of the week, gathering old potatoes and tomatoes from the floor. She tries to sell them for a living and begs the rest. Sometimes she recognizes me when I pass her and sometimes she thanks me for my *cinco* as if I were a complete stranger."

Luz pulled her knees to her chest and put down her head again. "There. Now you know about my people."

"But if you knew there was nothing, and no one here, why did you want to come?"

Luz looked at me, her eyes full of tears. "You did it for the others. I wanted to see if you would do it for me."

My face was tight with anger and hurt. I sat down beside Luz. Tears ran down my cheeks and a deep sob took my breath away. I looked up at the sky and let my face wrinkle up so tight that the muscles had nothing to do but release. I let myself sob again. It felt good.

The sky was turning orange. "Do you really want to die here, Luz?"

"No, but we'll never find our way out."

I took a breath. Seeing Luz for what she was put things in their place. I stood up and dragged Luz up with me.

"Let's go."

Through the branches I saw the sun setting on the horizon. So that was west. I thought we'd come from the south, so I headed that way, trying to stay on a straight course through branches and small trees. Nothing looked familiar. There was no sign of a path.

Luz didn't say a word but at least she kept pace with me. I thought of the tunnel back in Copan, but that had been different. We'd had Reinaldo to lead us. Still, I needed to summon the same confidence here. What was it that Reinaldo had said? The path is what it is...

We walked on, keeping a good pace, even though we had no idea where we were going. There was a clearing up ahead. My hopes rose. Could we have made it back to the edge of the forest? No. It was just a wide fork where two paths crossed.

"Which way?" said Luz.

It was getting dark. The bugs were starting to bite — the wooded paths would be thick with them. I had no idea which path led back.

"Let's stop here for a bit," I said.

"For what?"

"Maybe someone will pass. Someone who can lead us out."

We sat in the road, leaning against each other back to back, and waited.

I heard footsteps that sounded heavy, like a man or large animal. I braced myself to see what would come down the path. Then I saw a thin woman with a weather-beaten face, her steps heavy because she was carrying a bucket of water. I jumped up and rushed toward her so quickly that she jumped back.

"*Dios mío*," she said, catching her breath. "We don't see many strangers here."

"We're not strangers exactly," I said. "Luz was born here." I looked to Luz for help. "We came up from Juntapeque to find the farm where she grew up, but we got lost."

The woman sucked in her breath. "Sundown is not the time to go looking for a farm." She looked at Luz again. "You're from here?"

"*Sí.*"

"Who was your mother then?"

Luz looked down. "Lourdes Velasco, and my *papá* was Jaime Espinal."

"I don't know them. But there have been Velascos in these parts," she conceded. "You can't go back to Junta tonight — it's too far. I'm Doña Sebastiana. I live nearby with my daughter. You'll stay with us. In the morning I can take you down to Juntapeque myself."

"*Gracias,*" I said. "You're so kind. Thank you."

Luz took the bucket from Doña Sebastiana, and followed her down the path.

Doña Sebastiana's home was a small wooden shack hidden behind a cluster of trees just off the path. When we got closer we were welcomed by the squawk of chickens that pecked around the house. I wondered if we had passed other such dwellings along the way.

We sat on the low bench in the front room and shared tortillas and watery coffee. Doña Sebastiana apologized for the meager supper, and insisted that Luz and I take the hammock in back. She and her daughter would sleep on a mat in the front room.

We got in the hammock head to toe. I settled into the gentle rock of the hammock and felt fatigue roll over me. Things would be okay. We would be in Tegucigalpa by late tomorrow night.

"Do you have enough covers?" asked Luz.

I pulled Doña Sebastiana's thin blanket up to my chin. "Yes."

"I'm sorry," said Luz softly.

I was still too upset to acknowledge the apology. "You have to stop putting yourself in danger, Luz."

"These devils — I try so hard not to let them get inside."

"The devils and witches aren't real, Luz. You have to believe that."

"Are you trying to tell me that witch didn't cast a spell on the farm? It was a beautiful farm once, I didn't dream that. And then everything died," said Luz.

I felt Luz's legs tremble.

"When things went wrong on the farm," I began, "after your dad left...I know it was hard. Your mother couldn't do all the work, so things broke down. The farm failed, but it wasn't witchcraft."

"What about the fire? We were fast asleep and we woke up to find the whole kitchen in flames."

I imagined the scene in my mind. "Kitchen fires are accidents, Luz. Your mother must have been tired and fallen asleep before the fire was completely out."

"Maybe it was all accidents with my mother then," Luz said slowly, "and she went crazy — you'll say that was bad luck. But what about murderers who cut up innocent children, the soldiers who can come into a village and kill everyone, and the fathers who rape their daughters?" Luz shook her head. "I know I'm part crazy, but I didn't invent those. Don't they prove to you that there really are devils?"

I closed my eyes. This trip was wearing me down. Luz's demons were crowding in on me, making me admit they were real. I couldn't refute Luz's list. In fact, I could add to it. Why did children like Luz end up so alone? And Sister Paula's children? How could they be thrice damned by poverty, abandonment, and disability too? Was there really a kind God that was interested in this world?

"I'll never believe in devils," I whispered. "But if I did I would still believe that we can be stronger than they are. We have to say 'no' as loud as we can. Tell those devils that our God, our will, is stronger than they are. That we can beat them." I waited for another reply, another challenge, but Luz was silent. "Do you think you can do that, Luz?"

"I don't know," said Luz. "Maybe."

We woke in the thin darkness of the early dawn to the sound of Doña Sebastiana slapping tortillas into shape. She had already gone to fetch water. Seeing me awake she pointed to the bucket.

"You can wash," she said.

By the time the morning light was full we were ready to head down to Juntapeque.

"I'm going to take advantage of having you along," said Doña Sebastiana. She handed Luz a basket of eggs and gave me a sack of tomatoes to carry. Then she hoisted a large basket of potatoes up on top of her own head and led us back to town.

La Casa de los Niños
November

IX

I filed into the chapel with the girls. They all sat down together in the last pew, except for Katia, who took a seat at the end of the front row. She looked straight ahead, her hands folded, but visibly shaking.

Mother Maria had called them to her in the middle of the afternoon, on a Saturday, and the girls knew why. The school year ended on December fifteenth, just three weeks away. Mother Maria needed to make room in the *Residencia* for the younger girls coming up. Those who were continuing their studies or apprenticeships would stay, of course, but it was time for the others to go out on their own.

I looked from girl to girl. Despite their grumbling I could see that Mother Maria was right. Most of them were ready. We had already started looking into rented rooms in Las Estrellas, a modest but safe neighborhood not far from *La Casa*. The girls could afford to live there if they went out in pairs.

Katia was more nervous than the others and she had reason to be. She'd managed to keep her job, but she continued to drink and stay out late, and she seemed to have more money than she could possibly be earning as a seamstress. She somehow managed to keep up the ruse of going to Mass and receiving communion, but I was fairly certain that Mother Maria knew what was going on.

Katia was so troubled and hard, but she'd made us all laugh so many times. I wished I could go over and hug her, but of course, Katia would never accept an embrace.

Mother Maria came in, blessed herself, and recited the Hail Mary with the girls. Then she made the announcement that everyone expected.

"You have work you can be proud of, and we've made sure you all have your ID cards." She gave me a nod of recognition.

It was true. I had followed through and gotten papers for each and every girl, even Luz. After the trip to Juntapeque, I had sought legal advice. I found that, based on the trip, I could serve as a witness of non-documentation. That was enough to establish Luz as a "certified undocumented citizen of Honduras." As such, Luz was entitled to an ID card like everyone else, and after the usual waiting lines and stamps, she got it.

Luz's situation was far from settled though. She hadn't been able to pass sixth grade, and I knew Mother Maria wouldn't let her repeat again. She'd found part-time work as an assistant in a sewing shop, but I wasn't sure she could manage living on her own.

"And you'll always be welcome to visit here, to share the Mass with me, like daughters," Mother Maria was saying. Then she read off the names of the girls who could remain at *La Casa* for continuing "*formación*." The others would have until the end of December to make arrangements.

I listened as Mother Maria read the predictable list, but I was surprised when Mother Maria announced the last name. Mother Maria was allowing Katia to stay.

I took a quick glance at Luz, who was looking down at the ground, clearly upset. Then I followed Mother Maria out.

"Mother Maria? Could we talk about the list? I was wondering how many new girls there will be."

"They won't arrive until after you've gone home, Beth."

"I know," I said softly. "But I thought I might help you figure out how to make room for Luz, just until we're sure that her new job is working out... I don't think she has anywhere to go."

"She's a strong girl. She'll find her place."

"But..."

I searched Mother Maria's face hoping she would guess my question and answer it. But she stood before me impassive, waiting for me to speak.

"You were so kind," I said, "giving Katia more time. Why not Luz, too?"

Mother Maria looked at me. "Luz and the others are ready to be on their own. They're scared, but they're ready. We know where Katia would end up — the brothels or dead in the street. I can't send her there."

"She may never change," I said, more to myself than Mother Maria. "But at least she'll be okay for a while longer."

"She's been coming to Mass." Mother Maria put her hands up in submission. "God's mercy will lift her up or she'll bring herself down, but I'm going to keep her here with me until then."

Early the next morning I knocked on the screen door of Sister Paula's house then let myself in. Sister Paula was singing as she kneaded a large mound of dough, with Celina parked beside her to watch. On Sister Paula's other side Lola stood on a chair kneading her own small ball.

When Sister Paula saw me she didn't stop her song to say hello. Instead she split the dough in two and passed one of the halves to the other side of the table where I could work.

"Bett," cried Celina.

Lola acknowledged me by smiling and lifting her ball of dough in the air for me to see.

I showed Lola the bag of cinnamon and sugar I carried in my hand. "I'll need your help," I said.

Baking together had become a Sunday morning tradition. It had started with Sister Paula's big heart, of course. Ophelia deserved a break from cooking, so Sister Paula started getting up early on Sundays and making fresh bread for the children. With

Rosa gone, I decided it would be nice to treat the girls on Sunday morning, too. So I helped with a double recipe.

One Sunday, I offered to make my mother's cinnamon rolls and everyone loved them. We made rolls every week after that. The excitement of the children, Sister Paula's beautiful voice, and the smell of warm yeast and cinnamon had turned the Sunday chore into the high point of my week.

We finished kneading, then rolled the dough flat. The children took turns sprinkling the raisins and sugar and cinnamon. Then Ophelia led them out to the play yard while Paula and I rolled and sliced and set the spirals on the flattened oil tins we used for baking sheets.

Just as I placed the third sheet of rolls in the lukewarm oven to rise, Paula brought two cups and a pot of hot coffee with fresh cream to the table. This small luxury had become part of the Sunday morning tradition, too.

Paula served me then sat down and let out a sigh. Lola came in and climbed on Paula's lap, smiling out at me from beneath Paula's chin. Paula kissed her on the forehead and tried to smile, but I could see worry in her eyes.

"Is something wrong?" I asked.

Sister Paula looked frankly at me. "Mother Maria and I had words this morning after *matins*."

"About Theo again?"

"He's been difficult lately."

I looked around, suddenly aware that the house was relatively quiet. The usual thumping and rolling sounds of Theo moving about were absent.

"Where is he?"

"Just now I'm not sure," said Paula. "He left yesterday and didn't come home last night."

I knew that Tegucigalpa was a scary place for a beggar child on a Saturday night. I remembered how Theo had come home the last time. Filthy, with his nose bleeding. Sister Paula thought he'd been attacked, but of course he might have started the fight, too.

"He'll come home," I said. "He always does."

"She says he can't stay here any longer."

"You'll change her mind. You have before."

Paula shook her head. "She says I've lost him, that he's dangerous."

A part of me agreed with Mother Maria about Theo, yet Sister Paula had always been able to handle him. She had a special gift, I had seen that again and again. At some point though, he could become too strong, too difficult to handle. Sister Paula needed to think realistically about that.

I was saved from having to speak my mind because Ophelia was calling from the play yard. "Here he comes."

Paula set Lola down and went to the doorway. Theo was there on his skateboard outside the gate. He was dirty, his hair matted, and his lip was split and bloodied. He looked stunned and confused and numb.

"What are you going to do?" I asked.

Sister Paula wiped her hands, which were dusted with flour and cinnamon, on her clean apron. "He needs to know that he's loved. Even now. Even like this."

She went out to the gate and opened it. "Theo." She embraced him. "You're home."

Theo pulled himself up on one knee and nuzzled his head against her, groping for affection and wiping his nose. Sister Paula led him in, her apron stained with dirt and blood.

While Sister Paula saw to Theo, I set the rolls to bake. By the time I took them out of the oven and called everyone to breakfast Sister Paula had Theo bathed and in a clean shirt. When she brought him to the table he insisted on sitting on her lap. He was heavy, and Sister Paula was uncomfortable. Still, she held him there and hand-fed him a warm cinnamon roll.

When Lola came in with the others, she saw Theo in Paula's lap. Upset at being displaced, she folded her arms and took a step back away from the table. I called to her and offered my own lap as a substitute. Lola accepted with a shy smile. I was surprised how good it felt to hold Lola, the warmth of it. I gave her a hug, then kissed her on the forehead as I had seen Sister Paula do.

X

December 15th came quickly. As I zipped my suitcase shut I could hardly believe I'd be flying home in the morning. I had set aside the whole evening to pack, but it only took an hour. The truth was I didn't have a lot of bags, only a carry-on and a mid-size suitcase. I had traveled light when I came, wanting to leave materialism behind. Now I was returning home with even less. I'd given my things away one by one to the girls, my American jeans to Suyapa, an electric burner to Rosa, and the tape player to Katia. By the time I had to pack there was hardly anything left, as if my life was ending and I wouldn't need any earthly goods at all where I was going.

I looked around the room. There was no sign that it had ever been mine, just cinder block walls, a cement floor, and a small window with clumsy wooden shutters. The hook on the back of the door where I hung my yellow-and-white-striped towel was conspicuous now, a naked claw, and the metal bucket I kept filled with wash water was dry, already covered with a thin chalky film.

I felt warm from packing. I pulled my hair back to the nape of my neck, braiding it expertly without a comb or mirror, the way the girls had taught me. My hair had never been this long.

My skin was darker too. Over these months the tropical sun had turned my olive skin a warm brown. I blended in here now. I had to admit I enjoyed that, and the girls had liked it too — to stand beside me and say, "See, we're sisters," and then step back and giggle at their cheekiness.

I paced back and forth in the small room. Now that it was time to go home, I wasn't sure I wanted to leave. A knock at the front door pulled me from my thoughts.

"Is anybody home?" a deep voice called out. "May I speak with the *encargada*, please?"

The *encargada*. I smiled to myself. I had tried, for the past year, to be something else — a counselor, a sister, a friend — but it was no use, I was the *encargada,* at least for a few more hours.

I made my way down the hall to the *sala*. A man with a straw hat in his hand stood at the screen door. Behind him on the street was an old green pickup with *La Casa de los Niños* painted on the cab. I opened the door.

"I'm Don Roberto," he said, nodding a greeting. "I have a message for one of your girls." Then he looked down and spoke more softly, "It's for Vera — from her mother."

My heart jumped. Vera hadn't seen her mother in over ten years, not since her mother had left her at *La Casa.*

Before I could turn to call for Vera, the girls began to gather in the kitchen. It was too late to keep things private. They were already whispering the news. "Vera's mother. Vera's mother is calling for her."

Had Vera left for night school yet? I turned to ask but there were three voices ahead of mine. "Vera." "She's still here." "I'll get her."

Vera came in. "You called?"

Don Roberto bowed his head more deeply to Vera. "I've just come from Choloma. One of the drivers who hauls coffee near San Luis saw your mother there." Don Roberto waved his hand in the air helplessly. "She asked him to get word to you. She's ill, very ill, and she wants to see you, if you're willing."

Vera put her notebook down on the table. The crease in her brow went smooth. "I'm willing." Then she turned to me. "You'll come with me, won't you?"

I looked at Vera, then to the faces of the other girls. I'd made the same promise to all of them, and I'd made good on it for Felicia and Rosa and Luz. Now the girls looked at me expectantly. Would I let Vera down?

I found myself making a list — cancel the plane reservation, call home, pack a small bag for a trip to San Luis. I closed my eyes. No. I couldn't postpone my departure.

"Oh Vera, I want to, but I'm going home tomorrow. My flight leaves first thing in the morning — I can't." I looked helplessly at Don Roberto. "How will she find her mother?"

"She's working coffee on a *finca* outside of San Luis. I'm heading to San Isidro in the morning. I can take her that far."

"That's fine," said Vera. "I'll take the bus the rest of the way."

Don Roberto clicked his tongue and shook his head. "There is no bus. The roads are too rough. From San Isidro you'd have to hitchhike — and wait for a good sturdy truck. If it rains, you may have difficulty even then." He looked down in shame as if he were responsible for the rains and road conditions. "I'll give you a ride if you want, but it's not a trip that I recommend. Not alone."

Vera paced out nervous steps in a circle. "I'm going. I have to see my mother before she dies."

Don Roberto looked from Vera to me and back again. "When you get to San Luis you'll ask for Señor Macedo. He owns the farm. He can take you to your mother."

Back in my room I looked at my suitcase, packed, ready for the trip home. Tears welled up inside me. Should I have stayed for Vera?

I shook away that thought at once. My year was over. Of course I wished I could finish some things, do more. But there would always be more to do, no matter how long I stayed. Some days I could imagine staying forever. Planting myself here, letting my roots sink in, like Sister Paula had. But I could never be Sister Paula, and I had my other life to think about. My mother was counting on my being home for Christmas, and there was Jake. He'd be waiting for me at the airport in just twenty hours.

When my alarm sounded at five in the morning, I felt excited. Today I would finally go home. Then my heart grew heavy as I recalled Don Roberto's message like a bad dream, and remembered what day it was for Vera.

I had to be ready to go to the airport by six, but I wanted to take a last walk around before the girls woke up and the house was crowded with goodbyes.

I went into the *sala*, trying to memorize it. The gray cinderblock walls, the large wooden table that was covered with a red-and-white checked sheet of vinyl during meals, and the metal chairs that did double duty as kitchen chairs and sitting room furniture. Instead of using the colorful tiles made locally, someone had imported green linoleum, so that the floor would not crack or stain.

Later the *sala* would be full with the sound of chopping, the sizzle of refried beans, and the aroma of coffee. Now quiet and empty, the *sala* revealed itself to be a lonely place. It needs a mother, I thought.

At eight o'clock my plane would take off. Meanwhile the girls would gather here as usual, talking and fretting, their legs and arms wrapped around the backs or sides of the metal chairs, squirming like children, trying to be comfortable. When I first arrived I'd felt uneasy about the whispers and giggles that came from this room, certain that the girls were laughing at me.

Don't be paranoid, I had told myself, they probably have more interesting things to laugh about. I knew now that they really were laughing at me, at least some of the time. Katia had come to me the other day, to say goodbye and thank you, and to apologize for "all the times I made fun of you with the other girls." I smiled to myself now. To be mocked by Katia was to be expected, but to receive her heartfelt apology was a great honor.

The *sala* was where the girls argued about chores and called me in to referee, until they put up the chairs at the end of the day, and the sound of the mop declared peace with a swishswishswish, or a swish…swish…swish, depending on whose turn it was to wash the floor.

My thoughts turned back to Vera. Every evening Vera came into the *sala* after a long day in the sewing shop. She grabbed a bite to eat, went to school, then came back to the *sala* to do her homework while her roommates slept. She paid her own tuition, never asking Mother Maria for help. "I don't want any more debts, Beth, and the ones that you don't have to pay back are the worst."

I've refused her such a small thing, I thought. To help her through a rough spot, a few short days.

It wasn't safe for Vera to make the trip alone. Don Roberto had said as much. What would have happened if Felicia had been alone when soldiers stopped her on the way to Vista del Oro? And Rosa had thanked me again and again with the words "I never could have faced those things alone." Vera's trip would be even more difficult; with her mother sick, maybe even dead, when she got there.

I went back to my room and looked at my packed bags for a long moment, then I picked up the canvas carry-on and emptied the contents onto the bed. I re-packed the bag with a change of clothes, a canteen full of clean water, a toothbrush, shampoo that I would use as bath soap too, and a roll of toilet paper from the hall bathroom.

I picked up my Polaroid camera and weighed it in my hands. It was bulky, and I'd have to keep a careful eye on it all the way, but Vera would want a picture, and her mother would want one too. I tucked my journal and passport into the front pocket of my bag. Cancel the airline reservation, call home, and I'd be ready to go.

When I re-entered the *sala* later that morning Don Roberto's truck stood out front. Vera waited beside it, a large duffel bag slung over her shoulder.

I wrapped some beans in a soft tortilla, took a few gulps of coffee, and went outside.

"I'm coming with you." I opened my arms to Vera. "If it's not too late."

Vera's jaw dropped then regained its composure. "Beth, you can't do this for me. Oh, thank you!"

Grinning now, Vera climbed into the open truck bed and extended her hand to me. Don Roberto appeared, looked at me, gave an approving nod and climbed in the cab.

The road out of town was noisy with signs of morning business — traffic, fresh produce carried in baskets on people's heads, crowded bus stops. Finally we reached the town limits and left the city buses and traffic behind as we turned north onto the one well-paved road in the country.

"We're on our way," I said.

Vera smiled and nodded, then looked at my bag in alarm. "Did you bring your camera? I know she's sick — but I'll sit her up and comb her hair. You can take our faces, together..."

"It's right here." I patted the zipped compartment of my bag. "What's in your bag? It looks as if you're going away for a month."

"Just clothes," replied Vera, "and some things I might show my mother. My diploma from primary, and the tablecloth I embroidered. I'm going to tell her about night school, too."

Vera's hopes were running high. It's a good thing I came, I admitted to myself. The long trip north would allow plenty of time to talk, to help Vera have more realistic expectations, to hold her hand if she needed it. I breathed in the cool morning air and let it out. Just one more week and I'd be home.

Vera's Journey

Vera would have done what she did whether I had gone with her or not. I thought the trip could help her to be free, to make peace with the past and move on, but sometimes a journey changes things so much that you can't go back the way you came.

It didn't seem fair to me that Vera could be tethered down for life by the circumstances of her birth. Still, I wasn't sure what was right. If she chose herself that would lead to suffering, too. There were other innocents to be considered.

If I hadn't walked with Vera, I don't know if I would have known what I knew later, that freedom can't hold you in place and protect you from the wind the way the weight of love can.

I took that into account later, when I needed to find my own way home.

*   *   *

I sat beside Vera in the back of the truck, my jacket zipped all the way up so that the collar shielded my face from the wind. Hitch-hiking hadn't been what I'd expected. I had imagined sticking out my thumb, then being passed over by indifferent travelers until someone took pity on us and gave us a ride. Instead Vera and I had waited on the side of the road for an hour, during which time not a single vehicle passed. We started walking north, not that we could make any real progress on foot. Finally, a beat-up orange pickup with two men in the cab and one in the back came down the road. The driver slowed down just long enough for Vera to step up to the window and tell him where we wanted to go.

"We'll pass by there on our way to San Miguel." The driver tipped his hat back as he chewed tobacco. "Hop in back."

Vera climbed up on the rusty fender and swung one leg over the back of the truck and I followed suit. As soon as my second foot was off the ground the man in the back slapped the side of the truck as a ready signal to the driver. The truck lunged forward as I scrambled to sit down.

The truck bed was cold and its wide ridges made an uncomfortable seat. At first I gripped the side of the truck for balance, but after a mile or so I positioned myself the way Vera did, relaxed but braced for movement, as if I were in a saddle.

The sun came out and I leaned my head against the cab of the truck to take in the sky. Then the wind picked up and I had to tuck my face into my collar, leaving only my eyes exposed. Vera sat on top of her folded blue sweater and held her hair back to keep it from blowing in the wind. She stretched her neck to see what she could of the landscape. When the truck hit a bump she cried out in surprise, then laughed.

Later we came a to rocky patch of road and the truck slowed. It was finally quiet enough for the riders in back to hear each other speak.

The *campesino* who'd been in the truck when we got in spoke to us through stained teeth, offering us some hard rolls that he carried in a paper bag. "What brings you to these parts?"

"Visiting family," said Vera.

He looked into our faces and nodded. "Sisters then."

Vera gave an amused smile then snuffed it out. She raised an eyebrow at me. "*Sí, hermanas.*"

The man directed the next question to me. "Where are you from?"

I hesitated. "San Luis, *¿y usted?*"

"Not far. I'm getting off at Santa Ana."

I smiled at Vera, pleased with the game. I was happy to shed my *gringa* skin for a while, and Vera seemed glad to have left her *encargada* on the roadside, too.

As we rode toward Santa Ana, we talked some more. The rains had been early this year. The coffee harvest would be, too. We were making good time, the *campesino* assured us.

We pulled into Santa Ana around noon. The *campesino* waved and headed home. Then the driver got out to stretch and announced that we'd have lunch here.

Thick, chewy, tortillas were served with beans in their own rich broth and sour cream. I would miss these simple foods when I got home. I could try to cook them myself, of course, but the beans I bought at home wouldn't carry the flavors of this life, this soil. I could never replicate the hunger I felt after a long ride in the open air, the warmth from the clay oven, the taste of hot coffee from a tin cup, the sound of tortillas as they were slapped into shape, or the ease and pleasure of eating with my hands.

As we rode from Santa Ana to San Luis, the strong wind carried away the words that we shouted at each other, making conversation impossible. The movement of the truck, bumpy and arrhythmic, and the lapping of the wind, fenced me into my own private world. I looked at the mountains and breathed deeply, trying to inhale them. Every few minutes the clouds were changing into new and splendid arrangements. I turned away from my fellow riders and sang into the wind. I couldn't even hear myself.

Near San Luis the road became rugged again. I hadn't believed the driver when he told us that the two-hundred-kilometer trip would take four hours. We had breezed through the first half of the trip, but the last leg was hilly and narrow and rocky, and we couldn't go more than about fifteen miles per hour. As we got closer, Vera talked about life in the country, how she helped her mother in the fields when she was a little girl.

"One *lempira* a bucket," she said with authority. It had never occurred to me that Vera knew how to pick coffee, or break the neck of a chicken, or eat sugar from the raw cane.

We came to a fork in the road where a turnoff marked with tire tracks led to a narrow road, more of a footpath, though a truck could probably pass. The path to San Luis made a dusty line up the gently sloping hill that led to the town. The driver slowed to a stop.

After the truck drove away neither of us moved for a moment. The spot where we'd been dropped off seemed safer, closer to the world we knew than the hill before us, and the places beyond.

Vera looked toward the path. "I do remember picking coffee," she said. "I used to wake up in the morning and find her gone, already in the fields. I'd be covered in her *bata*; she'd put it over me before she left. Her smell would keep me asleep. Then she would come at breakfast time and bring me a biscuit, and we would go back to the fields together." She smiled at this and then whispered, "But I can't remember her face."

I tried to imagine Vera's mother. I pictured eyes like Vera's, but when I altered the image to make them duller, more full of suffering, their essence was lost. I erased the eyes and drew high cheekbones that had become hard from the sun and wind. I looked at Vera for another clue, but Vera's face was too soft to hold a wrinkle or the weight of regret.

"We must be close," I said. "Let's go."

The hill was just steep enough to hide the town that lay beyond it. We walked at a steady pace, impatient for the moment when we could see what was on the other side. Finally, we came over the crest. We saw a square with a church and a small cluster of houses.

Between us and the small town was a blanket of low brush with a road down the middle. Small houses grew up around the road and a few dotted the more remote spaces. In the distance, on the other side of town, we could see trees in neat rows, all about the same height. I shaded my eyes with my hand and squinted. The trees appeared to be frosted with a light layer of snow.

"What's that?" I asked.

"That's coffee," said Vera. "It grows like that, on tall shrubs. After a few weeks of rain they're covered with those white flowers. When I was a little girl I used to fill my hands with the blossoms that fell to the ground and throw them up into the air. Like confetti."

I looked out at the trees. My year in Honduras was almost over and I'd never seen a coffee plant.

"What do the flowers look like?" I asked.

"They're white. Why?"

"How big are they? How many petals?"

"They're just simple flowers, like any other," said Vera, as if I was a child asking too many questions.

We came upon a few small houses — people who lived outside of town and probably worked in the coffee fields during the harvest. As we walked by, some children who had been playing in a small pack ran to the roadside. They stared with their mouths open as we passed.

"*Buenas dias*," said Vera, and I repeated it with a wave.

A few of the children had the courage to giggle while the others ran in the house. In the background I could hear the sounds of women's work, the brush of a broom, the clank of pans, the thud of wet laundry hitting stone, feet shuffling back and forth.

Toward town we saw more signs of life. A man passed by leading a mule laden with goods — a large sack of beans on one side, a crate of plantains on the other, and a case of Coke, artfully strapped on top of the saddle. He greeted us with a "*buenos dias*" that was paced to fit his steady gait.

It was quiet in the square, except for a few pigs that snorted and scavenged in the street. Two women in kerchiefs and long skirts sat outside the town clerk's office.

Vera greeted them and asked if they knew Don Macedo.

The first woman laughed. "*El patrón*. Everyone knows him."

"He lives in the big house in the square." The second woman pointed the way.

Beyond the church I saw a house that was much larger than the rest. It was the only house with a stucco wall around it and an iron gate at the entrance.

When we drew closer, I saw a rose garden inside the gates. The patio was paved in stone and swept clean, as clean as an indoor room might be. The gardener, who was trimming a rosebush at the edge of the yard, came to open the gate. He led us toward the heavy wooden door and knocked for us.

The maid opened the door. When Vera explained why she had come, we were invited inside. Don Macedo was taking his *siesta*. He'd see us shortly.

Don Macedo appeared after about fifteen minutes. He was taller than most Hondurans and had a beard and moustache. With sharp eyebrows, pale skin and a long nose that wasn't at all flat, he looked like a full-blooded Spaniard. He wore a starched shirt and his hair was freshly combed.

He greeted Vera with a kiss on both cheeks. "Your mother is out at the *finca*. Her fever has passed, at least for the moment."

Then he turned to me. "A foreigner," he said. "Where are you from?"

"The United States."

As he moved toward me the strong odor of cigars made me step back. But he didn't try to embrace me as he had Vera. Instead he offered me his hand. "I could tell by your shoes," he said.

He looked around himself uneasily, then smoothed his shirt, which had a straight hem at the bottom and was worn on the outside in deference to the heat.

"It's a pleasure to welcome you to San Luis, and an honor to receive you in our poor country. We don't have all the comforts of the United States, but I have a telephone if you need to make a call." He searched for something else to offer. "I am at your service," he said finally.

"Thank you," I said. "Your garden is beautiful."

"Oh, this is nothing," he said modestly. "I have plans for more. Imported rosebushes. And I'm going to plant violets from Africa in the window boxes. They are bright purple, like velvet."

"Those will look lovely," I said. "My grandmother used to cultivate them on her windowsill."

"You know them then," he said. "Of course in your United States everything is common."

Then he turned to Vera. "Well, *señorita*," he said, "and lady," he added in heavily accented English, "you are in luck. I am heading out to the *finca* this afternoon. I can take you to see your mother."

*   *   *

Don Macedo's truck was the only one in town, and it was much nicer than the one that had brought us to San Luis. The upholstery was clean and not torn, and three people could fit in the cab. I was glad not to have to ride in the truck bed.

Outside of town Don Macedo pointed to a field of young coffee trees just a few feet high.

"I'm starting over," he said. "That was my first coffee field. The people from town used to help out at harvest time. Even the grandmothers. But the harvest got smaller and smaller. After twenty years the plants gave nothing. I chopped and burned, and then I let it rest. Last year we planted the new trees. In a few more years we'll harvest near town again."

As we rode toward the *finca* Don Macedo showed us his fields. The patches of land that he owned were spread out, but each told the same story. Small coffee growers had suffered misfortune, and then were saved by Don Macedo, who bought their land so they could leave town and settle somewhere where they might find work. I squirmed in my seat beside Vera. Don Macedo made it sound like he was doing these farmers a favor by buying them out so they could head for the cities to look for jobs that didn't exist.

"And the fields where my mother works," asked Vera, "are they far from here?"

"About forty kilometers. It takes all day to walk but we'll get there within the hour. I've had good crops there for the past ten years, and I bet she has another good ten years in her."

"And my mother has worked for you all these years?" Vera asked.

"Just about. At the beginning I went out there twice a week. To check for pests — the coffee flower is fragile. And squatters, too. If you don't shoo them away you end up with ten families there in no time." Don Macedo chuckled to himself. "But it's a long way, like I said, and when your mother came looking for work I thought I would help her out. She knew coffee, and seeing that she had a small boy to take care of..."

"A small boy?" Vera looked confused.

"Yes, your brother." Don Macedo took his eyes off the road to look at Vera. "You have two now."

Vera swallowed hard and faced Don Macedo. "At least she wasn't alone, then, when she was sick."

"She wasn't alone. When your brother Enrique came and told me she was ill, I sent Sylvia to care for her and cook for the boys. She stayed with her for a few days. A week."

Vera nodded, taking it in. "So my mother is the caretaker out in your fields. Does she pick for you, too?"

Don Macedo laughed uncomfortably. "She and the boys make the rounds with their buckets. For the fun of it really. There's not much to do out on the fields. And I pay them a little something."

"How much?" asked Vera.

"Fifty *centavos* a bucket," said Don Macedo, "taking into account the housing they live in here, too."

"How much was it when I was a girl?" Vera was concentrating hard. She seemed to be trying to remember, but I knew she hadn't forgotten. It was one *lempira* — twice as much. Vera had said so on the ride in to San Luis.

When Don Macedo stopped we seemed to be in the middle of nowhere, but a footpath zigzagged up a steep hill. He got out of the truck.

"Blanca," bellowed Don Macedo in the sharp cadence of a command. Then he seemed to remember the purpose of his visit. "I've brought you your daughter," he called out in a kinder tone.

"Over here." Blanca's voice rose up above the coffee tree and down the hill to greet us.

At the sound of her mother's voice, Vera ran up the hill. I wanted to race up the hill after her, but I held back.

I heard the sound of a woman's voice rise up in delight. Then Vera's voice saying, "Me too." They were embracing now, I imagined. I looked up the hill but couldn't see them.

By the time I got to the top Vera had dropped her bag and found her mother. They were standing between two rows of coffee plants, which were about a foot taller than me, but I could hear their voices.

When I looked around the end of the row I saw Blanca, with a bucket in hand and two boys by her side. Blanca was smiling, but her fatigue was obvious. She was thin and her cheekbones cut hard lines around her eye sockets. The bones on her hands and limbs were prominent too. Although her skin was brown from the sun, I detected a gauntness that would have manifested itself as pallor if Blanca had the luxury of staying indoors when she was ill.

The brothers were barefoot and covered with a crust of dirt that looked as if it had been baked on by layers of wind. The taller one, Enrique, was old enough to stand back soberly and assess Vera, while the younger one, Paco, embraced her and smiled lopsidedly around a sore on his upper lip.

I looked out at the field that lay beyond us, and reached out to touch one of the small stubby branches of the coffee plant. The blossoms of five white petals looked like stars. The blooms sat on shiny green leaves, amid clusters of red and green berries — as if the plant was in several stages of ripeness at once. Which of these is picked, I wondered. And where is the bean?

I studied the plant, trying to memorize the shape of its leaves, its sheen. I wanted to take home some authentic knowledge of this plant, this field, this world. Would I forget it, even after holding it in my hand? Would I have to look it up some day as if I had never been here? I didn't want to let go of the plant, or to leave this country and the part of myself I had come to know here.

Vera found me. "Come and meet my mother," she said. And then to her mother, "Beth lives with us at *La Casa*. Today she was supposed to be on an airplane to the United States, but instead she came here."

"*Gracias.*" Blanca embraced me lightly. She apologized for her dress, her dirty hands, her unpreparedness for the visit. "And the sun is so strong here, forgive me."

"I'm glad to meet you," I said, taking her hand. "Your daughter —" I faltered. I couldn't very well say she's told me so much about you. "Your daughter is so special to me. To all of us at *La Casa.*"

I looked at the red berries in Blanca's bucket.

"Here is our coffee," said Blanca with pride, as if she owned the plantation herself.

"Is it harvest time?" I asked.

"We're always harvesting some," said Blanca. "I pass through once a week to gather the ripe berries. Don Macedo doesn't want to see them spoil on the ground. But the big harvest is later. Then we have lots of people working here. This row right here would be full of *gente.*" She gestured to her boys, "Children, too. Mine do a lot, the low branches so I don't have to bend."

"Ha," said Vera. "He told me you were just the caretaker. And he has you working like a mule in the fields."

"Shhh," said Blanca. "He took me in when I had nothing."

"But look how he keeps you, and you keep this whole farm working for him," said Vera, not afraid of being heard. "And how is it that you have these boys?"

"Things happen," said Blanca. "I couldn't manage here without them now." She looked at Vera. "I did you a good turn sending you away."

Vera looked at her brothers. "They should be in school."

Don Macedo passed nearby, inspecting the field. When Blanca heard his footsteps she turned to work again, picking coffee as she spoke.

"Don't punish me, *hija*," she said. "Things were difficult for me. With your father. And later too."

Vera fell in with her now, picking coffee and placing berries in her mother's bucket as she listened. I watched Vera's hands fall in rhythm with her mother's. She was as fast as Blanca, and steadier.

"I married your father because my mother wanted me to. We were poor. I was old enough. With Jaime they'd have one more person working. He could work for *La Compania*, for the *gringos*, like my father. Picking bananas. They gave lodging. So we'd get another room and I could take some of my brothers and sisters with me. More comfortable for everyone. But then your father—"

Blanca shook her head in exasperation.

"What did he do?"

"It didn't suit him to work there. He had to pick a fight with the supervisors. We were treated like slaves, he said. And he made sure everyone heard him."

"Maybe he was right," said Vera.

"He didn't grow up in *La Compania* like I did. It was hard work, but they took care of us. I always had shoes and notebooks for school. All the children did, but not from their fathers. Half of the men drank their pay. *La Compania* put us in school and bought our notebooks until we were big enough to work. I finished third grade. I could read. Now I've forgotten. No newspapers come by here anyway. But I'm still good with sums. Remember that, Vera. Your mother isn't stupid."

Blanca stood up straight like a proud schoolgirl for a moment, then bent over to pick up a berry that had fallen to the ground. She rose from under the plant with difficulty, bracing against pain, but carrying on. "So don't talk to me about *La Compania*. There are two sides to it. Your father never wanted to listen.

"When you were three we came to these parts, to work coffee. Your father always talked about buying land, but he drank the

181

money. So there I was. I never loved him, but I stayed with him until you were five. Then I gave you to Mother Maria and I left."

Blanca leveled off the berries in her bucket, assessing the quantity that she had collected before moving on. "Almost half a bucket," she said to Vera, as if they were partners in this.

She sighed as she settled in by the next tall shrub and continued her story. "I had nowhere to go. I couldn't stay with my family — when my father was too old to work they lost the housing at *La Compania*. With his last paycheck they went to San Pedro. They were suffering there, and there was no room for me. No one wanted to give work to a *viejo,* an old man. My mother took in washing and my brothers worked a little. Everyone blamed Jaime for getting them thrown out. Usually when a man is old they give his work to his sons, but they didn't want my brothers. All troublemakers like Jaime, they said."

"How did you end up here," Vera asked, "with these boys?"

"I found work in San Pedro for a while, and then I got pregnant." She pointed to Enrique. "When his father left, I had the luck of meeting Don Macedo and he brought me here. That was nine years ago."

"But you only had one child then, what about the other?"

"It gets cold here at night," Blanca laughed, "that's how I got the second one."

Vera frowned. "So here you are raising the sons of irresponsible men."

"They're half mine. More than half. And they're your brothers."

Vera looked at the boys again and sighed. They were throwing berries at each other and laughing. "Stop it, you monkeys," she said. "You're supposed to help your mother. Don't you know she's been sick?"

The boys stopped for a moment and looked at Vera, and then resumed their play. A moment later Don Macedo's boots could be heard again, crunching down in the row behind the one they were working. The boys stopped their antics and scurried over to their mother, working the lower branches and dropping berries into her bucket.

"How is your reunion going?" said Don Macedo with an open grin.

"Fine, thank you," said Blanca with a slight bow. "The field is looking clean, isn't it?"

"Everything looks fine," conceded Don Macedo. "I'll be heading back to San Luis, now. I'll come back tomorrow with some pesticide for the back quarter."

"But I didn't see any pests," said Blanca.

"You did fine," Don Macedo said. "This is just prevention."

He turned to me. "You can ride back to San Luis with me. There is a truck that's going to San Pedro in the next few days and I can arrange for you to go along. At least you won't have to hitchhike. As for tonight, there is a comfortable hotel in town if you like, or you are welcome at my home. We have a guest room and Sylvia will take care of all of your needs." He finished with a chivalrous bow.

I looked at Vera. I was glad about the ride to San Pedro, but I hadn't planned to stay in town while Vera was here with her family.

Vera looked surprised too, and turned to her mother. "Beth can stay with us, can't she?"

"She can't stay here," Don Macedo said. "There's no proper bed, and it will be cold at night."

Blanca lowered her gaze. "You're welcome here," she said, "but you will be cared for so much better in Don Macedo's house."

I turned to Don Macedo. "I'll be fine here for tonight, but we'd be very grateful if you could arrange for the ride to San Pedro."

"Very well," said Don Macedo. "I'll try to send some blankets and food — nothing fancy but maybe I can manage a little cooked meat," he glanced at Blanca and added, "for everyone. That way you can celebrate having your daughter here at last."

Don Macedo set off down the hill and when we heard the sound of his truck door closing. Blanca set down her bucket and hugged Vera again. "Welcome," she said. After a few moments she turned back to her work. "If he's coming back tomorrow I'll have to finish this," she said.

*　　　*　　　*

It was suppertime and there was no sign of the provisions that Don Macedo had promised.

"I'll fix something," said Blanca who prepared a meal of eggs, tortillas and fried plantains.

Blanca and the boys ate from one plate, and Vera and I shared the other. The boys ate vigorously, looking at their mother in disbelief every time they reached for more.

"Yes, go ahead," said Blanca. "All you want."

They ate until there wasn't a scrap left. Had they eaten a week's worth of food? I made a note to myself to send something through Don Macedo. A bag of beans, maybe, and a tin of coffee.

After dinner we sat outside for a while. Blanca seemed quiet and her eyes looked heavy.

"Pardon me," she said, "but I need to lie down."

Vera put her hand to her mother's head. "You're feverish," she said. "I'll fix your bed." She turned to Enrique. "Can we get some more water before dark?"

Enrique picked up a bucket and went out. He carried his shoulders high, already used to small burdens, whatever could fit in a bucket. He seemed glad to have Vera taking charge.

I stayed outside with Paco so that his mother could rest. Paco amused himself with a stick. First it was a horse that he was riding, then it was a machete that he used to slash at imaginary crops. Then the game changed. Paco was angry.

"If you don't behave yourself, this," he threatened, pointing the stick at an imaginary child.

"Paco, what are you doing?" I asked.

"Nothing," said Paco. His face fell back into the shape of a little boy's and he laughed shyly at being caught. "I was just playing," he said, dragging the stick in a line around himself on the ground now. "I was the boss," he said proudly.

A few minutes later I heard the sound of horse's hooves. It was Don Macedo's gardener coming up from town.

"Don Macedo sends his apology that he couldn't come himself." He handed me some blankets and a small bag. "*Maize* for your breakfast," he said, looking around. "Do you need anything else?"

"It seems that Blanca is ill again," I said.

"That's how it is," said the gardener. "The fevers go up at night." He looked toward the door. "Her daughter is with her?"

"Yes."

"I'll head back to town, then. It's getting late."

Vera came to the door, waved goodbye to the gardener, then called to her brother. "Paco, it's time to come in, it's getting dark."

I looked at Vera, still in her mother's apron after doing the dishes. At *La Casa* she had seemed like a girl, needing my help and protection. But she wasn't a child anymore. Now I was in her care. Everyone here was.

Enrique came back carrying the bucket awkwardly in front of him, taking stumbling steps and changing hands, trying not to spill. I held the door for Paco, then Enrique, and stepped inside myself before closing the door for the night.

The house was dark inside. As my eyes adjusted to the darkness, the thin candlelight spread out to the ceiling and walls. The ceiling was about ten feet high, and there were rows of shelves on all sides. The structure must have been intended as a storage shed originally.

Blanca's belongings were kept on one of the open shelves in an odd assortment of burlap sacks and plastic bags. Straw sleeping mats were spread over the dirt underneath the lowest shelves, which hung over the simple beds like a dark canopy. Was it like a womb, or a coffin? Both, I decided.

Vera was still in her mother's apron. She pressed her finger against her mouth when she saw us enter. "Shhhh, she's sleeping."

Paco tiptoed over to the sleeping mat that he shared with Enrique, ready to lie down beside him. But Vera went over and placed her hand on his shoulder.

"Go and wash your face first." She directed him to a bucket that was set on the sill of the small window by the front door, and set a stool in front of the window so he could step up and wash his face, letting the water spill to the outside.

"Quickly, we don't want to use up all the candles," said Vera. She looked to me. "These are the last ones."

I splashed water on my own face and went over to the mat in the far corner, where Vera had set down my backpack and placed a folded towel for a pillow.

I decided to sleep in my clothes. Even with the blanket that Don Macedo had sent I would need them to stay warm.

Vera washed her face and put out all the candles but one, which she carried to the sleeping mat beside her mother. Before she lay down she braided her long hair tightly.

She laughed self-consciously as she looked in my direction, "I always wear it down, but not if I'm going to sleep on the floor."

She turned to blow out the candle, but stopped herself to be sure that the book of matches was near the candleholder. She studied the remaining matches.

"Only three left. These will run out before the candles. We can manage without coffee, but no light?" She threw up her hands. "And there's hardly any *maíz* left for the tortillas."

I reached into my bag. "The gardener brought some *maíz*, and I have a book of matches. When we get to town we can have some coffee and beans sent up. I hadn't thought of candles. We can send those, too. That way they'll be all set."

Vera took the matches and set them by the candleholder. "For a few weeks. Then they'll be back to nothing." She blew out the candle and lay her head down.

I lay awake, surrounded by planes of blackness that distinguished themselves from one another only at the seams. The solid blackness of the shelf above me contrasted with the black air that was filled with the sound of breathing. Even Vera's worried sighs had fallen into the regular pace of sleep by now. She and her brothers made a predictable chain of sounds, counterpoint rhythms that eventually drifted together. It was like a round gone wrong, with everyone singing in unison, looking at each other helplessly for a way out.

Blanca slept restlessly, tossing and turning and letting out an occasional moan. The fever was penetrating the peaceful barriers of sleep. I turned away from Blanca and faced the dark wall on the other side of the room.

It was probably ten o'clock. I would have been home by now. I watched my mother hug me and cry. Then my sisters encircled me with smiles and laughter. I imagined the tall blue spruce twinkling in the corner of the living room, full of the ornaments that my mother had collected over the years. I glanced up at the shelves of the shed again. All of Blanca's belongings fit on one shelf, with room to spare. The shelf in the basement at home where my mother kept the Christmas ornaments was about the same size.

I lifted my head to re-fold the towel that I was using as a pillow. At home my bed was probably made up for me with an extra pillow and cotton sheets. I took a long shallow breath, careful not to breathe too deep. I didn't want to let the feelings that were collecting in my chest rise into quiet sobs, not here with four other people in the room. A part of me wished I could fly out the window and be home. And another part wanted to stay here by Vera for as long as it took, until things were okay.

I awoke later to the sound of moans. I pulled myself up onto my elbows. Vera was in the shadows lighting a candle.

Vera heard me stir. "She's getting worse," she said. "The fever is back and she's shaking."

"Sylvia." Blanca cried out the name of Don Macedo's maid-servant, half word and half moan.

Vera put her face close to her mother's. "It's Vera, Mother."

"I'll get a cup of water," I said.

"Oh Sylvia, I must be dying," said Blanca. "I'm seeing Vera's face. She's so beautiful. She looks like my mother, only young, fresh..."

Vera took the water with one hand and propped up her mother's head with the other. Blanca drank a few sips and her voice came in stronger. "God forgive me."

I delivered the cup of water. There was nothing more I could do, so I lay back down on my sleeping mat. As I faced Vera and Blanca with my eyes open, I saw how much darkness surrounded them. The sun had been down for hours, but now the moon had rotated away too, leaving us in a deep blackness that is reserved for the sleeping and the dead. Vera set the candle above Blanca's head, so there'd be enough light to tend to Blanca without disturbing her sleep. From where I lay the candle illuminated their faces indirectly from behind, erasing Vera's rosy cheeks and the lines on Blanca's face. Tight braids cut similar lines around both faces, and their noses and mouths cast the same shadows. Their eyes distinguished them, though. Vera's were full and wet enough to catch a little light. Blanca's were dry. Dark sunken holes. The fever even denied her the relief of her own tears.

She moaned again. "Oh Sylvia, she'll never know that I cried for her. She was the jewel of my life."

"Mother, you're not dreaming, I'm really here. It's Vera. Don't you remember? I came to you this afternoon in the coffee field. You told me everything."

Blanca sat up. "Vera," she said, but dizziness made her fall forward. She rested her elbows on her knees, letting her head hang down.

After a moment she lifted her head for another sip of water. "Oh Vera, I've always regretted it."

"I know," said Vera, letting out a sigh. "Now save your strength. Don't talk."

"There's one more thing—"

Blanca had used all her energy to form her words. Vera helped her to lie down again.

"What?" said Vera. "Tell me, then you have to let yourself rest."

"When the fever takes me," Blanca began then paused to gather strength for what came next. "Promise me you'll take care of your brothers."

So that was why Blanca had called for Vera. I closed my eyes and waited for Vera's reply. "Don't promise," I wanted to shout. Instead I willed the message over to where Vera sat, hoping that it would surround her and keep her from being trapped here.

Blanca sensed Vera's hesitation. "Please..."

"You're going to get well," said Vera. "Now let's have a little more to drink." She propped up Blanca's head again, then held the cup of water up to her lips. Vera watched her drink intently, as if this small comfort, water from the nearby spring, could cure.

After the cup was empty Vera sat holding it a while. Blanca's breathing became regular. Finally Vera lay down. I heard her tossing and turning, then a stifled sob. I pulled my sleeping mat next to Vera and placed my hand lightly on Vera's shoulder.

"Are you okay?"

Vera sat up and hugged her own knees. "She's going to die. If not now, soon."

"I know it's hard to see her like this, Vera. When we get back to San Luis," I winced as I heard herself say 'San Luis' too firmly, "maybe we could arrange for a doctor to see her."

"We'll have to. I can't leave her like this," said Vera.

"Of course not," I said. "You'll see her through this fever. But remember, Vera, some of the things your mother said, the things she asked you to do, were because she was delirious with fever. She wasn't herself. She wouldn't want you to sacrifice all you have -- your schooling, your work. That's the life she wants for you. She'd say that if she were well. I know she would." I waited for Vera to reply. "You don't want to throw away everything you've worked for, do you?"

"No," said Vera, turning her head in the direction of the mat where her brothers slept, "but what about them?"

"It's sad, I know." I felt confused myself. "But Enrique is already eleven, and they have Sylvia and Don Macedo."

I looked over at Paco as I listened to my own words. I thought of his stick. I forgot Vera and wanted to hold him. Then I saw Vera's life becoming like Blanca's and I put him down again.

"You have a right to think of yourself, Vera," I whispered.

Vera lay down again. "I need to go to sleep," she said, her voice small. "The boys will be awake and hungry in a few hours."

When I opened my eyes Vera was making tortillas by the window. Blanca was sitting up on her mat, exhausted, but lucid.

"Vera, let me do that." She lifted her hand and then watched it flop down to the mat again.

The boys sat quietly on their sleeping mats staring at me. They must have been watching me sleep. Now that my eyes were open their silence was broken.

"I'm hungry," said Paco.

Vera set the warm tortillas on the table. "Just tortillas today. But I'm going to have some food sent up, so you can have eggs and beans every day."

"How will you?" asked Enrique.

"I brought a little money with me," said Vera. "In Tegucigalpa I'm a seamstress."

That was a switch. Vera usually said she was a secretarial student, even though she worked as a seamstress all day to pay her tuition at night school.

"I'm going to buy shoes, too, so that you can go to school."

Enrique gave her a nod of gratitude and looked down.

"And don't you be embarrassed to be the oldest." She waved a finger at Enrique. "You'll learn fast."

"School?" said Paco with an incredulous grin. "But how will I get there?"

"Enrique will take you," said Vera.

"It's two hours," said Enrique.

Vera thought that over for a minute. "You'll have to walk," she said. "Now eat."

The boys finished their breakfast and ran outside. Vera served Blanca, who drank a little, took a bit of a tortilla, and settled back down for a morning nap.

It was almost nine when Vera and I sat down to our own breakfast, a cup of weak coffee and tortillas. Vera took a sip of coffee and looked out the window at the boys.

"Look how wild they are." She shook her head.

"They'll have trouble sitting down in front of a desk at first," I said. "I'll have to visit the teacher," said Vera. "To explain."

"You're taking on a lot," I said. "Be careful you don't make promises that you can't keep. Shoes. School fees. Those are expensive. Remember how little you have left over now, after you pay for your own clothes and school fees."

"I'll keep my promise." Vera looked past me out the window. "I was living high before — with store-bought clothes. I'm a seamstress, I have no business buying ready made. Most people in my country make their own."

My country, I thought. The wall had gone up so quickly.

"I may have to leave school for a while," Vera added.

"But what about your career? It's important to you."

Vera's face hardened and she looked away. "A lot of people would be proud to be a seamstress. My brothers are here. I can't pretend they aren't."

"I'm not saying you shouldn't help." I reached out to touch Vera's arm. "Maybe Mother Maria could take them."

"She's already done enough." Vera looked over at her sleeping mother. "They need *me*."

"What about Raoul?"

"He'll have to accept it. Maybe he can teach Enrique carpentry. That might be easier."

Helping with school fees at first, then bringing the boys to Tegucigalpa later. Families here did things like that all the time. Maybe it could work. I sighed, confused. Even if the plan was realistic, it wasn't fair to Vera. Yet putting Vera first, when the needs of her brothers were so great, didn't seem right either. What would Sister Paula do? I knew the answer to that. For Sister Paula everything was possible. She'd have planted a row of beans by now. I gulped the coffee, hoping it would wash away the fatigue and help me to focus.

A few minutes later Don Macedo appeared in the doorway. He knocked on the doorframe, entered, and looked over at Blanca. "Is she ill again?"

"Yes," said Vera, standing to greet him. "Last night she was crazy with fever. But she's a little better this morning."

Don Macedo shook his head. "Fevers this close together — she must have Jungle Fever."

Vera nodded seriously. "Is that truck you told us about still leaving today? Beth would like to go to San Pedro."

This time I didn't offer to stay. I'd agreed to go ahead to send up the food and supplies and contact a doctor.

"I'm going to stay on a few days until the fever passes," continued Vera. "And I'd like her to see a doctor."

Don Macedo turned to Vera. "You're leaving? I thought you came to find your mother."

Vera's eyes widened as she took in the shape and size of the misunderstanding. "I came to visit," she said. "I have to go back to Tegucigalpa."

Don Macedo cast a glance at Blanca and lowered his voice. "I took care of her when she had no one, but now she has a daughter."

Vera looked down and spoke quietly. "With medical care she'll probably be better in a week or so. She'll be able to work again..."

He put a heavy hand on Vera's shoulder, holding her to the spot where she stood. "The Jungle Fever will kill her. Who will raise your brothers?"

"I'll be here when the time comes."

Don Macedo's face was hard. "I can't have an *enferma* minding these fields. She's old and sick. Caring for her is the job of her own flesh and blood."

"I'll be leaving at ten-thirty, miss," Don Macedo said to me. Before he walked outside he turned to Vera again. "You're a grown woman now. It's time to forget your illusions. In the end blood is thickest. You have to obey that."

After he left, Vera sat down in her chair and covered her face with her hands.

I put my arms around Vera, who was still silent, but shaking. Then Vera was no longer able to hold her breath to keep her cries inside. She gasped for air and sobbed into my shoulder.

I was crying, too. "What will you do?"

Vera sobbed some more, then sat up and dried her eyes with her apron. She poured herself a cup of water and took a sip. She looked out the window, her back to me. "I'll stay. What choice do I have?"

"But how will you manage?" I lowered my voice. "You can't trust Don Macedo to help you."

"I know, but I may have to work for him. Just for a while."

A few minutes later Don Macedo appeared at the door, ready to go.

Blanca began to stir.

"Go ahead," said Vera. "I'll be down to see you off in a minute."

As I walked down the steep hill, I felt myself pulled faster than I wanted to go. I knew I was saying goodbye to Vera for the last time. A knot of sorrow lodged in my throat, then Vera called out to me.

"Beth, what about the photo? I still want it."

I was glad to have an excuse to go back. I took the Polaroid camera out of my pack and put it around my neck. It bobbed back and forth as I walked up the hill.

Vera untied her hair and combed through it with her fingers. Her mother sat up and Vera brought her a blouse.

"Just the faces, Beth. That way you won't be able to tell she's in bed."

Vera sat beside her mother and smiled as if it were her first communion or her fifteenth birthday. Blanca managed to open her eyes all the way and form a closed-lipped smile, her life a small triumph after all.

I snapped the picture and took it out of the camera, careful not to touch the wet surface. An outline was already starting to form. Shadows emerged and took on light and color, as if the image of Vera and her mother had been there, ready to unfold, all along.

"It's coming out well," I said, surprised that the flash had worked so well inside the shack. I handed the photo to Blanca.

Blanca looked at it and shook her head. "It's like a miracle."

Vera touched her mother's shoulder and took the picture, setting it to rest on a shelf where it could dry. "I'm going to see Beth off, then I'll be back."

"You're not leaving?"

"No, I'm going to stay here and take care of you."

Blanca opened her mouth to protest.

"And the boys," added Vera.

"Oh, no, *hija*. I can manage for a while. Don't do this." Blanca laid her head back and closed her eyes.

We stepped out into the sunlight. "I wish there was something more I could do," I stammered through tears.

"Would you take another picture of me, for Raoul?"

I wiped my eyes and nodded, wishing I had thought of it.

Vera took off her apron, smoothed her skirt, and smiled.

I took the picture out of the camera and blew on it. I put my arms around Vera and hugged her one more time, careful to hold the picture away from us, so it wouldn't smudge. I walked down the hill and got in the truck, still holding the picture in my hand. When I looked at it again the image was crisp. Vera, with a row of coffee plants and her mother's house behind her.

La Casa de los Niños
Late December

XI

I dropped my backpack at the foot of the bed, sat down, then flopped back on the thin mattress. After the long truck ride I'd taken the bus from San Pedro. There was dust from the road in my throat and my nostrils, even my pores. I needed to rest, but first I wanted to bathe if there was water. I might even heat some water on the stove. I lay still a moment, trying to decide whether the pleasure of warm water was worth the effort.

I sat up and reached in the front pouch of my pack for the picture I had taken for Raoul. I looked at Vera. What else could I have done?

Mother Maria would blame me. She'd say that Vera would have been better off if she had never gone to San Luis. It was true that Vera had taken on responsibilities that were too much for her, but there was something right about it, too.

I heard voices from the *sala*. "Raoul is here," then "I'll get Beth."

There would be no warm bath, no time to think.

I took the picture to the *sala*. Raoul stood in the doorway, his hands in his pockets. He was an awkward teenager when I met him a year ago, but now he had the bearing of a man. He had been recently named a master carpenter in the wood shop, making finished pieces for sale and supervising the work of the younger boys. After a year he would likely graduate to a job in one of the best carpentry shops.

He extended his hand to me.

"Vera decided to stay in San Luis for a while," I began, "until her mother is stronger."

"But what about her classes and her job?"

"Her mother needs care," I said helplessly. "There are two other children. Young boys. There was no one else."

Raoul winced and put his hand back in his pocket.

I remembered the photo. "Vera asked me to give you this."

Raoul looked at the image in disbelief. There was Vera with the coffee farm and her mother's shed behind her. "Whose house is that?"

"That's where her mother stays," I said.

"How will she manage? She left here without a *centavo*." He pointed at the shed. "She can't live like that."

"Don Macedo will let her work in the coffee fields until she gets work as a seamstress."

"Picking coffee for Don Macedo." The hardships of Vera's situation — her mother, her brothers, her *patrón* — registered one by one on Raoul's face.

"I should be with her," he said. "If I had the money I'd go right now." He made a fist with one hand and hit it into the open palm of the other.

I looked at Raoul. Did I dare interfere with the delicate balance of random acts that bring people together or tear them apart?

"Wait here a minute," I said. I went to my room and got all the cash I had. I went back to the *sala* and held it out to Raoul. "I think there's about fifty *lempiras* here."

Raoul started to shake his head no. He wouldn't take a handout.

"It's for Vera," I said.

He paused, then took the money. "I'll pay you back someday."

"It's not much," I said. "The bus fare is ten. Vera has food and provisions for now, but they'll need more."

"I can pick coffee, too, if I have to."

I watched him walk away. By the time I was back in the U.S. he would be in San Luis with Vera. Had I done the right thing?

Mother Maria would be upset that one of her best boys had left the woodworking shop, and I didn't know what kind of reception Raoul would get from the people in San Luis. He would face the same fate as Vera, I supposed. Whatever that would be.

Raoul came by again a few hours later.

"I'm leaving in the morning. I came to take the rest of Vera's things," he said.

I walked with him to Vera's room. Suyapa packed Vera's clothes in a plastic bag, while Katia got some food from the pantry for Raoul. By now all the girls knew about Vera, and about Raoul, too.

"I have some material that I bought last week," said Felicia. "It was for a skirt, but Vera can have it." She looked at the silky floral print, realizing it was too fine to wear picking coffee. "Or she can make it up to sell," she said softly.

After Raoul left, the roommates and I looked at the empty bed in silence. Vera was gone.

Suyapa turned to me. "Will you take my picture, like you did for Vera?"

"Me too," said a few of the others.

The girls rarely got a chance to get their pictures taken. I might as well use up the last rolls of Polaroid film. I'd take two pictures each. One for each girl to keep, and one for me to take home.

Felicia called the others while I got the camera. I heard a flurry of movement in the hall, as the girls changed their clothes and combed their hair. I took the opportunity to splash some water on my face and change my shirt. I would take the pictures out by the gate. The light was good there and Sister Paula's garden would be in the background. In no time I had the pictures laid out on my bed to dry. I looked at the girls with their smiles and serious expressions. A few leaned against the gate like models, while others stood up straight and clasped their hands together like nuns.

They'd each had a turn, but it felt as if someone was missing. Then it dawned on me. I hadn't seen Luz since I got back.

I went to her room but Luz wasn't there. I went to the *sala*.

"Has anyone seen Luz?"

Felicia looked at the clock. "She should be home from school soon."

"But her notebooks are on her dresser."

Katia looked up and shrugged. "I thought you said we would have to be responsible for ourselves now that you're leaving us."

"You're right, I did. And you will. But I'm worried about Luz."

Lately Luz had been skipping school and closing herself in her room. Sewing, she said.

Katia looked at Felicia then Suyapa, then finally, me. "I wasn't going to say anything, but I'm worried too. Luz didn't sleep here last night. Maybe she was with someone — but that's not like Luz."

"Do any of you know where she might have gone?" I asked, grateful for Katia's confidence.

Katia shook her head no, but Suyapa spoke up slowly. "She said she was going to see her uncle yesterday afternoon. I don't know if she came back after that."

I knew what that meant. Luz had gone looking for her father.

I went out to the main road and waited for a bus that was headed downtown to the public market. All I knew about Luz's uncle was that he sold vegetables in the *mercado*. He would be there for a few more hours.

The bus was already crowded when I boarded. I held my purse firmly against my hip with my hand over the zipped opening. With the other hand I grabbed the bar above my head, steadying myself in the aisle as the bus lunged and jerked towards its destination.

Most people got off at the *Parque Central*, but I stayed on for two more stops to look for Luz's uncle in the *mercado*. I had been in the market many times before, but always with the girls, who I relied on as guides. Now I looked at the maze of densely packed stalls. Where would I find vegetables?

I entered by the pots and pans. Stacks of plastic dishes and washing pails. Shiny tin pots just like the one we had at *La Casa*. They were so thin they could be dented with a spoon, but they boiled water just the same.

"*Señorita*, how can I help you?"

"*Señorita*, we have tablecloths, napkins, matches."

I knew better than to make eye contact. That would encourage the vendors to pull me over to their stalls, desperate as beggars, to show me their goods.

"Just five *lempiras*," said a women.

"No, thank you. I don't need any," I said, without stopping.

"I'll take three then, or whatever you'll give me."

I tried to keep my head down as I continued on.

Out of the corner of my eye I saw a table that displayed brightly colored *nicas*, plastic chamber pots with handles that were used to toilet train children. I remembered seeing them when I came to the market for the first time. Not knowing what they were I'd bought one right away. The little pot seemed perfect for dunking into my bucket at bath time, it held just the right amount of water, and had a handle, too. The girls had laughed at me and I didn't know why. Finally Luz told me what it was. I remembered Luz's smile now as I moved toward the back corner of the market, where the fresh produce vendors were clustered together.

They displayed their wares on straw mats, with small tables here and there for weighing, cutting samples to taste, and making change. The smell of papaya, mango, and banana hung in the air.

There were fewer walls and partitions in this part of the market. From where I stood I could scan the stalls for Luz's uncle. But what did he look like? Not many of the vendors were men, so that narrowed it down. And since he was Luz's father's brother his last name should be Espinal, like Luz's.

"Excuse me, *señora*," I said to a woman in a kerchief who was selling the herbs. "Could you tell me where I could find *Señor* Espinal. He sells vegetables."

The woman looked at me with suspicion, glanced at my purse, then pointed to the stall to her right. "My sister has carrots, tomatoes, onions. Good prices too."

"Thank you, but I need to speak with Mr. Espinal." The woman folded her arms, and looked beyond me.

I lifted a bunch of *manzanilla* to my nose. The scent of chamomile gave me momentary relief from the nauseating sweetness of the fruity smells. "I'd like to buy some *manzanilla*, for tea."

"That's fifty *centavos* for a bunch," said the woman as she wrapped it in paper.

"And *Señor* Espinal?"

"Wait here a moment." The woman walked over to consult her sister who shook her head and called over another vendor. About ten minutes later the woman returned.

"You'll find him over that way," she said pointing with her lips as she lifted her chin. "Ask that man who is selling the melons, he'll tell you where."

I went back and asked the man. After being referred to three different vendors I found myself face to face with *Señor* Espinal, who sat on a stool surrounded by three large baskets, which were almost empty.

He was dark like Luz, with the same prominent facial bones and hollows around the eyes. He greeted me with a smile that carried the resemblance further.

"I'm looking for Luz Espinal. Are you her uncle?"

"She's my brother's child." He folded his arms and waited for me to explain myself.

"I work with Mother Maria at *La Casa de los Niños*. We haven't seen Luz since yesterday morning. One of the girls said she might have come to see you."

"She came to see my brother. He's here from San Cristobal, just for a while." He shook his head — half puzzled, half pitying. "She's a little crazy, isn't she?"

Just what I was afraid of — Luz was in one of her moods when she'd gone to see her father.

"No, she's not crazy," I said. "She's a good girl, one of Mother Maria's favorites."

Luz's uncle said nothing, but he looked concerned.

"I need to talk to her. Do you know where I can find her?"

"She came to my house last night, but she only stayed for a little while. She fought with my brother and then she left."

"Was she upset when she left?"

"My brother says she's a little touched — like her mother."

My shoulders straightened defensively at the criticism of Luz.

"Anyway, I don't really know her." Luz's uncle shrugged. "She never visited me until yesterday."

"What did they fight about?"

"You'll have to talk to my brother."

"Can you take me to see him? It's urgent that I find Luz."

I saw the conflicting demands of courtesy and family loyalty play against each other in his brow. He placed his hand on his hips and looked from side to side, as if he were listening to two sides of an argument. "What does it matter to you?"

"I want to help. Luz has no one else."

"What about Mother Maria, if she loves her so much."

I felt caught. "I'm here on Mother Maria's behalf," I said carefully. "This kind of argument — I'm not trying to blame anyone — but it could be dangerous for Luz." I felt tears of frustration rising up, but, realizing they might help, I didn't try to hide them. "I just want to bring her home to Mother Maria."

"Very well then." He pointed to a small stool behind a table. "Sit here, please, while I get ready to go home. My brother is there and you can ask him whatever you want."

I sat on the stool and watched as the market closed for the day. Vendors dragged the tables across the floor and rolled up the large mats. They stacked their baskets inside each other, three or four high, with the leftover produce in the top one. As they carted their belongings home the vendors were mostly hidden behind their loads, which though light now, were still bulky and awkward.

From a distance it looked as if the mats moved themselves, marching home at the end of the day.

Luz's uncle stacked his baskets and motioned to me. I started to follow him, then remembered the stool and picked it up.

"Let me," said the uncle, but I insisted.

I carried the stool awkwardly through the narrow rocky streets near the *mercado*. Finally I tried placing the stool upside down on my head. The Hondurans were right, it was easier this way.

Luz's uncle laughed. "You look like a real Honduran woman. Now let's take you to see my brother."

The area around the *mercado* was known to be dangerous at night. I felt relatively safe with Luz's uncle, but it was getting dark and I didn't know where I was. Did I have enough money for cab fare if I needed it? Probably not since I'd given most of my cash to Raoul. And I hadn't told anyone where I was going.

Luz's uncle turned onto a dirt path that led down a hill, away from the road. The darkness hid the houses below. He shifted his baskets to one arm and took the stool from me, slipping his arm through the rung on the bottom. Then with the hand that reached through he took my hand and helped me down the rocky path.

After a few moments my eyes adjusted to the darkness. I could see the path and rows of one-room shacks on either side. People sat in doorways, sharing the dim light of the moon as we walked past.

"My *señora* is just ahead," said Luz's uncle. "Consuela, we're here," he called as we approached a small house.

We entered through the low doorway. A candle on a small table illuminated the room. A framed picture of the Sacred Heart of Jesus hung crookedly on one wall, with a long cross made of braided palms tucked behind it.

On seeing me, Consuela Espinal looked around with alarm. I recognized the look. Not an unfriendly gesture, but the shame of having visitors when there was no food to offer.

"One moment. I'll prepare some *aguita*."

I knew the word from my visits to the countryside where people prepared weak tea from herbs. I remembered the chamomile in my bag and pulled it out. "For you, *señora*."

Consuela smiled shyly and took the herbs, offering me a seat. Then she looked to her husband for an explanation.

"Beth is from the United States. She's with Mother Maria." He paused a moment for his wife to react.

"You know her," Consuela exclaimed. "They say she's like a saint."

"She wants to talk to my brother. They are looking for Luz."

Consuela wrung her hands together. "He left."

"Do you know when he'll be back?" I asked.

"He took his things." Consuela cast a meaningful glance at her husband, as if she would prefer to discuss this privately. "He came here drunk this afternoon. I think he went back to the village."

"He's like that," said Luz's uncle with an apologetic shrug. "He comes and goes."

I was half relieved at not having to confront him. "I still need to find Luz. Is there anything you can tell me?"

Luz's uncle thought for a moment, then pointed to a chair. "Sit down."

I took a seat across from them. He waited for me to take the first sip of tea. Then he began.

"Luz came here yesterday afternoon looking for her father. She sat in that chair where you are now, waiting for him. He spends the afternoon in the *cantina*." He looked at me to be sure I got his meaning.

"He drank too much, even before he was married. My mother begged him to stay away from the *guaro*. When we heard that Luz was with Mother Maria — it was a shame."

"We wanted to take her," interjected Consuela, "but we are so poor and we thought our own children would come some day. See how God answered us? We never had our own."

"When my brother came in Luz changed," he continued. "She was angry, and she looked just like her mother all of a sudden. My brother was scared. We're Indian, so we believe in spirits. My brother — he was drunk already — said he saw a ghost coming at him."

"'*Hola Papi.*' That's how she started — but without respect. She spoke to him in a way that I would have been afraid to. He's my older brother — I was taught to obey him.

"She kept at it. 'You don't recognize me, *Papi*?'" Luz's uncle imitated her high-pitched taunt. "'Didn't you know I would grow up? Did you think I would dry up and blow away just because you didn't want me? I've changed, but you're still a drunk. You told everyone my mother was crazy, but now I'm big enough to say it isn't true.'"

"Now she was yelling. I told her to be quiet, to respect her father a little. She looked at me like she was possessed. 'I'm going to respect myself,' she said.

"My brother was angry. He cursed her mother and called her a *puta*. Excuse me, but that's how he said it. He looked like he was going to hit Luz, but then he was quiet. I thought he was going to pass out from the drink, but she sobered him. Seeing her. The shock. I think he felt sorry for all that happened. Leaving her, mistreating her mother. God knows that was true.

"Then she started again, more calmly, but with lies."

"What did she say?" I asked.

"That he came to her at Mother Maria's secretly, in the night. That he tried to rape her, but she cried out for help and he ran away." He shook his head in disgust. "It couldn't be true. She would have been a child."

My heart ached for Luz. Now I understood why Luz had pretended not to recognize her father later, when he came to *La Casa* and tried to take her away.

"How can you be sure she's lying?"

"My brother would never do that."

"But you said yourself that when he was drunk he did terrible things." I knew I shouldn't argue, but I couldn't help myself.

"It's not possible," Luz's uncle insisted.

"But why would Luz make something like that up?"

"You have to remember, *señorita*, that her mother was crazy too. Luz — it's not her fault — but these things are passed on. Luz is *loca*."

Until now Consuela had sat beside her husband, quiet with her lips pressed together. Now she spoke. "Angry and disrespectful maybe, but I'm not ready to say she was *loca*. She had a right to speak to him that way. The way he treated her mother."

"What are you saying, woman?" said Luz's uncle. "Do you believe that my brother did the things that Luz said he did?" He shook his head and pointed his finger at both of us. "You have to remember that he wasn't always like that. When he didn't drink he was better. He left his wife alone, and he worked a little."

"That's true," said Consuela, her defiant energy spent.

"What happened then?" I asked. "What did he say when she accused him?"

"My brother was broken-hearted. He cried to see her crazy like that. He asked her, what do you want from me now? 'I don't want anything from you,' she said. 'Just know that you have a daughter in this world who knows what you are, and that when you die, I won't cry for you.'"

"That's what she said." Consuela nodded. "'I won't cry a single tear.'"

"But he said he was sorry," Luz's uncle interjected. "For a man like my brother that is difficult. She's almost a woman, she should know how to forgive. But she left him there like that. She broke her father's heart. When she left we didn't think to follow her. We knew she lived in the city with Mother Maria, so we thought she'd gone home. Now you tell us she didn't. I don't know what to say."

"Do you have any idea where I might find her mother?" I asked.

"She moves around a lot. I haven't seen her in over a year. And you couldn't talk with her like you're talking with us. She'll just look at you without saying a word. She's a sad woman..." his voice trailed off and he made a final helpless gesture. That was all.

"I'll just have to hope that Luz comes back," I said softly. I rose to leave then sat down again. I didn't know how to get home.

"I'll accompany you to Mother Maria's," said Luz's uncle. "It's too late for a woman alone."

He stepped outside and held the door for me, then offered me his arm to help me through the dark. As I let him lead me out I felt grateful, then angry. 'Why didn't you take Luz home?' I wanted to ask him. 'What did she do to be unworthy of your protection?' But I was quiet because I knew the answer. Luz had dared to express her rage.

Someone was pulling me out of a thick sleep. I saw Luz, laughing, washing herself in the river that ran through Juntapeque. Had there been a waterfall? I didn't remember that, but now it ran down behind Luz into a clear pool.

"Beth, wake up."

Oh, I didn't want to leave that dream. Luz was okay. She had found a place that was clean and bright and safe. But the voice continued to call me.

I opened my eyes and saw Mother Maria's face over mine. She was shouting and shaking my shoulders. That couldn't be. Mother Maria would never come to my room. I could tell by the morning light that Mass was long over, it was past seven.

"Beth, something terrible has happened."

I rubbed my eyes. Mother Maria must have found out about Luz.

"I know. I went to see her uncle yesterday and —"

"Her uncle? What are you talking about?"

"Luz. She went to look for her father, and —"

"I'm not talking about Luz," said Mother Maria, her eyes bulging. "You're dreaming. Wake up. I want you to be dressed before I ring the bell to tell the children."

I sat up in my bed and looked around. It was day. Mother Maria had come to wake me to tell me something terrible.

"What happened?" I asked finally.

"Sister Paula is dead."

XII

"When I went out back to fill the *pila* I heard Theo shouting."
Ophelia spoke quickly as she stirred oatmeal in the large pot. "You
know how he yells when he is angry.

"They were down by the *abonero,*" she continued. "Sister Paula
wanted to bring soil up to use in the garden. She liked to go in the
morning before her bath, and she sometimes took Theo with her
to help. I think she did it to help me really. He was acting up that
day, running and banging his fists on the floor. She took him so I
could get breakfast ready in peace. The others were all sleeping.
She didn't want his shouting to wake them up."

Who cares about making breakfast in peace, I wanted to say.
What happened? But I had to let Ophelia tell it her own way.

"So when I heard shouting, it didn't worry me. It seemed nor-
mal — that's how we live here. Then I heard her scream. I knew
something was wrong, but I'm not allowed to leave the children
alone in the house. That's one of Sister's rules. When I heard another scream, and then a thud, like a *golpe,* I went out. It must have
been the shovel, banging against her head. He hit her again and
again. God forgive me, I was afraid to go near. It was like the devil
had come to earth. Then I saw her on the ground."

Ophelia started to cry, uncontrollably sobbing out the words,
"I couldn't help her."

I put my arm around her and cried too. Ophelia blew her nose
on her apron, then made herself finish the story.

"I called for the watchman. By the time he got there Theo was crying and saying, 'Wake up, wake up.' He thought she was sleeping."

Composed now, she began filling the children's bowls with oatmeal. "If they don't eat soon, they'll be howling with hunger. Oh, Lord, how are we going to live without Sister Paula?"

I ran to the compost ditch behind the house. The watchman was there, guarding the scene, and two policemen stood by, making notes, speaking to each other in hushed tones, then pointing to the body. Theo sat in a lump under the tree, his arms tied behind his back. No one knew what to do with him.

Sister Paula lay on a stretcher by the ditch. The sheet underneath her head was drenched with blood, and the back of her head seemed flat. Her face was covered with mud, but not blood.

Sister Paula's mouth was set in pain and her eyes were wide open, as if at the very end she had seen that she could not quell Theo's rage with her love, and it shocked her.

I held in my tears until they made me shake. I leaned my head against a nearby tree and let out a cry. The air around me felt too thin to hold me up. I waited, hoping to wake up in a sweat, heart pounding as my brain gave my body the message — it's okay, it's only a dream.

Then I heard the chapel bells ringing.

I ran toward the big house. Mother Maria would want me to be there first.

When I got to the top of the steps I stopped to catch my breath before I went in. Looking out I saw the girls gathered by the *Residencia de las Señoritas*. Even from here I could hear the confusion and alarm in their voices. Then Theo was carried out of the woods by one of the watchmen. Sister Paula's stretcher did not follow. They must have taken her out through the *Camino Viejo*.

I entered the chapel to find Mother Maria praying alone. It seemed strange to see her without Sister Paula. In spite of their differences the sisters prayed together every morning. I took the seat next to Mother Maria and bowed my head.

Mother Maria shook with sobs. "I should have helped her with him."

"It's not your fault," I said.

"Paula knew how to love him like Jesus would have. But I never could. I made her carry him alone."

"I think she would have said that it was God who carried them both," I said, surprised at myself.

The girls came to the doorway and stood at the back. I went over to them and told them to come in and sit down. I looked over at Mother Maria who struggled to control herself. "We're going to pray a while."

The girls whispered to each other.

"Is it true that Sister Paula is dead?" said Suyapa.

"They're saying that Theo did it," said Katia. "He raped her and chopped her up with an ax."

"It wasn't like that," protested Felicia. "The boys said they saw Sister Paula's body on a stretcher. It was whole, and she had her clothes on. It was a head wound. Oh God —" she cried, putting her hand over her face and sobbing.

The other girls were starting to cry, too. Mother Maria stood up to speak and they held their breath, as if her words could reverse what had happened.

She stood up and motioned to the watchman in the hall outside the chapel.

"Bring him here. And untie him."

She made the sign of the cross and bowed her head in silence for a moment. The watchman carried Theo to the altar, then set him down on the kneeler where Mother Maria had just been praying. Seeing this Mother Maria motioned to Mercedes to bring a chair. Once he was positioned on the chair he fell forward a bit, his eyes droopy.

"I have tragic news," she began. "This morning Sister Paula was killed out by the *abonero*. You'll hear rumors, but I want to tell you, what I told the policemen outside. What I saw from my window." Mother Maria gestured to her room above the chapel, the highest point in the *La Casa* compound.

"I saw a *ladrón* come up from the *Camino Viejo*. Before I could open the window to shout a warning he attacked Sister Paula with her own shovel. He started to run away, but then he stopped and put the shovel in Theo's hands. He hoped that no one had seen. He wanted us to blame the one who loved her most for what happened." She embraced Theo.

I was numb with shock. Hadn't Ophelia said that she heard Theo shouting? But she hadn't actually seen him strike Sister Paula... I looked around now. No one questioned what Mother Maria had seen with her own eyes.

"Later this morning we'll make a *caminata* to the *Virgen de Suyapa*, that she may take Sister Paula into her care. Those of you who are older, I hope you'll fast with me, too."

Mother Maria stood by the foot of the stairs near the big house, ready to lead the procession. She looked old, bent over, with dark rings around her eyes. There must have been at least fifty people gathered around her in a loose line. One hundred if you included the children on their way up from the Children's Village, giggling because they could not understand. Sister Paula's children were missing, though. Mother Maria said most of them couldn't make the walk, and she didn't want them to disrupt the Mass. She had asked Ophelia to keep them inside. All except Theo, who hadn't been sent back to Sister Paula's house since the tragedy.

He was beside Mother Maria now, strapped into a wheelchair, secured across the neck and chest, and around the wrists. His one leg shot back and forth, as if he was still scooting along on his skateboard. His eyes were dull and far away — not somewhere else, just lost. He had been medicated, I was sure of it. Sister Paula would have hated that, but what was the alternative? No one else could manage him.

Mother Maria looked pained when her eyes met mine. "Like this he can rest. He misses her terribly."

Mother Maria held on to Theo's wheelchair, leaning into it for support as she began the procession. She intended to push him all the way to the Suyapa shrine. She led the Rosary, her Hail Mary's loud at first, and slow enough to remind everyone that they should be concentrating on every word. Once the rhythm had been established her voice became softer. Everyone felt the inevitability of the prayer cycle now, and all their voices rose on the sung refrain, as if the song could be made big enough to match Sister Paula's spirit. *"Ven con nosotros a caminar, Santa Maria, ven."*

"Walk with us, Holy Mother, come." I said it to myself in English. My voice rose with the others, almost breaking. I so wanted the company of that large woman-spirit who could love everyone perfectly, give life, answer prayers.

I took a place beside Mother Maria. I let myself be surrounded by the pulse of the prayer until I was sure it was strong enough to keep me steady. Then I opened a door, a valve of my heart, just a bit, to look at the feelings inside. Afraid that oxygen might make me burst into flames, I held my breath until I convulsed into a sob. Then the sung refrain was over, and the Hail Mary picked me up again. I controlled my breathing, focused on saying the words, kept walking.

By the time we had been walking for forty-five minutes the sun and heat were weighing on us. Mother Maria's face was wet with tears and sweat. Wet marks could be seen under the arms of her navy blue habit. Her breathing was strained to the point that she was no longer saying the prayer out loud, just 'Hail Mary' then 'now and at the hour of our death, Amen.'

I felt the shape of Sister Paula's death in my mind as she prayed. Every time the song lifted me higher, then brought me down lower when I exhaled. I could see the Basilica in the distance.

"She gave her life for nothing." I hadn't let these words form in my mind until now.

All the anger that I had kept at arm's length poured into me like so much salty water. I had to swallow before I could try to come up for breath. Sister Paula didn't deserve to die, and she hadn't been "willing to." She would never have left her children alone, her garden untended. Her death knocked the God of Justice right off his chair, for sleeping on the job, for forgetting someone who loved him.

The road that led up to the Basilica looked out over a poor urban shantytown. I imagined Sister Paula standing at the foot of the church steps, shaking her head in disapproval, measuring out the Basilica's size and cost in bowls of rice, converting it to tin and brick for simple homes. She was never a hilltop kind of nun, but now she'd be honored up there.

Mother Maria was panting visibly now. She caught me looking at her. "Can you help me for a while, *mi hija*?"

I took the wheelchair and began to push. Mother Maria kept a hand on one side, and held onto me for support. After a few moments our movements were synchronized. Mother Maria leaned into me as she said the first half of the prayer, then leaned away to pull her own weight while I said the other half. The song lifted us for a moment, then we fell again, and moved to the next bead, repeating the cycle.

Having Theo in my hands and Mother Maria at my side made me feel strong. Sister Paula was close, trying to breathe the faith back into me, but I was angry and scared, I pushed her away.

"I don't have to believe what you believed, or live like you lived," I said. Then I begged her to come back, "But I wanted to, I wanted to."

We started up the hill that led to the large Basilica. On either side of the path vendors spread their wares on blankets. They called out to the pilgrims in loud irreverent voices. "Save yourself with the cross of Jesus," and "Cleanse yourself — pray with the Immaculate Mother."

A fruit seller sat at a low table cut an orange into quarters and held it in the air, "Oranges, refresh yourself here."

He repeated his sales pitch three times. By the fourth time I was expecting it, his offer had the same beat of inevitability as our rote prayers.

I looked up at the orange. The dark hand that held it glistened with juice. I can't break my fast, I thought.

I looked down at Theo, who was asleep now and seemed heavier because of it. The orange was pulling at me, making the dryness drier. I closed my eyes for a moment and willed myself forward.

There must have been at least twenty stairs. How would we get Theo inside? I turned to Mother Maria, continuing the prayer.

"We're going to the little Chapel in back," she said. "The Virgin is kept there."

Once in that chapel, we took our turns kneeling before the little Virgin, the children first, then the *encargadas*, then me, then Mother Maria. Afterward the children were shepherded into pews. Theo woke and began to cry in soft sobs that worked up to moans. Sister Paula was not there to hold him close. And she never would be again.

I rubbed Theo's shoulder and stroked his head. "Easy now, it's okay."

Theo let his arms go limp by his side and stopped crying long enough to form a few words through his dry lips. "I want a drink."

I turned to Mother Maria, "Has he eaten today?"

Mother Maria put her hand to her mouth. "Oh God, in my fast I forgot him."

"I'll get him something. I can be back before the Mass starts." I started off then turned back to Theo, taking his face in my hands the way I had seen Paula do it.

"Theo, I want you to wait quietly for me while I go get you an orange. Do you understand?"

"I'm hungry," he whined, but softly. He understood. He'd wait.

I ran down the hill to the orange seller with the wet hands.

"One orange, please," I said, and then I looked down at the crate of oranges, one of the voluptuous pleasures of this land. I picked one up. My fingers looked thin and pale around it, as if a few hours of fasting could cause me to waste away. I handed it to the vendor. "And one more," I said softly, "quartered."

I put Theo's orange in my pocket and looked at the sweet orange flesh in my hand. I should fast for her, I thought. Then I bit into the fruit and pulled it away from the rind with my teeth.

The sweet juice reached deep into my throat, and I felt the cool wetness move all the way down to my chest. A few bites eased my discomfort. Wrap up the rest and go back to the fast, I thought. But my hands were wet and I wanted more. I ate up that whole sweet life.

I entered the church again, alongside the priest who had just arrived. A coffin had been placed at the back of the church.

The reality of Sister Paula's death hit again, producing a dull ache. I bowed my head and walked quickly to Theo's pew. He tossed his head from side to side and let out a low moan. I peeled the orange and put the rind carefully in my pocket. I fed him the orange sections neatly, so every bit of juice went inside him, so nothing would be dropped.

"Now he can't receive the host," said Mother Maria, "what a shame."

"I think Paula would want him to have it anyway," I said, "just this once."

Mother Maria nodded uncertainly. "But not the wine. He'll spill the blood on the floor, and that can't be."

XIII

After the funeral I went to my room and lay down. I knew I should sit in the *sala* for a while, in case any of the girls needed to talk, but I was tired, and I didn't have any answers for them anyway.

I heard a loud cry from Sister Paula's house. That, in itself, wasn't unusual. I often heard such cries in the early morning as clothes were pulled on over limbs that wouldn't bend, and children who couldn't understand the ritual of washing had their faces splashed with cold water. Things usually settled down by eight o'clock, though. By then the children were seated before bowls of Ophelia's oatmeal, and, more often than not, Sister Paula's singing could be heard.

But it was late afternoon, and this thin wail was different from the others, a voice I didn't recognize.

Poor Ophelia. She was patient with the washing and feeding, but Sister Paula had provided the love. The kids would forget, like kids do, and take comfort from lollipops, but Ophelia had a huge burden now. I lay there a few more minutes, then felt ashamed to be listening from a distance when I could be helping. I pulled myself up and went over to give Ophelia a hand.

When I went into the house most of the children were in the *sala*. Theo wasn't there, of course, Mother Maria was keeping him in the big house for now. Without him the house seemed still, lifeless in a way.

The wailing was coming from Paula's room. I went down the hall.

Lola's tiny body was rolled up into a tight ball on the end of the bed. Her face was pressed against her thighs, and her arms were wrapped around her knees, her hands bloodless and pale from the effort of squeezing her own elbows. She sobbed as Ophelia tried to unlock her hands, to separate her knees from her chest.

"She's been crying all day," Ophelia said. "She won't eat."

Lola wailed again.

I had never heard Lola's voice before today. I didn't think anyone had.

When Lola saw me she quieted, just the aftershocks of her cries were left, breathy sighs and little hiccups. She slowly let herself unknot, then she came over to me and wrapped herself around my leg. There she closed her eyes and sucked her thumb, rocking herself.

"I'll stay with her a while," I said.

After Ophelia closed the door, I led Lola over to the rocker. I lifted her into my lap and held her tight. Clinging to each other in Sister Paula's chair was fine — I needed it too.

I rocked gently as I looked around the room. Everything was as Sister Paula had left it. Her hairbrush was on the edge of her dresser, ready for use, and the pillow she slept on still held the impression of her head. The room smelled clean, a faint scent of flowers, the way she did. I closed my eyes for a moment. Sister Paula was still here.

Maybe Mother Maria would agree to keep the room this way for a while, but that wouldn't change anything. I was leaving. We all had to go on.

Lola's hair was a little tangled. With Sister Paula gone no one had thought to brush it this morning. I started to cry again. I thought I'd cried myself dry at the funeral, but these were fresh tears, from a different place. Sister Paula was dead, gone from the world, that was bad enough, but now I saw the smaller places no one thought of, places where the hole that Paula left behind was as deep as a canyon.

I'll comb Lola's hair, I thought, and I'll put a bow in it. Not that the bow itself mattered; but I wanted Lola to have what the children with bows have. I wanted her to have a mother who sets it in place.

Lola's head felt pleasantly heavy on my shoulder now that she had relaxed a bit. She still clung to me, even though she was on the brink of sleep. I stroked her back lightly with two fingers. We rocked together until she fell asleep. Then I kept rocking, because I liked the way it felt.

A few days later, Mother Maria sent Mercedes for me. I was glad to be summoned, I wanted to say goodbye to Mother Maria and tell her the good news about Luz.

I had never been upstairs in the big house. I went up and found Mother Maria sitting on her bedside chair. The room was small, but stuffed with comforts, a double bed with two pillows covered with a white chenille bedspread, an electric space heater, and a tall wardrobe that hung open to reveal a row of freshly pressed navy blue habits. The curtains were open, and the bright sunlight made small dust particles visible in the air.

"I wanted to come to see you," I began from my place in the doorway. "But I wasn't sure when..."

Mother Maria nodded that she understood. "Please come in," she said.

I went in and sat on the bed. "Luz came by yesterday," I began. "She's found sewing work, and a room for herself and her mother. It's by the *mercado*, but she says she feels safe there, that it's okay."

Mother Maria nodded again. "That's good," she said. Then she looked up at me. "You're leaving at the end of the week?"

"Yes." I felt ashamed, but I wasn't sure why. I put my head in my hands; tears overflowed onto my cheeks. "I'm sorry."

Mother Maria came over and sat beside me on the bed. "There's nothing to be sorry for. You were kind to come here for a year, to be with us."

"But I hate to leave with everything so unsettled, the girls going out. And Sister Paula gone."

Mother Maria folded her hands in her lap. "Forgive me for speaking about what is between you and God," she began. "But you have a special calling, Beth, a gift for caring. You're like Sister Paula in that way."

I stood up and walked toward the window. I didn't want Mother Maria to see how deeply she had touched me.

I looked out over the *La Casa* compound, toward Sister Paula's house, as if I might find Sister Paula there waving, giving me a sign. Then I tried to look beyond, but the view was blocked by trees. How could that be? The view of the compost heap, the site where Sister Paula was killed, wasn't visible at all.

"You lied about the murder," I whispered.

Mother Maria looked down at her own hands. "Not entirely. After all, Theo is innocent, like I said. And I did see the devil that caused all this ahead of time. The only real lie was when I said I didn't know in time to save her. I knew she needed help with him, but I was so busy with donors, running this place..." Mother Maria sighed deeply. "I left her to walk alone."

We sat in silence for a moment then I stood up to go. Mother Maria stood up too. "Think about staying, Beth. Until they find someone to replace Paula. Perhaps another year?"

I opened my mouth to say no but Sister Maria raised her hand in protest. "Consider it at least," she said. "Let God guide you."

I imagined staying at *La Casa*. Was there really a difference between one year or two? Five or ten? It was just time. Home, the life I'd be letting go of, seemed far away. At times it seemed possible that I'd never go there again. Then, when I thought about calling home to tell them, to explain things, that world sprang up from its flat place in the past, green and full. People needed me and loved me there, too. As much as I wanted to stay at *La Casa*, I also wanted to live my life, the life I'd always expected to have.

I should stay, they need me here. By Friday I could admit that to myself. But I couldn't give up everything like Sister Paula had. I wanted to go home where I belonged, to my mother and sisters. And there was Jake's quiet love. I couldn't leave that gift unopened.

La Casa would have to go on without me. The girls were more or less settled, at least for now, and Sister Paula's order had sent word that they would send a replacement in January — not that Sister Paula could ever be replaced.

On my last day at *La Casa* I went out to Sister Paula's vegetable garden. Things were still in order, except for a few overripe tomatoes, but Ophelia and I had agreed that it would be best to harvest what we could, preserve the tomatoes and dry the cilantro, rather than letting the garden go to ruin.

I worked for an hour or so, picking everything I could, then pulling up the green stalks and stacking them in the back corner of the plot.

As I was about to head up to the big house, Lola came out to the garden. She had Salto on one arm, and reached out to me with the other.

Poor Lola. She was lost after Sister Paula died, with no one to follow around. She had taken to walking around with Salto, carrying him back and forth to my room, or the *sala*, or wherever I happened to be going. We had spent a lot of time together in the past week. I felt Sister Paula's absence keenly, but thinking about her was less painful when Lola was around. I had gotten in the habit of rocking Lola to sleep in Sister Paula's chair at bedtime.

What would Lola do when I left? I bit my lip. I hadn't yet told her that I was going home.

Lola looked at the empty garden and the freshly disturbed earth that remained, then frowned accusingly at me.

The bed look abandoned. I wished I could plant something. It would have to be half-wild, something that didn't require much care. I thought of the hibiscus that grew around the big house. Paula had planted the first plants years ago and now they grew thick and strong as weeds. That would do.

I turned to Lola, "Do you want to help me plant some flowers for Sister Paula?"

Lola nodded yes, and hugged herself.

We worked quietly by the big house, with me pulling up the plants by the roots and handing them to Lola, who laid them carefully in a basket.

"I'm going home tomorrow," I began. Then I realized that to Lola home meant *La Casa*, nothing more. "Away, I mean."

Lola didn't look alarmed, she just shook her head "no" and tugged on my arm the way she did when I said it was time to go back to Ophelia's house. These tugs were always good for five more minutes and Lola knew it.

But those five minutes had to stop sometime. Otherwise they would add up to forever, and I was decided. I was going home.

I started over. "I'm going back to the United States. To my family."

But Lola didn't know what another country was, the world was just one place to her. Did she even understand the word 'family'? I doubted it.

"I'm leaving," I said. "I have to go."

Lola seemed to understand, but she didn't cry or cling. She just looked down at her basket and placed her small hand on the clumpy vines as if to say, "We're still going to plant these, aren't we?"

We continued working quietly. Once the basket was full we headed down the hill again to transplant the vines. Lola handled the plants with care. She knelt beside me and pressed them into the soft holes that had been left by the plants that were pulled up, then she pressed the earth gently against them.

I watched Lola and almost started to cry. What would become of this child who said nothing, but seemed to understand everything?

"I wish I could take you home with me," I said aloud, but in English, so there'd be no chance of Lola understanding.

That night I stood before my suitcase, packing for the last time. I took out the pouch that contained my letters. I wanted to pack the Polaroid shots of the girls there, to make sure they were protected. When I opened the pouch the picture of my mother that Jake had sent slipped out.

I took it in my hand and stared at it for a long moment. I thought of all I had done for the girls. Could I somehow do the same thing for my mother? Did I want to continue the search I'd begun? After all I had been through, the questions didn't seem as urgent, and the face that looked up at me seemed answer enough. It smiled at me, familiar, even though I didn't actually remember my mother looking that way, and foretelling love. It was my mother's face, my mother's story. I was going to respect that. I put the clipping with the photos of the girls. They belonged together.

As I was about to zip the suitcase shut, Lola came to my room and stood in the doorway, Salto under her arm.

I smiled and waved Lola into the room. This was going to be a difficult goodbye.

Lola saw my things in the suitcase and smiled. She put Salto on top and gave him a pat on the head.

"No." I took Salto and pressed him into Lola's hand. "He's yours to keep."

Lola smiled and placed him in the suitcase again. She was accustomed to speaking with gestures, and this was a new a game.

I felt a catch in my throat. I put the puppet on her hand. "I love you, I don't want to leave you," said Salto to Lola.

Lola, serious now, put Salto in the suitcase for the third time. She looked up at me, and then reached down and took off her shoes and placed them in the suitcase, too.

I took them out, crying through my smile. "I can't take these," I said softly, "you'll need them here."

Lola's face fell, then crumbled into tears.

Oh God, she misunderstood. She thought I could take her with me. My composure and resolve, my confidence in my decision melted into tears.

Then Lola opened her arms. She was asking to be held. She was offering comfort. "Bett," she said.

Lola's Journey

"*Yellow next, Mama.*"

Lola is beside me. It is early spring and the lake is shining with clean light. We are planting pansies by the oak tree, which is tall enough this year to provide the little bit of shade they need. I dig the hole, then Lola places the flower, bright yellow beside deep purple.

Does she remember Sister Paula? I wonder that myself. I've tried asking, saying Sister Paula's name, but Lola just shakes her head with a puzzled smile and goes back to whatever she's doing.

She remembers the songs though, the songs that Sister Paula sang. Sometimes she wakes up in the early morning, before the sun is up. She lies in bed singing to herself. Jake and I slip out of bed quietly and sit by her open door, listening to the miracle of her voice. When she sings Sister Paula's songs, her words are clear. It's as if Sister Paula is alive.

Her speech therapist tells me that the songs are clear because the singing relaxes her, positions her mouth muscles just so. But I think it's because the songs come out of the surest place, the place none of us can remember, the place where we first know love.

Acknowledgements

*   *   *

I am very grateful to the writers, friends, and family who supported me during the process of writing *Caminata*. Kate LeSar, Faith
Mullen, Shelly Kirilenko and the Writer's Center in Bethesda,
Maryland created a nurturing space for me as I began the process
of putting pen to paper. Elizabeth Letts, gifted writer and, more
importantly, treasured friend, provided valuable advice and support, intensely during the period when I was finishing the first
draft, and steadily over the years, to this day. I am also grateful to
Fred Brown and Lisa DiPrete for their readings and insightful editorial suggestions, and to Ethel DiPrete for her excellent proof-
reading. My husband Kirk has provided every kind of love and
support over the years. One advantage of taking nearly twenty
years to complete this novel is that I can also thank my children
Evan, Elise and Kristen, for reading and commenting on the
book! In recent months Evan has served as my editorial assistant,
expertly guiding me through the publication process.

I especially want to thank the girls who shared their lives with me
for the two years that I lived with them in Honduras. Although
this is completely a work of fiction, it is informed by the things
that they taught me, and if what I have written has merit or truth,
it is because of their willingness to let me into their world.

About the Author

*   *   *

Lori DiPrete Brown served as a Peace Corps Volunteer in Honduras, where she worked in a home for orphaned and abandoned teenage girls. Her experiences accompanying the girls in her care on their journeys to find their birth mothers provided the inspiration for this novel. She is a graduate of Yale and holds graduate degrees in public health and theology from Harvard. She studied writing at Yale and at the Iowa Summer Writer's Festival. Currently, she teaches global health at the University of Wisconsin-Madison, leads international field experiences for students, and consults with international global health organizations. She lives in Madison with her husband and three children and is a Benedictine Oblate of the Holy Wisdom Monastery. Her writing focuses on spirituality, social justice, and personal transformation. For more, visit her blog at globalhealthreflections.wordpress.com.

39026082R00142

Made in the USA
Charleston, SC
23 February 2015